fifteen weekends

Christy Pastore

Copyright

From the Desk of Author Christy Pastore

If you need some tunes while you read Fifteen Weekends, check out the Spotify playlist.

Join my mailing list at https://geni.us/NewsFromChristyPastore for the latest news on new releases, exclusive bonus material, sales, and other bookish stuff you don't want to miss. Always spam free!

If monthly newsletters and the occasional extra aren't your thing, follow me on BookBub for preorder and new release alerts.

fitteen weekends

Christy Pastore

Chapter One
Ashleigh

Ashleigh Preston sat with her legs crossed, hurriedly typing her notes while waiting at Gate Eight in London's Heathrow airport. She had just spent the last five days visiting the newly restored Great Northern Hotel, sipping couture cocktails at the GNH Bar and enjoying the luxurious comforts of the Cubitt room. Ashleigh was in the city to review the hotel's sleek and sophisticated redesign, which combined timeless elegance with modern touches. High ceilings hosted glamorous circular hanging chandeliers. Lustrous etched glass mirrors lined the walls, while sweeping staircases and expansive wide curved corridors seemed to go on for miles. Grand floor to ceiling and sash windows allowed light to flood nearly every space of the building. These features are most likely what she will highlight in the final draft of her review for the travel and lifestyle blog, *The Business Travelers' Wife*.

Looking at her phone the time read 8:45 P.M., reminding her of what she was doing at that exact moment only twenty-four hours ago. Pulling her dark hair up into a tousled bun, her mind lingered, taking her back to the corner booth at Plum + Spilt Milk where she could see the candles flickering and hear the music playing softly in the background. As she imagined the radiating glow from the gorgeous hand-blown pendant lights, Ashleigh felt her skin getting warmer. For a moment, she could smell seared olive oil on wood with a hint of garlic and felt her mouth begin to tighten, remembering the taste of the Yorkshire pudding and lemon posset with fresh raspberries.

"Excuse me, is this seat taken?" someone asked in a low voice.

Ashleigh snapped out of her daydream and saw a petite woman holding a large leather handbag dressed head to toe in black. With her brown eyes narrowed, the woman pointed at the seat next to Ashleigh.

"No it's not taken, you can sit there," she replied moving her own handbag next to her suitcase.

2

Ashleigh couldn't help but smile glancing at the shiny Union Jack flag keychain dangling from her Michael Kors handbag. Retrieving her iPhone from the side pocket of her carryon she clicked on the Foursquare app checking in to Heathrow Airport.

The keychain was a gift from Liam, just one of many tokens she could add to her collection. Liam Oliver Frost— her handsome Englishman, although he's not officially "hers," technically Liam's not even English. Liam is actually Welsh, and yes there's a difference just ask anyone in the UK. They're just friends and sometimes more, but never a couple. Ashleigh was in love once, deeply in love. When it was over, she was completely gutted. She made a promise to herself that she would never allow that kind of pain in her life again. Serious relationships are not in Ashleigh's repertoire. But it doesn't hurt to have a good looking friend with benefits. For the past few years, Liam has been that friend.

Terminal four was busy and the empty seats at all the gates were quickly filling up. Tired families were dragging heavy shopping bags from last minute stops at Harrods and

Burberry, while kids pulled their small rolling suitcases behind them in one hand, clutching bags from Caffé Nero and Simply Chocolates in the other. College students with headphones around their necks hurriedly made their way to power stations to recharge their electronics as overstuffed backpacks slid down their shoulders, most likely filled with all of their belongings and souvenirs.

Stretching her legs out and crossing her ankles, Ashleigh hoped her flight was not full. She definitely needed to relax after her exhausting few days in London, days that were full of both work and play.

The metal of the keychain felt warm as she rubbed it between her thumb and index finger. She gently grazed her thumb over the top of the glossy Union Jack design. Hearing a familiar vibrating sound coming from her purse, Ashleigh retrieved her phone and saw it was a tweet notification from @EMMYGREENE15.

@ASHMPRESTON15 SAW YOU CHECKED IN AT HEATHROW. SAFE TRAVELS HOME.

She laughed to herself, knowing her friend, the social media maven, never missed a beat.

@EMMYGREENE15 SO TIRED. I HAD SUCH A GREAT TIME, BOARDING IN FORTY MINUTES.

@ASHMPRESTON15 GOOD! DRINKS WHEN YOU GET BACK?

@EMMYGREENE15 ABSOLUTELY! I WILL TEXT YOU WHEN I GET HOME AND WE CAN MAKE PLANS.

@ASHMPRESTON15 PERFECT!

Ashleigh decided to check Facebook while she still had the chance before boarding the flight home. Scanning the news feed she saw: Amanda Parsons had checked into the boutique, My Sister's Closet. Ashleigh rolled her eyes, but hit "Like" begrudgingly. Emily Greene's status said: CANNOT WAIT FOR THE WEEKEND. She already had half a dozen comments and twelve "Likes." Make that thirteen now.

Liam Frost's last posting was a check-in at Starbucks earlier that morning with a comment that said: NEED TO RE-CHARGE THE BATTERIES. Ashleigh giggled to herself, knowing she was partly responsible for his much needed caffeine fix. With that Ashleigh went to Liam's status and hit "Like." She commented with only a smiley icon then closed the Facebook app on her phone.

While Ashleigh was looking forward to sleeping in her own bed back in Grand Rapids, she was always sad to leave London. Her love affair with the city began at an early age. Her father frequently travelled to Europe on business, and she, her brother and mother would accompany him. When Ashleigh was in high school she dreamed of living in London one day. She pictured herself shopping at Selfridges and enjoying afternoon tea at Claridge's where she would run into her then style icon, Princess Diana.

A few years ago when Ashleigh left *Maison Bleue Magazine* to begin freelance work, writing and taking photographs, her first assignment was to review the Corinthia Hotel's grand re-opening in London. This is when she met Liam.

A smiled crossed her lips as she began thinking about him. Liam was quite tall, about six foot three, with a slender fit build, gorgeous thick dark brown hair, and soulful deep brown eyes. He always looked like he stepped out of a fashion editorial in *Details* magazine. The man could wear a suit like no one else, thank goodness for fine English tailoring.

Liam grew up in a hotel, rather a castle that was renovated by his parents into a hotel. Since the renovations, Frost Castle has become a popular spot for tourists vacationing in Wales. Meeting new people and hearing stories of where they had traveled from to visit Wales was a major contributing factor to why Liam eventually became a Travel Writer.

Ashleigh's thoughts were interrupted by an announcement over the loud speaker.

"We will now begin boarding our first class passengers for flight nineteen with non-stop service to Detroit."

Slowly pushing to her feet, she gathered her items, including her now empty coffee cup, and walked to the nearest trash can throwing it away. Gazing out the windows of the airport and then back down Terminal four, she noticed a handsome man with dark brown, slightly curly hair standing by Costa Coffee. He was wearing a soft grey sweater and dark denim jeans holding a silver coffee mug with a black trench coat draped over his left forearm. He looked familiar to Ashleigh. Could he have been someone she knew from college? As he walked by, a dreamy expression appeared on Ashleigh's face. All of a sudden a small boy with blonde hair ran in front of the guy, who in turn accidently knocked over Ashleigh's carry-on.

In an American accent Ashleigh heard, "Whoa, there young man."

The little boy smiled and ran towards his parents who were sitting down near Harrods Food Hall. The mother had her nose firmly in a book, while the father was looking around seemingly unaware of his son's whereabouts at that moment.

"Here you go," the guy said, propping Ashleigh's suitcase right side up on its wheels.

Captivated by his steely greyish-blue eyes, Ashleigh found herself lingering a bit too long with her words.

Finally, after several seconds, which felt more like minutes, she coolly replied, "Thank you very much for the help."

The man smiled and nodded to Ashleigh, her gaze followed him as he was swallowed up into the mass frenzy of people.

Familiar indeed, she thought to herself. But, how did she know him?

The loudspeaker came on again.

"We will now begin boarding our Business Class passengers for flight nineteen with non-stop service to Detroit."

Ashleigh made her way towards the gate agent and handed him her boarding pass.

Chapter Two
Emily

Emily Greene grabbed her iPhone, favorite ink pen along with her organizer case, and quickly walked to the executive conference room for her weekly management meeting. Per usual, she was the first one in the room. She was a stickler for two things: punctuality and organization. Looking around the room she noticed that someone had left a bunch of file folders and sales brochures sprawled across the conference table, and the back table was in complete disarray. Pens, loose blank papers and dry erase markers were all haphazardly left laying out instead of placed back in the cabinet.

Doesn't anyone take pride in being neat?

Finally, her co-workers began to file into the room.

Upon further inspection of the files, Emily's blood began to boil. These were the first revisions for the retail store infographics Emily thought she'd misplaced two weeks ago. The completed files vanished from the database, and the hard copies were missing from her filing cabinet.

Emily had to stay and work overnight to re-do everything in order ready for her presentation the next day.

This had her former colleague Morgan Allen's passive aggressive stench all over it. Morgan had just been fired and was furious with Emily as a result. Needless to say, security had to escort Morgan off the property—she did not go quietly.

Her boss, Clark Reynolds began by saying, "How's everyone doing today?"

Susan Baker replied, "Doing very well."

Ethan Carlson pretended to be interested in something on his phone only giving a polite nod to Clark. Mike Landry shuffled his notes while a few of the other executives grabbed coffee and water.

"Glad to hear. Let's get started with our retail numbers report. Ethan you have the floor."

Emily glanced at her phone, and her mind began to drift. The very word "numbers" was a sometimes emotional trigger for her. It was so silly. Why did such a common word drive her crazy? Oh yeah, because of *him*.

11

Trying desperately not to let her mind go there, she shifted in her chair and focused on the report in front of her, but then her boss asked for last week's "weekly net income statement." It was too late. Emily's thoughts had already drifted to him, Craig Walker. She felt her cheeks begin to change color. Gripping her pen tightly she glanced out the window, spying a robin perched on the large pine tree outside.

Emily met Craig during her last year of grad school at University of Chicago—tall, dark and handsome. He was funny, intelligent and incredibly charming. The perfect specimen, Craig Bennett Walker met every desirable cliché on the "What Women Want in a Man" list.

Numbers, stats and stocks were his passion, and for some odd reason, even though at first Emily could only relate to about a quarter of what Craig was talking about regarding the stock market, it was a total turn on for her. Emily had been in The Loop district interviewing for a position at The Bath Shop's corporate headquarters when she stumbled into an out of the way bar called Mulligan's.

Feeling pretty good that she had most likely landed the job, she wanted to celebrate with a cold beverage.

It was a hot afternoon in Chicago, about eighty-six degrees, and there was a wonderful breeze coming off the lake which made it slightly tolerable outside. Hiking along Wacker Drive wearing black pants and a black suit jacket was no easy task. Her back was soaked, and her feet felt sweaty and numb from her narrow kitten heels.

The smoky bar was packed wall to wall with suits, mostly men with a few women sprinkled throughout. Suddenly, Emily felt twenty pairs of eyes dart in her direction. She did feel like a fool standing there all by herself in the doorway, sweat beading at the back of her neck. That was the moment when Emily first saw Craig, the most handsome guy she'd ever laid eyes on. He reminded her of a cross between a young Paul Newman and JFK Jr., very all American gorgeous.

Aside from the current awkward feeling, Emily felt especially pretty that day. Underneath her blazer was a cream colored sleeveless blouse that showed off her glowing, warmly tanned skin. Emily had been on the lake the weekend before giving her just enough color to say, "I'm ready for summer."

Shrugging off her jacket, Craig caught her stare. She smiled at him, and he motioned to the bartender. Craig scooped up two beers and headed in her direction, never taking his eyes off of her as he weaved in and out of the crowd, gliding closer to where she was standing. Craig had the best smile, and it was only amplified by his frosty blue eyes and warm complexion.

Emily's heart skipped a beat, and she jumped in her chair. Her colleague Susan had clumsily dropped her accounting binder on the floor, and Emily realized she was back in the boardroom not at Mulligan's bar.

"*Sorry* everyone, I am so very sorry," Susan stammered.

"It's okay Susan. It happens to us all," Clark replied trying to make her feel less embarrassed.

Emily bowed her head and rolled her eyes so no one could see her reaction to Susan, the bumbling idiot.

"Emily, how are things in the Marketing Department this week?" Clark inquired.

"Things in Marketing are going well. We're finalizing the logo graphics for the new line, The Huntington Collection," she stated firmly. "Those graphics should be ready for my final revisions next week along with the updated retail infographics."

Lowering his dark rimmed glasses, Clark praised, "Outstanding Emily, keep up the good work." Closing his iPad, he looked around the table and said, "Good work everyone. Meeting adjourned. Have a nice evening."

Pushing to her feet, Emily gathered her items and walked down the hallway to her office. She looked at the clock hanging on the wall which read 4:35 P.M. Before she could depart the office and end her work day, she had some paperwork to finish. A text from Amanda Parsons popped up on Emily's phone: HEY LADY, DO YOU WANT TO GO OUT TONIGHT AND HAVE A FEW MARTINIS?

Emily did not want to go out with Amanda because she knew that Amanda would hold her hostage until at least two in the morning and make her pay for all the drinks. Knowing she had to be in the office promptly at eight the next morning, Emily had a good reason not accept Amanda's invite. Emily ignored the text for about twenty minutes then replied: NO, I AM SO SORRY I HAVE PLANS TONIGHT. THANK YOU FOR THE INVITE.

As she started filing paperwork into the folder labeled *The Huntington Collection* her phone buzzed again. It was another text message from Amanda, pleading with her to come out for drinks. Emily read the text and sighed. *Why can't Amanda just take no for an answer?*

Locking her computer she double checked her day planner viewing her Friday schedule, gathered her things and walked towards the door of her office. Her phone lit up again, and she rolled her eyes thinking what more could Amanda have to say? It was not Amanda. It was a message from, her trainer Andy, whom Emily referred to as "Annoying Andy." He wanted to know if she was going to work out at the gym tonight. She ignored the text and proceeded to the door. Emily knew in her current state of mind her workout would be a waste of time.

"A moment, Emily," she heard a man's deep voice say.

Emily looked up and saw Ethan Carlson, the Director of Retail Operations standing there coolly darkening her doorway. Ethan was one of the best looking guys at Cooper Bentley. He had gorgeous tousled brown hair, thick dark eyebrows that were perfectly manicured framing his deep brown eyes. Usually Emily prefers men to have a clean-shaven face, but Ethan had just enough scruff that was appealing. Like his eyebrows, this too was perfectly manicured, not an untamed wild mess. Standing about six foot two, with a swimmer's build, rumor had it Ethan swam every morning, six days a week. Apparently it was part of his strict workout and diet regimen. If that was true, it showed.

"Oh, hi again Ethan. Did you need something from me?" she asked, feeling her heart thump wildly in her chest.

"Yeah, I just spoke to Clark and we decided that the retail infographics need your final revisions by Tuesday."

Emily felt her neck and face become flush. She turned away from Ethan's gaze and rolled her eyes. Ethan Carlson certainly had a knack for getting under Emily's skin. *Arrogant…confident…handsome…arrogant…lethally sexy. Why was he so damn good-looking? Oh, but don't forget how big of an ass he can be.*

"Are you serious Ethan?" she inquired sharply. "That means I'm going to have to work the weekend. And in case you didn't know Ethan, it's a holiday weekend."

Emily was now directly in front of Ethan, close enough to smell the subtle scent of lemon mixed with warm leather. Emily knew this fragrance well. It was Yves Saint Laurent L'Homme Libre cologne. He wore it every single day.

God he smells divine.

"You can do it Emily, I have faith in you," he replied smoothly.

What a crock of shit.

Her hand drifted up the wall to turn the light off. The office was now dark and she was moving towards the door's threshold. Ethan inched back allowing Emily to cross giving her just enough space to shut the door to her office. The air between them shifted as she caught Ethan raking his eyes over her. Sweat began to form on the back of Emily's neck.

"Can I walk you out?" he inquired. His voice was smooth and sultry.

While she would rather Ethan just fuck off and leave her to stew about having to work the weekend, Emily nodded, and he motioned for her to walk first. She took a few small steps, but Ethan ended up right beside her, matching her pace. As they walked down the hallway side by side passing the reception desk, Emily felt something hit the small of her back. It was just Ethan's hand, leading her out the door. A pleasurable shiver moved through her entire body as a ghost of a smile crossed her lips.

"Plans tonight Emily?" Ethan asked, while opening the door and allowing her to walk outside first.

The warm spring breeze was incessantly whipping strands of her long brunette hair across her face. Emily shook her head to the left and pushed the tousled strands back behind her ear. Emily caught Ethan's deep brown eyes gazing at her with intensity as she smoothed her hair back into place.

"Yes, big plans," she replied. "Thanks to you, I have to rearrange my weekend schedule."

He said nothing, only arching one of his dark eyebrows at her while the curve of his mouth turned upward.

Emily could tell he was irritated with her comment. She decided she'd rather not piss him off, that could be a mistake. Careful with her tone, Emily replied, "Okay, Ethan, so tell me this, why the rush with the paperwork?"

"Emily," he began, his jaw tightening. "We're still trying to piece together the mess left behind by your former assistant," he snapped. "Those infographics should have been done two weeks ago. Your department is a wreck, and we have a major presentation with LA Business Design coming up in a matter of days."

Emily blanched, and her temper flared. It wasn't her fault that Morgan was a complete fuck up, but as the Director of Marketing she had to assume some responsibility where Morgan's less than stellar job performance was concerned. Emily had pushed for Clark's approval to fire Morgan weeks ago, but Morgan somehow dodged every bullet that came her way and avoided getting fired until Emily was finally left with no choice.

They crossed the parking lot and arrived at Ethan's black Lexus LS 460. He pressed the button on his car keys and smoothly opened the door of the sleek sedan. As much as Ethan irritated her, Emily couldn't deny she was physically attracted to him. She imagined for a moment what it would be like sliding into this beautiful work of luxurious machinery with Ethan. With one of his hands on the wheel, the other clutching her knee they would drive up the lakeshore to his beach house for the weekend. Biting her bottom lip at the delightful thought, she quickly pushed it out of her mind feeling a bit embarrassed.

The sun was shining directly in Emily's blue-green eyes, so she placed her right hand on her forehead to shield the blinding light allowing her to see Ethan looking back at her. *God he's good looking. Why did he have to have a girlfriend? Better yet, why was he such an arrogant prick?* Emily spied her silver Audi two rows over from Ethan's car. Pivoting on her heel, she began to walk away.

"Well, Emily I would hate to know that your job was interfering with your big weekend plans," he called after her. "Why don't you meet me back here around seven and we'll work on the infographics together?"

Emily's blood sizzled in her veins. Shifting her gaze back to Ethan, she replied calmly, "Fine, Ethan, thank you for the help. I will see you at seven."

Chapter Three
Amanda

Amanda Parsons had only been up for four hours and decided to finally shower. She was out partying the night before with her co-workers from The Bath Shop. They had completed the floor set by midnight and they were totally wired. Amanda was, of course, the one to suggest they hit the bars. Finishing her shower, she decided she would hit up her favorite designer discount boutique, My Sister's Closet, and see if she could find some stylish clothes to sell in her eBay store. She had sixty dollars to her name at the moment and probably should not have been shopping, but she told herself she needed to go. Payday was tomorrow, so she felt she could make it until then with just a short money supply. Besides, if she absolutely needed the cash, she could always manipulate her roommate Daniel for Starbucks or a meal.

Daniel and Amanda had met a few months ago when he travelled to her store at Woodfield Mall to fill in for one of the managers who had gone on vacation. The pair became fast friends with their love of spa products and iced cappuccinos. Daniel and his boyfriend of four years had just broken up, and he found himself needing a roommate. It worked out well for Amanda because she had been living with her divorce lawyer, and he had just taken a job in Boston.

Amanda did not want to move nor continue the affair. Sleeping with your divorce lawyer should only be rewarded if he wins you an exceptional amount of money, which he was incapable of doing for Amanda. However, since he was a much better fuck than a divorce lawyer, she broke her rule rewarding him with the pleasure of taking her to bed nearly every night.

Amanda slid into her white Nissan Altima, sweeping aside the empty coffee cups and bags from Wendy's and McDonald's to make room for her purse on the passenger seat. The scent of grease hung in the air, which was amplified by the heat from sitting outside in the sun. She quickly rolled down her windows. The smell was almost unbearable.

Listening to the radio, she wondered what semi-glorious fashion treasures she would find. Last week she found a vintage Chanel purse, a pair of lightly worn Jimmy Choo pumps and an off-white strapless chiffon gown with slight fabric pulls, probably from the previous owner's fingernails.

It was in this moment that Amanda felt sad having to shop at lower end and bargain shops. It was only a short time ago when she was shopping in the finest stores in the world—Dior, Chanel, Prada and Louis Vuitton. A few years ago she never would have stepped into a place like The Bath Shop or My Sister's Closet, but now, this was her reality.

After Amanda had dropped out of Notre Dame in October of her junior year, realizing college was not her thing, she packed her bags and jetted off to Milan for a few weeks, then onto Paris, London and finally Monte Carlo. Her time in Europe was thrilling, spending Thanksgiving with friends in the South of France talking about wine, current events and literature. She spent Christmas skiing the Alps in Switzerland and drinking wine by the fire with her then boyfriend, Matthis at his cozy chalet.

One day while in Monte Carlo she went to the ATM machine to pull out some cash and found she had insufficient funds. That was her father Jack's doing, who was furious with his daughter upon finding out that she had dropped out of college without so much as a word. Amanda was ordered to return to Bloomfield Hills immediately. If she didn't want to go back to school she would have to get a job.

While she would rather not work at all, Amanda knew her father would help her find a suitable job. With all of his contacts she was certain there was someone who owed him a favor. That favor was a job at WWSK 950 AM in Detroit where she landed her own talk show. Surprising even herself, Amanda was elated about this career opportunity. It turns out she had a real talent for engaging guests in interesting and thought provoking topics. The Amanda Parsons Show generated the second highest ratings at the station, only behind the very famous syndicated news talk host, Brian Rush.

Beep…Beep…Beep.

Pulled from her thoughts, Amanda realized she was stalling traffic. She gave a gentle wave in her rearview mirror to the person behind her saying, "Sorry, sorry. I'm going!"

She arrived at the boutique finding a parking spot near the entrance. Amanda took her phone out of her purse and checked into the store from her Facebook page. She'd lost most of her country club and society friends from the fallout of the scandal. Her Facebook friends list was limited to those few hangers on, new people she had met and her co-workers. While she had her phone out Amanda sent a text message to Emily Greene to see if she wanted to go out for drinks later. Emily was one of her few friends who had a lot of money, and she could take advantage of that opportunity, getting Emily to pay for all the drinks. She would tell Emily to put the drinks on her credit card and Amanda would tell her that she would give her cash once she got paid, which she would never do.

Emily replied saying she had plans for the evening and could not make it. Amanda sighed, thinking to herself, *yeah right*. Amanda had a feeling that she was being lied to.

Despite her animosity towards Emily, Amanda needed to keep her as a friend. Emily had resources and connections that could help Amanda achieve certain personal and career aspirations. Amanda knew that Emily's assistant was just fired, and even though Amanda couldn't really see herself working for Emily it was a better alternative than the mall.

Amanda walked over to the wall of shoes adjacent from sportswear section. There, amongst the worn tennis shoes, snow boots and gently scratched patent heels, sat a pair of black spiked Christian Louboutin heels. Amanda checked the size. She could not believe her good fortune that they were an exact fit. Amanda's green eyes began to widen and she ran her index finger over each one of the spikes affixed at the toe. Sliding her sherbet colored ballet flat off her right foot she delicately eased into the gorgeous shoe, feeling her stomach tingle at the sensation of her toes as they hit the supple leather lining.

"Those stilettos look quite lovely on you," a velvety smooth voice complimented.

Amanda turned around, slightly startled. With the height difference in the shoes, she needed to balance herself carefully. Looking up through a few of her golden blonde waves that had fallen in her face she saw the man, approximately in his early-forties, standing there smiling at her. He was insanely good-looking, tall with dark brown hair that was almost jet black, and sparkling blue eyes, the kind of blue eyes that a girl could get lost in if she stared long enough. Placing his hand on his hip, moving his grey overcoat back, he revealed his lean physique under a fitted black shirt paired with sleek black dress pants.

Wow just...wow...he's completely—beautiful. He doesn't need to know that, yet.

"Thank you. I think they're pretty fabulous," she replied sweetly.

"I'd love to buy them for you."

"You want to buy me shoes? I don't even know you," Amanda stated while slipping off the flat on her left foot and putting on the matching heel.

"My name is Vince." Introducing himself casually, while he ran his hand through his dark hair, he asked, "What is your name?"

"Amanda," she said while gazing at her reflection in the mirror carefully examining the shoes. She stood sideways with her left-side closest to the mirror so she could view the entire heel. Amanda then switched to her right side, hyperaware that Vince's gaze was carefully affixed on her body.

"What, do you have some sort of weird ass foot fetish?" Amanda inquired sharply as she turned around to face Vince.

Vince laughed as he took a step toward her with his shiny black oxfords. "No, I do not have a foot fetish. I simply thought the heels looked nice on you."

"This is bizarre, this is discount style boutique. Not Bergdorf Goodman's. I would expect this sort of scenario to happen in a nice department store, but *not* here."

Inquiring seductively, Vince gave her a sly smile.
"Shopping at Bergdorf Goodman's, would that make you
happy, Amanda?"

Amanda, still wearing the Louboutin's looked Vince
squarely in the eye and said, "Yes, that would make me *very*
happy Vince."

"Well, as much as I would love to charter a private jet
to New York City and take you shopping Amanda, I cannot
do that for you today. I have a dinner meeting tonight."

"What makes you think I would let *you* jet *me* off to
New York City for a pair of shoes?" she asked coldly. In
her mind she was doing backflips and screaming that a
handsome man with money wanted to buy her shoes!
Amanda knew this game and she had no shame about it.

"Wouldn't you?" he asked lifting one of his dark
eyebrows.

Stepping away from the mirror, she turned her back to
Vince. She felt his eyes watching her as she worked her
body in the most appealing way while bending down to slip
off the shoes, placing them back on the rack.

"Maybe, how about you take me to dinner first?"

Vince reached into the inside of his jacket pocket and retrieved a business card. Amanda felt her hands begin to sweat, this hasn't happened to her in months. He took a pen and wrote something on the back. He leaned closer to her. She felt the crackle of electricity as Vince's fingertips grazed her hand as he pushed the card into her palm. The textured card read: VINCE L. EVERETT, FOUNDER + CEO, EVERETT STERLING AVIATION. She flipped the card over and saw a ten digit number that said, "PERSONAL CELL".

"You can call me anytime at that number. I look forward to hearing from you, *Amanda,*" he said with a smile. He turned and walked towards the door.

"Thank you Vince Everett. I *might* be in touch," Amanda called out.

Still walking, he turned his head over his left shoulder and held up his right hand and gently waved.

Walking hurriedly towards the door she removed the car keys from her Gucci handbag, one of the few things she was able to keep from her divorce. She looked left and then right making sure that the intoxicating and handsome man she had just met was no longer in the parking lot to see her get into her old beat up car.

She was grinning from ear to ear. *If this works out, I won't need Daniel, Emily, or that bitch Ashleigh anymore. Goodbye shitty mall job. Hello Sugar Daddy and new Louboutin's.*

Dating a guy who could charter a private jet at a moment's notice made Amanda's insides churn with excitement. The mere thought of having money again made her feel giddy all over. Now, all Amanda needed was the perfect outfit for seduction. In her mind she already had the dinner date planned for Saturday evening.

Chapter Four
Ashleigh

Ashleigh walked down the aisle of the plane eyeing where she thought her seat was located and saw the row was empty. Only a young curly haired blonde girl wearing a University of Michigan sweatshirt and a twenty-something brunette wearing a yellow tank top paired with a black cardigan were seated in the row in front of her. To her right there was a young Saudi-American couple, or possibly Persian, sitting very close to each other looking at photos on a cell phone. By their happy glow, Ashleigh suspected they were newlyweds returning home from their honeymoon, plus their rings were quite shiny, which was another sign that they were probably newly married. No one was seated behind her, and everyone seemed to be filing back to coach class.

Ashleigh settled into her seat grabbing the iPad and headphones out of her handbag. The flight attendants closed the door and began their preflight checks. After several moments, the loudspeaker came on: *"Flight*

attendants, please prepare doors for departure, crosscheck and all-call."
The plane began to back away from the gate and then
headed to the intended runway for takeoff. Ashleigh could
see the London skyline in the distance lit up so beautifully
against the night sky.

See you later London. Until next time Liam.

The plane sped faster and faster down the runway.
Ashleigh's heart began to beat rapidly. Feeling her body
tense up, Ashleigh grabbed the armrests on both sides of
her seat as the plane began to ascend into the night sky. She
sighed deeply, releasing all the anxiety from her body.
Suddenly the rain began to fall, hitting the windows. She
closed her eyes remembering the smell of the rain on that
spring night.

The Corinthia Hotel's grand re-opening was a lovely
affair. The two-hundred ninety four room hotel was once
home to the Ministry of Defense. It was hard not to notice
Liam standing at the end of the sleek marble bar in The

Northall. He was wearing a midnight navy suit with contrasting notch lapels and ordered a martini "shaken not stirred." *He walked right up to the bar and ordered the martini James Bond style. That just happened!* Seated two seats away from where he was standing, Ashleigh found this to be amusing and laughed quietly to herself while looking in Liam's direction. He caught her eyes on him and winked. Liam approached her smiling, but Ashleigh spoke first. "Why Mr. Bond, I would have never guessed you'd order a martini."

"Why Mrs. Kensington you know it's my bag baby," his voice purred with a gritty tone.

The pair of strangers found this exchange of Hollywood cinematic quotes to be quite humorous. Ashleigh took a sip of her cocktail, the Northall Bramble, a gin sour drink with a sweet mix of blackberries, raspberries, orange and lemon juice.

"My name is Ashleigh. It's nice to meet you," she said, giving him a sweet smile with her hazel eyes beaming.

"Liam, Liam Frost," he said adjusting his ink black tie, in his very best James Bond voice (Connery not Brosnan).

He extended his hand to meet hers. A wave of heat rushed over Ashleigh's skin. Electric pulses radiated through her core at his touch. Her eyes darted to the sculpted curve of his mouth, and she wondered what it would be like to kiss this tall drink of water.

Listening intently as Liam talked about the hotel's history in his Welsh accent, Ashleigh was utterly enraptured with everything about him. Everything he did was so smooth and sexy, even the way he picked up a cocktail napkin and placed it in front of her.

It should be illegal to be that charming.

Liam, who was leaning casually on the bar with his right forearm, gracefully shifted and picked up his martini with his left hand never taking his eyes off Ashleigh. Ashleigh was feeling especially sexy and confident that evening wearing her newly purchased long-sleeve white Issa dress with a sexy slit down the bodice. Signaling the bartender with his index finger, Liam ordered two more cocktails.

Yep, that was even sexier than picking up the napkin.

"Would you care to join me on the patio?" Liam asked, his brown eyes blazing with intensity.

"What patio?" she inquired, feeling the knot in her stomach begin to tighten.

"The one that sits just off the Hamilton Penthouse."

"The Hamilton Penthouse?"

Liam leaned in closely. "Where else but the Penthouse would be best suited for James Bond?" he said, smiling coyly.

"I...I'd love to join you," she replied feeling the knot in her stomach began to release slowly.

Ashleigh finished the last sips of her drink and grabbed the refresher that Liam ordered, along with her clutch. Liam slid her chair back and offered his hand. Ashleigh stepped down and felt Liam's hand touch the small of her back directing her body to the exit. As the pair walked down the hallway past the concierge desk, Ashleigh said, "That was some cocktail reception tonight."

"Yes, it most certainly was."

"How did you end up in the Hamilton Penthouse, Liam?"

"Well, I have a friend who works for the company that manages the Corinthia," Liam stated as he hit the up arrow at the elevator corridor. Ashleigh smiled and said, "I guess it's good to know people in high places."

"Or have attended University with your best mate and then later introduced him to his future wife. That way he always feels as if he owes you one," Liam replied as he reached into his jacket pocket and took out the keycard inserting it underneath the HPH button.

"Miss," a nasally voice pricked at Ashleigh's ears. "Miss what would you like to drink?"

Ashleigh lazily looked up from her seat and saw a young flight attendant smiling at her with a pen and paper ready to take her order.

"I'll have a club soda with a twist of lime."

The flight attendant nodded at Ashleigh and continued down the aisle. Ashleigh unlocked the tray table of the empty seat next to hers. The captain came on the loudspeaker saying,

"We have now reached 10,000 feet. You may turn on all electronics. However, due to the slight stormy weather we are experiencing, I'd like to leave the seatbelt sign on.

Our total flight time is eight hours twenty-five minutes. We will be arriving in Detroit at approximately at 1:05 A.M. local time. The weather in Detroit is a cool fifty degrees with mostly cloudy skies. We are happy to have you aboard Delta, and our flight attendants will be sure to take good care of you during the duration of our flight. Thanks again for choosing Delta Airlines."

Ashleigh reached for her handbag under the seat in front of her and pulled out her day planner, opening it to make sure her hotel confirmation number was easily accessible. She was going to stay the night at her favorite hotel near the airport. She really disliked the one hundred and sixty-one mile drive from Detroit to Grand Rapids. She had chosen to book a hotel room overnight, which would give her plenty of time to rest before her 12:15 P.M. flight home. The flight attendant returned handing Ashleigh her drink and a bag of peanuts.

"Thank you very much," Ashleigh whispered to the flight attendant, who smiled and then proceeded on her way delivering the remaining drinks. Ashleigh put her headphones on, and the sound of Michael Buble's sexy, smooth as silk voice, crooning the song "Feeling Good" went pulsing through her ears. She took a sip of her drink and placed the cup back on the tray table. The refreshing bubbles from the club soda coupled with the smooth jazz sounds coming through her ear buds returned her to her earlier thoughts of Liam, and she closed her eyes.

Chapter Five
Emily

Arriving home shortly after five-thirty, Emily quickly unloaded her car and grabbed the mail. It was a fairly quiet evening in her neighborhood. A few kids were riding their bikes down the sidewalk as the warm spring breeze gently rustled the newly blooming leaves on the oak trees that lined her street.

Emily lived in the historic Ottawa Hills neighborhood in Grand Rapids on Pontiac Road in a lovely four bedroom, three and half bath home. Purchasing the home fairly inexpensively and renovating it to suit her modern contemporary taste took about three months. Nearly everything was white except for an accented color palette mostly made up of Spanish Grey, Dark Vanilla, Grullo and Classic Black. The vanilla hues made the space feel warm and welcoming, while the grey and black tones gave it a polished finished. Emily thought the expansive dark hardwood floors throughout the kitchen and hallways, beautiful crown molding and marble counter tops in the kitchen and bathrooms added a touch of glamour.

Placing her Tod's indigo leather handbag and that day's mail on the glass console table in the foyer she kicked off her heels. Emily padded into her kitchen and opened the right side door of her stainless steel refrigerator pulling out all the ingredients needed to make a grilled chicken salad. She placed the items on the center island beside the double sink. Emily loved her kitchen but hated to cook. Craig, he loved to cook, and Emily always enjoyed watching him as he prepared delicious exotic meals. His favorite culinary works were Middle Eastern and Mediterranean dishes. Since Craig had been gone Emily had to learn the art of cooking for one, though her meals were far less culturally influenced.

Switching on her iPod, music from a 1980's mix poured through the speakers. While chopping an avocado into cubes her feet began to move in rhythm with the sounds of "Kiss" by Prince.

Great, everything's reminding me of Craig today.

Emily began to sing the chorus out loud while laying a halved chicken breast lightly brushed with olive oil, pepper and salt on the grill top. A few feet in front of the island sat her round kitchen table that had seats for four. She dropped her utensils at one of the place settings and pulled a bottle of Stinson Vineyards Monticello Chardonnay from the wine cooler located underneath the island.

The white wine was illuminated by the pendant lights hanging above causing a prism of colors to reflect through the glass. Tearing the already washed lettuce, she placed it carefully in the bowl, adding grape tomatoes, the cubed avocados followed by diced carrots, mushrooms and the chicken that she had cut into small strips. Blue cheese crumbles poured from the measuring cup, each one bouncing off the bed of greens as if a snowball fight had broken out between the leaves of lettuce.

As the sink filled up with warm water, Emily took a final sip of her wine. She heard her phone ring and went to retrieve it from her handbag that was still sitting on the table. She rolled her eyes at the sight of Ethan's name appearing on screen.

"Hi Ethan, what's up?" Emily answered the call casually, trying not to come off overly annoyed.

"Emily, I was calling to see if you'd like me to order dinner for us tonight?"

"Oh. Sorry Ethan, I've already eaten."

"Very well, Emily." He cleared his throat. "I'll see you in about an hour. Don't be late."

"It was thoughtful of you to consider me for dinner, Ethan. See you then."

The phone call with Ethan reminded Emily to text Andy, saying that she had plans with a friend and that she would catch up with him at the gym soon. She set her phone down on the table, picked up the dishtowel and hurriedly began wiping down the counters. All the dishes were washed, dried and put away.

Emily ran upstairs to her bedroom to slip into some jeans and her favorite electric blue, silk blouse from J. Crew. Looking at her reflection in the mirror she decided to touch up her makeup, lightly. She brushed her teeth, put on some more deodorant, glossed her lips with her favorite nude lip color and spritzed some perfume. The clock read

6:33 P.M. With a final check of her makeup in the living room mirror she grabbed her purse and glided out the door.

Staring at Ethan, Emily took note of his appearance. He was wearing a light blue button down shirt that had faint pinstripes paired with dark jeans. He rarely wore anything casual. She was used to seeing him in suit and tie. Even on Friday's when the dress code was relaxed it was rare that Ethan would come to work wearing jeans. For a guy he accessorized well, nothing too flashy, but he did occasionally style his suits with a pocket square, shiny cuff links or a sterling silver tie clip from Tiffany's. And he loved watches, Cartier, Burberry, Gucci and Movado. He probably had at least ten different styles he could circulate and mix and match through his wardrobe.

Ethan was now standing next to her. "You smell nice this evening," he remarked, his voice silvery.

"What a lovely compliment. Thank you, Ethan."

Why can't he be this nice all the time? Or maybe he was suggesting that I don't normally smell nice.

Running his hand slowly across the top of the conference room table and tracing the edges of the paper with his index finger, Emily imagined those strong hands were on her face, with that index finger tracing her jawline to her lips. Suddenly, Emily felt her whole body become hot, and she sipped her water.

A million thoughts began to rush into her mind. *This guy is your co-worker and don't forget a total ass. As hot as you think he is, you have to control yourself.*

Snapping out of her silence Emily asked, "So, what do you think?"

Shifting to an upright position, Ethan replied, "I only see the need for a couple of changes, Emily."

Emily smiled politely feeling relief curl through her thinking she could go home soon and not have to work the weekend.

"Oh, wait," Ethan scowled. "This is incorrect, totally and completely fucked up."

Emily leaned over the table to see what had Ethan so worked up. "Emily, tell me why you're using last year's percentages for the path to online purchases? That doesn't help us here and now," Ethan chided. "These numbers are a lot higher this year."

Ethan folded his arms across his broad chest while staring at Emily. Fire danced in his eyes as he waited for her to answer. Emily stood there motionless and stared at Ethan blankly. Confusion, anger and fear all coursed through her body. *Is Ethan trying to intimidate me?*

"I'm...I'm sorry Ethan, this is the numbers report that was given to me by Morgan," Emily replied, feeling her throat thick with anger and possibly tears.

"I don't need your excuses, Emily," he huffed. "And no, it wasn't. I emailed Morgan the current numbers. Check your records again."

Her fists balled up as she felt hot tears begin to prick her eyes. There was no way Emily was going to let this egomaniac bully her, causing her to cry like a frightened little girl.

"Just once I wish someone in this damn office could get something right and finished on time. Taking time out of my schedule to do other people's work is not something I'm fond of doing," he lectured. A glint of gold flecked in his brown eyes and he ran his hands through hair inhaling sharply.

"Excuse me Ethan, I'll be right back," Emily said firmly.

Pivoting on her heel, she walked to the door and turned the corner. Once she got far enough down the darkened hallway, assured that Ethan wouldn't hear her cries, she sprinted for the stairs. When Emily reached her office she closed the door and leaned against the cool wood trying to calm her jolted nerves. Morgan had left her in such a bind with all of her screw-ups.

Pulling up the email from Morgan, she saw that it was last year's numbers, but the email was not forwarded from Ethan. Morgan had just attached the wrong copy.

"Fuck me!" Emily blurted loudly. "Why didn't I fucking catch this mistake?" She was merely yelling for stress release for her own sake into her dimly lit office.

Emily slumped down in her chair and sat there for a moment staring at the email. Replaying the conversation with Ethan over and over in her mind and hearing his grating words wash over her, Emily felt like a scolded child who had done nothing but disappoint her parents. Ethan and Emily were equal colleagues, yet somehow he seemed far superior in his role with the company than she did.

"Who does Ethan think he is to treat me this way?"

A shudder moved through Emily as she heard the thunder and lightning wickedly cracking outside. She peered out her window and saw the rain coming down in sheets. Emily wrapped her arms around her shoulders and sighed deeply.

Knock…Knock…Knock

"Emily, is everything alright?" Ethan asked softly.

Emily would rather crawl under her desk and hide than face another berating from Ethan Carlson.

Chapter Six
Amanda

Lying in bed staring at the ceiling Amanda felt restless. She looked at the time. It was nearly one-thirty in the morning. She contemplated reading the latest issue of *Maison Bleue* magazine or finishing a chapter in the book she was reading. Flashes of lightning illuminated her bedroom, and seconds later, thunder rumbled in the distance. Startled by the noise Amanda sat up quickly, got out of bed and padded into the living room. Unlocking the sliding glass door to the balcony she felt the spring breeze hit her body. *Why was it was warmer now than it was earlier today? That's funny.* Only in the Midwest was running both the air-conditioner and heater in the same day considered completely normal.

She felt cold raindrops sporadically hit her skin like tiny needles. The skyline over Grand Rapids was especially colorful tonight giving it an iridescent glow from the lightning. The intense illuminating flashes and loud thunderous claps reminded Amanda of another stormy May night. A loud bang and jolt of lightning that seemed to be very close to the condo sent Amanda retreating back inside, closing the door behind her.

Crossing the living room, she peeked to see if Daniel was in his room. He was not. She wondered what bar he was in downtown, no doubt dancing the stormy night away. Opening the fridge she pulled out a bottle of coconut water and headed back to her bedroom. Perusing her well assorted collection of books, stemming from literary classics to murder mysteries and a few dirty novels for just plain fun, she saw the purple floral print box located on the top shelf.

Pulling the box down carefully, she slid the top back and started rifling through its contents. There were tons of photos, pictures of her days at Notre Dame and tailgating with friends before the big game. There was one of her standing with her father on the eighteenth green of the golf course at the club in her wedding gown. She sometimes really missed her father, but he wanted nothing to do with Amanda. All her life, Amanda was the apple of both her mother's and father's eyes. She excelled at so many things, swimming, tennis, volleyball and academics. Amanda was incredibly smart. She would have preferred school to be more social rather than studious, though.

She touched the photo, glossing her finger lightly over the image of her in the dress, remembering the feel of the duchess silk satin. Laughing to herself, she picked up the picture of her and Julie waving sparklers and wearing patriotic yet cheesy light-up Uncle Sam hats from the club's Fourth of July party. Finally Amanda found it, the photo she had been looking for, the one that shattered her entire world after being uploaded to the Bloomfield Buzz online gossip blog with the caption, "Amanda Ford's Rainy Night Rendezvous with a Mystery Man."

The man in the photo was not her then husband Brandon Ford. Nope, it was Andrew Langston. Andrew was the 21-year-old bartender at the country club with whom she started an affair four years ago. *How could I have been so careless? Brandon gave me everything I ever wanted and more.* Then, she remembered the loneliness she felt during her marriage. Brandon worked nearly every night and sometimes on weekends at the law firm.

Amanda heard the door to the condo open. She quickly leapt off the bed and shut off the light. Sweeping up the box of photos in her arms, she jumped under her covers with them pretending to be asleep. She did not want to be up another two hours listening to Daniel rambling on about all the young guys he met while out dancing. Even though she'd love to go toe to toe with Daniel and tell him about meeting Vince, she knew that she needed her sleep to function properly at work. Stretching out her legs and yawning, she grabbed her phone from her nightstand. The time was 2:10 A.M. She had an alert from Foursquare, Amanda signed reading the notification. *Looks like Ashleigh's in Detroit again. I miss Detroit.*

Getting out of bed quietly she tip-toed to her bookshelf and placed the box back on the top. Amanda took a quick few sips of her water and crawled back into bed, wrapping the sheets around her as the lightning flashed four times outside. There was a loud crashing boom that caused her to screw her eyes tight. Amanda pulled her blanket over her head and tried to shut out the noise.

Chapter Seven
Ashleigh

"Ladies and Gentlemen we are now in our final approach to Detroit. Please put your seats and tray tables in the upright and locked positions. We do have some weather in the Detroit area… some light rain showers. The local time is now 1:32 A.M. The Temperature at Detroit Metropolitan Airport is surprisingly warmer than usual, currently it's fifty-seven degrees. We're so glad you joined us, and thank you for flying with Delta Airlines." Ashleigh's eyes fluttered open slowly. She glanced out the window into the blackness of the night sky.

"Do you have any trash, Miss?" asked the flight attendant as she held out the garbage bag in Ashleigh's direction.

"I do not. Thank you," she replied.

The plane had a pretty smooth landing despite the rainy weather. Taxiing to the gate Ashleigh turned her phone back on to check her messages. A few Foursquare check-in notifications, a couple of Facebook updates and a tweet from @LIAMFROST15.

@ASHMPRESTON15 IT WAS WONDERFUL TO SEE YOU. {SMIRKS} HOPE YOU ARRIVED SAFELY IN DETROIT.

She typed a quick message to Liam.

@LIAMFROST15 ENJOYED SEEING YOU AS ALWAYS. I JUST LANDED. GOING TO THE HOTEL NOW. XO

The ride to the hotel from the airport was quiet except for the low hum of the radio in the cab which was set to WWSK 950 AM, Amanda's former place of work. The conversation was regarding the safety practices of the textile industry, recalling the horrific building collapse in Bangladesh that killed more than two-hundred and thirty people. Gazing out the window of the taxi she thought about all those poor people who lost loved ones, and she felt a deep sadness wash over her body.

The rain was beginning to fall at a faster pace now, and the few cars that were on the streets at this hour began to slow down. People in the Midwest seem to forget how to drive when it rains or snows. Ashleigh stretched her arms and yawned. She collected her belongings as the taxi came to a stop under the glass awning of the hotel.

Arriving in her room Ashleigh took off her coat and began to unpack her toiletries placing them on the vanity in the bathroom. The clock read 2:20. Ashleigh unzipped her suitcase finding her pajamas and slipped into them. After brushing her teeth and washing her face, she began to plug in all her electronics including her iPad and iPhone. Making sure the door of the room was locked and latched, she turned off the bathroom light and then climbed into bed. As she was just drifting off to sleep her phone lit up with an alert, it was a tweet from Liam.

@ASHMPRESTON15: GLAD TO HEAR YOU MADE IT TO YOUR HOTEL. WISHING YOU A RESTFUL NIGHT'S SLEEP.

A smile slid across her pale pink lips as she read the message from Liam. Placing the phone back on the nightstand, she closed her eyes. Suddenly, she found herself standing in the elevator lobby of the Corinthia Hotel with Liam.

The elevator car dinged alerting the pair that they had arrived on the floor of the penthouse. Holding the shiny chrome door for Ashleigh he gestured for her to exit the car. Liam led her through the beautiful conservatory style entrance which hosted a grand marble staircase. A flowing floral motif was etched in the walls of the stairwell and a stainless steel handrail with decorative detailing guides the way as you ascend to the second level. There was so much light in the space, showcasing the striking marble counter tops, impressive tailored furniture and glossy silk wallpaper.

When they arrived upstairs in the master suite Ashleigh turned to Liam and said, "Just like Bond, you've already managed to get me to your bedroom. Impressive, quite the place you have here."

"Why thank you, but you haven't seen anything yet."

Liam walked to the center of the room and drew back the curtains revealing the London skyline and spacious rooftop terrace, hardly what Ashleigh would consider a patio. In Grand Rapids, most people use their patios to take care of their herbs in small plastic orange flower pots and host summer barbeques with friends and family. But *this* was a terrace, and this particular London rooftop terrace was especially posh with its open fire pit, stylish furniture and inviting vitality pool. One could easily imagine hosting charity galas and cocktail receptions in a space such as this.

"Can I pour you some champagne?" Liam asked holding up a bottle of Laurent-Perrier Brut.

Still clutching her cocktail from the bar in her hand she replied, "I'd love some champagne, but may I finish this first please?"

Smiling back at her Liam popped the cork and began pouring two glasses.

"You can, but you must take a sip of this champagne," Liam directed while handing her the crystal flute.

Ashleigh took the glass in her hand which held the pale golden colored liquid. Taking a sip of the drink the bubbles tingled in her throat. She immediately noticed the fresh crisp mix of citrus and ginger. It was lovely.

"So? What do you think of the champagne?"

"It's delicious. I don't usually care for sweet drinks, but this has a crispness that is very pleasing," she replied.

Liam chuckled politely and said, "Very good description. I'm going to guess that you're a food and wine writer?"

"Close, I write mostly about hotels and the amenities they offer—the details of the rooms, the spas, the restaurants and bars in the hotels. I also include places to shop and points of interests when visiting cities and locations. My specialty is writing reviews directed at working women and women who travel with their husbands on business, features that have suggestions giving the wives something to do while their husbands are in meetings."

Liam took a drink of champagne and smiled at Ashleigh replying, "That sounds quite interesting."

"Why are you here Liam, besides the fact that your best mate made sure he put you up here in the penthouse?" she asked. Her hazel eyes watched intently as he took his jacket off. Removing the jacket gave her a better view of his toned arms and slender build. He was even more delicious in just a dress shirt and tie.

"I'm the Managing Editor for *Wanderlust Magazine* here in London. Our focus is food and travel. Not such an international man of mystery anymore, now am I?"

Ashleigh replied with a soft laugh, "I guess not."

"Shall we adjourn to the terrace?" Liam inquired while loosening his tie.

He grabbed the ice bucket with the bottle of champagne off the marble top bar, and Ashleigh nodded as if actually uttering the word, yes. Liam and Ashleigh walked onto the terrace. It was a cool night. There was a breeze in the night air, and from Liam's penthouse view she could see Lord Nelson's column. Liam lit a fire and refreshed Ashleigh's champagne. He crossed the terrace back to the bedroom where he picked up a cashmere throw and brought it out to Ashleigh. She kicked off her strappy sandals, stretched out her legs and covered them with the blanket.

Liam and Ashleigh talked until nearly three in the morning, getting to know each other and sharing stories from their childhood, including a sweet story about how Liam inherited his Grandfather's Scottish Deerhounds after he passed away. She told Liam about growing up in Troy, Michigan, her college days spent at Central Michigan University and why she chose News Editorial Journalism as a major.

After one and a half bottles of champagne and a bottle of sparkling mineral water, the sky unleashed a downpour of cold water over the city. They quickly sprinted inside the penthouse. Noticing that Ashleigh had forgotten her heels, Liam raced back out to retrieve them. He nearly fell on the glossy marble tile before turning back, prize in hand. Liam darted inside and was completely drenched. Ashleigh giggled the entire time.

"Oh you find this to be funny do you? Americans you're all the same, laughing when someone nearly gets injured," Liam said while smiling from ear to ear.

Doubled over and laughing Ashleigh tried to catch her breath saying, "I'm sorry, Liam, but you have to know I would have helped you up if you fell on your ass."

Ashleigh walked into the master bath and pulled a fluffy white towel off the rack.

Liam called after her, "Yes that might be true but, only after you had a good laugh at my expense."

Handing him the towel, she replied, "You should take those clothes off Liam before you catch a cold."

"I think you're right, and it's very late. I have a 10:30 A.M. meeting with the Executive Chef at Plum + Spilt Milk."

"Oh...oh right...absolutely," Ashleigh muttered watching Liam carefully as he slipped off his soaked shirt revealing his chiseled abs. Her cheeks flushed and she swallowed hard at the sight of his perfectly sculpted body.

It seemed that time along with Ashleigh's breathing stopped for a moment. She was visually stunned at the sight of Liam's nearly naked body. Feeling all her muscles convulse at once she began to rake her eyes over every inch of him. From his precisely cut biceps, her gaze trailed to the defined muscles on Liam's chest, and finally to his trim waist which showcased those "pure sex lines" women always talk about. Standing in front of her wearing only a pair of trousers, Ashleigh noticed just how long Liam's legs were. Ashleigh's eyes darted to the bed that was inches from where she stood, visualizing the two of them rolling across the satin sheets together in a tangle of limbs.

Catching her stare, Liam shot Ashleigh a wolfish grin. She managed to snap out of her lustful thoughts and say, "I'm sorry. I definitely wouldn't want you to be tired for your meeting tomorrow."

"Ashleigh, darling I had such a lovely evening in your company. May I see you again tomorrow?" Liam approached Ashleigh slowly. He slipped his hand around her waist kissing her gently on each cheek. Ashleigh could feel the heat radiating from his bare skin. Her knees weakened and her heart raced. He released her from his grip and she managed not to lose her balance.

"I would like nothing more Liam," she said while looking up at him through her long lashes. "Thank you for a wonderful evening. I am so glad I met you."

They exchanged business cards and made plans to meet for lunch before attending the rest of their scheduled events for that day.

Bang!

A loud thunder clap awoke Ashleigh from her slumber. Lightning flashed, illuminating the entire room. Climbing out of bed she padded to the window and drew back the sheer curtains to view the spectacular light show. Thunder and lightning volleyed like Rodger Federer and Andy Murray during a match of the Wimbledon finals.

Ashleigh stood in silence clutching her arms entranced by the beauty of the dark cloud formations. Adrenaline began pumping through her system as she counted the time between each intense rumble of thunder waiting to see where the next bolt of lightning would strike in the ominous blackness. The anticipation was almost too much for her to handle as her eyes darted around the skyline. Ashleigh's throat went dry, her breathing increased and a sharp pain slashed across her arm. The sound struck with the force of a giant bass drum raging through her entire body.

Stumbling slightly, her back hit the wall; Ashleigh released the tight grip she had on her arm feeling the warmth of blood flowing over heated skin. A sharp exhale escaped her lips as she slid down the wall. Reaching for the desk Ashleigh tore away a piece of paper from the notepad and covered the mark she dug into her flesh. Hot tears pricked her eyes as the white paper turned dark crimson. Burying her face in her hands Ashleigh allowed herself a good cry.

Choking back the sobs as the bleeding stopped, calmness spread over her when the rain began to fall, loosening the tension knotted in her stomach. Forgetting the pain of that dark afternoon, she jerked her phone from its charger flipping to a photo of him. A ghost of smile crossed her lips.

Some people like rumbling sound of thunderstorms. Ashleigh used to enjoy them, but they had become a continuous painful reminder of what she'd once loved and eventually lost.

Chapter Eight
Emily

Emily sat with her legs curled under her on Ethan's black couch, the warm buttery leather felt heavenly to touch. His office was warm yet masculine and smelled like cedarwood mixed with vanilla. A sleek dark espresso desk occupied the space in front of the back wall with a black leather high-back chair, both from Cooper Bentley's Classic Collection. Tucked into the corner was a minibar, gorgeous etched crystal drinkware delicately lined the countertop. A separate conference table, with seating for six, sat a few feet to the left of his desk. Black and white photographs, mostly of landscapes and nature, lined the walls in dark espresso colored frames. A large flat screen television sat on the wall across from his desk streaming various sales and marketing videos, world news - especially the BBC, or sometimes one of the music channels. Ethan's choice of music ranged from seventies rock, frequently playing tunes by Led Zeppelin, The Rolling Stones and The Who, to anything by

311. Tonight, Ethan had decided to watch the local news to monitor the storm.

Ethan suggested to Emily that they would be safer in his office, rather than on the second floor completely surrounded by glass. She couldn't argue with his logic. Emily brought the three-wick candle from her office, in case the power went out at least they would have some light.

Ethan had come to her office and actually apologized for his brash tone with her over the infographics, admitting he was quite stressed with the upcoming proposal for LA Business Design. Landing this account was going to be huge for Cooper Bentley. LA Business Design was one of the world's leading retailers in home and office furniture. In October they will open their first flagship store in Hong Kong followed by a location in London. If Ethan and his team manage to score the account, Cooper Bentley will finally be sold internationally, positioning their small company to gain exposure from a vast new customer base.

"Emily, I've sent you the revised numbers for the shopping habits of men and women when shopping for furniture, and our national retail numbers report for all stores. You should have everything you need to complete your project."

"Great, my team and I will have it done by the end of the weekend," Emily replied cheerfully as she closed her laptop.

"The storm is still pretty strong," he said pushing to his feet. "I don't think it's safe enough for you… either one of us to drive right now." He stood with his back to her as he peered out the window. Ethan stood tall and powerful, allowing Emily to view his deliciously sculpted shoulders and back. Emily was fixated on his silky brown hair that fell just above the collar on his shirt. She wondered what it would be like to run her fingers through the dark waves. Ethan turned to face her placing his palms flat on the conference table asking, "Would you care for a drink while we wait for it to blow over?"

Emily blinked and felt her chest tighten, "Sure, Ethan, that sounds nice."

Ethan handed Emily what appeared to be whiskey, she could tell by the dark color and the smoky aroma. When she took a sip, it instantly warmed her belly. Ethan moved to the black leather club chair that sat in front of the couch. Placing his glass on a leather coaster, he took his right arm and unbuttoned the cuff on his left sleeve. Emily watched him intently as he repeated the same action with his opposite hand and rolled his sleeves up on each arm.

The silence between them was unnerving. All Emily could hear was the sound of rain shrilly tapping the windows and her heart thundering in her ribcage. Emily shifted her body, blurting out, "So, Ethan I heard you and Libby broke up?"

Fuck! Panic swept through Emily. It was just office gossip. It wasn't like Emily and Ethan were buddies, although, she had gone with him to lunch on occasion, and she met Libby a few times. But discussing the intimate details of each other's lives was not something to which the pair was accustomed.

Ethan's eyes narrowed as he picked up his glass. He took a sip and replied, "Truthfully, she and I just didn't see eye to eye on some things, and after a while we were just going through the motions of being a couple. I honestly fell out of love with her months before we actually broke up. I shouldn't have stayed with her, but I felt bad."

Emily couldn't believe that Ethan was opening up to her so casually about something deeply personal.

Why did you feel bad?" she said quickly. *Fuck, now that does make me sound nosey.*

Ethan cleared his throat, "Libby had some emotional issues and was seeking treatment at the time. I guess I stayed with her out of guilt because I was losing interest, not because of her issues, but because we both wanted different things. Big picture stuff, you know?"

"Yes, I can certainly understand that being an issue. Sorry to hear that, Ethan."

Emily could definitely relate. She often wondered if that was the reason why Craig disappeared from her life one night never to be heard from again. Was it big picture stuff, or was it because of life in general? Craig's job at CME Group was highly stressful. Dealing with the day to day pressure made Craig high strung at times, some people just don't manage their stress well. Emotions take over, and you become lost inside your own mind.

71

Ethan asked if he could freshen up her beverage, and she said yes. The shadows from trees swaying outside danced across the walls of Ethan's office. Sweeping her hair up into a quick ponytail, coldness brushed over Emily's neck sending a chill down her spine. Shivering, she pulled the soft blanket that rested over the back of the couch across her legs. A smile slid across Ethan's lips. Curious, Emily wondered what could have melted Ethan's seemingly hardened exterior.

"What are you smiling about Ethan?"

He paused for a moment and handed her the glass, "You're cute, Miss Greene."

"That's two compliments you've bestowed on me this evening, Mr. Carlson. I'm not really sure how to take that," she replied arching one of her eyebrows at him. "You don't seem to really like me, and you don't seem very impressed with the level of my work."

Bang!

Emily jumped about a foot off of the couch and spilled a bit of her drink on Ethan's coffee table.

"Fuck! I'm sorry Ethan," her voice broke. "I didn't mean to, spill my drink."

She was visibly shaken by the onslaught of thunder and lightning that continually raged outside. Ethan walked towards her, removing the glass from her trembling hand, placing it on the table.

"Emily, it's okay," he mumbled softly rubbing his hands over her arms. Ethan eased her back to the couch and wrapped the blanket around her shoulders.

"Do you want to watch a movie or listen to some music, Emily?" Ethan asked softly, his brown eyes intensely fixed on her. "I know it's kind of late, but once the storm passes I can follow you and make sure you get back to your house safely."

"That's awfully nice of you Ethan, but I know you have better things to do with your time tonight than worry about the safety of a grown ass woman."

Flipping to the hard rock channel on the TV, Ethan chuckled softly and replied, "Emily, your safety is my *only* priority tonight."

Seriously, "When The Levee Breaks?" This song is so fitting for tonight. Emily felt her heart thump in her throat as Robert Plant's sexy voice crooned the chorus.

Taking a seat next to Emily on the couch, Ethan lightly grazed the back of her hand with his fingertips. Electric sparks ignited shifting the mood.

"Emily," he muttered softly sweeping her long bangs off her cheek.

Emily's breath hitched, and her body trembled a bit when his hand found its way to the curve of her jaw and his lips found their way to hers.

"Ethan," she pulled back breathless. Her heart was racing. That kiss was everything she imagined it would be.

Gone were the cordial conversations, exchanged pleasantries and the lukewarm flirtations. She felt it. He felt it. Now…the "it" that existed between them was pure desired attraction, and it was as charged as the vibrating jolts of lightning crashing outside.

"Shhh, no more talking Em," Ethan whispered. He dipped his head, brushing his lips to Emily's. Emily inhaled his oh-so masculine and fresh scent causing her mind to dizzy. Her lips parted allowing Ethan the sensual pleasure of delivering lush rolling licks to her tongue. Emily's head was spinning. Mere hours ago she was cursing this handsome man who had her on the edge of a meltdown, and now she was wrapped up safely in his arms kissing him.

Emily wished the storm outside would never quit.

Chapter Nine
Amanda

Amanda was slightly exceeding the speed limit, she had just been to her monthly waxing appointment at Studio Smooth in East Grand Rapids. It was nearly nine and she needed to hit up Macy's before she went to work at ten. Today, the mall was open an hour early for the holiday weekend sales. Arriving at the mall she had about forty-five minutes to shop for a dress for her yet to be confirmed Saturday night date with Vince.

Knowing exactly what it was she was looking for she made a beeline to the Misses section, in search of red and black dresses. Something sexy, yet sophisticated, she thought. Amanda carefully explored the racks containing numerous poly-cotton, rayon-spandex blends and sifted through the endless amounts of somewhat appealing Jessica Simpson and Style & Co. designs. Some days she still couldn't believe she was shopping off-the-rack, but hopefully those days would soon be behind her and then she could call up Courtney at Gucci and have her pull designs for her special dates and events once again. It was so depressing how her life had fallen to pieces, but she managed to stay upbeat outwardly. Of course, Amanda sometimes helped herself put on that happy face by taking a Zoloft or the rare Lithium which helped with her moods and depression.

Finding a few red and black dresses that were suitable to her taste, she walked to the dressing room and tried them on. Ultimately she decided the sleeveless red Calvin Klein sheath was the winner, plus, it was on sale so that made the decision easier. Desperately wanting to peek in the shoe department, Amanda looked at her phone for the time. She had about twenty-three minutes to pay and be on her way to work. She knew she already had a pair of nude Jimmy Choo patent peep-toes in her collection that would go perfectly with the dress, there wouldn't be enough time for new shoes today.

While still in the dressing room, Amanda pulled out a silver and pink flask with some vodka in it. Taking her happy pills, as she called them, out of her purse and washing them down with two gulps. She popped two

Altoids in her mouth while making her way to the checkout counter.

A woman with short dark hair and glasses, whose nametag said, "Angie" was standing behind the counter placing dresses back on hangers.

"Did you find everything you needed today, Miss?"

"Yes, I did. Thank you very much."

"Will you be putting this on your Macy's charge today?"

"I will not," she stated firmly while handing Angie her debit card. "Oh, I'm also a mall employee. I work at The Bath Shop."

"Do you have your ID on you to prove that you work there?"

Already a step ahead of her, Amanda flashed her nametag and handed Angie her Driver's License. Glancing down, peering over her glasses at the nametag and then Amanda's license, Angie smiled as if acknowledging they were both sisters in the customer service industry.

"Very good. Thank you, Mrs. Parsons. We are offering all mall employees an additional fifteen percent off today.

So, you will get twenty-five percent off your entire purchase with us."

Thinking to herself, it's actually *Miss* Parsons you bitch, she didn't have the time or energy to correct her.

"Would you like your receipt with you or in the bag?"

"I'll take the receipt. Thank you, Angie."

Walking away from the checkout counter, Amanda pulled her phone from her purse and dialed Vince's number, which she had already put on her favorite's list. The phone rang four times before she heard Vince's voice, but it was his outgoing voice mail message.

"Hello, you have reached Vince Everett. I am currently away from my phone. Please leave me a message and I will return your call as soon as I can."

Exiting Macy's and entering the main part of the mall, Amanda spoke into the phone saying,

"Hi Vince, this is Amanda Parsons. We met yesterday at the boutique, My Sister's Closet. I was hoping that you were free tomorrow evening for dinner and drinks? This is my cell number. I will be at work until about seven this evening, please call me when you get the chance and let me know if tomorrow evening works for you."

Arriving at work and on time for once, Amanda headed to the back room placing her things in her locker. Grabbing her handbag she walked to the bathroom and took out her flask. She took a few swigs of vodka. The liquid burned her throat, and her stomach became hot. There was a knock at the door.

"Just a minute and I will be out," Amanda stated calmly while pressing toothpaste to her toothbrush.

"Okay thanks," the chirpy voice replied.

Amanda didn't recognize the voice on the other side of the door. Once she finished brushing her teeth she reached for her favorite lip gloss and applied a fair amount. She unlocked the door, but whoever knocked was nowhere around.

Amanda's phone began to ring as she was placing it into her locker. She quickly retrieved it and saw it was Vince calling. She immediately walked to the back corner past the bathroom and answered.

"Hello," she answered cheerfully.

"Hello Amanda. This is Vince."

"Hi Vince. How are you today?"

"I'm doing very well. I was calling to tell you that I am free tomorrow evening for dinner. I'd like to take you to a French restaurant that I am quite fond of. Do you like French Food?"

Amanda loved French cuisine. Her favorite dishes were tartiflette and truffade, but like most, she loved French desserts. She paused, she didn't know of any French restaurants in Grand Rapids.

"I adore French food. Where is the restaurant?"

"It's in New York City," he replied.

Amanda was floored, after a few moments of silence she managed to muster the question, "Did you say New York City?"

"Yes, I did. Is that okay? Do you have to work Sunday?"

"Nope, my schedule is clear." Amanda's insides were screaming, and her heart began to beat wildly in her chest.

"Good. My driver will pick you up at your apartment at 5:30 tomorrow evening. He will bring you to the airport, and we will leave promptly at 6:00 o'clock. Pack what you like, but you really won't need anything that I cannot readily obtain for you. We will be staying the night in the city."

"Oh…okay. See you tomorrow Vince."

"Goodbye Amanda."

Amanda ended the call and smiled from ear to ear noticing how easy it was to slip back into her country club mannerisms. The conversation, while casual gave her the opportunity to present a refined demeanor. She walked out of the backroom onto the sales floor, butterflies danced in her stomach. Maybe she wouldn't need the rest of that vodka after all.

Chapter Ten
Emily

The sidewalk was still wet from the early morning's severe weather that had rumbled through the city. Careful not to get her pants wet, Emily walked slowly avoiding any pools or puddles of water. Surprisingly, she was awake and ready for the day despite only getting a few hours of sleep. A bigger surprise was Ethan admitting he had wanted to ask her out for some time. She confessed her feelings to him as well, and they ended up talking until well after midnight.

After dropping of her stuff in her office, Emily entered the conference room and immediately smelled the rich aroma of delicious blends of fresh-brewed coffee. On the table were three to-go boxes, and as luck would have it, one of them was the Kona blend. She filled her cup and picked up one-half of a plain bagel, while looking around for light cream cheese. She found the container on the opposite side of the table. Just as she was about to spread the bagel Ethan walked in the room. She noticed he was wearing dark denim jeans paired with a collared shirt under a light blue V-neck cashmere sweater. *He was wearing jeans on a Friday.*

Stopping behind her, he whispered in her ear, "Good morning Em." The sultry tone of his voice sent a pleasurable shiver through her body, and she felt her nipples harden. Ethan reached over and ran the back of his hand down her bare arm. Frazzled, Emily accidently dropped the knife and the bagel she was holding. Both hit the table at the same time. The sound of the knife clanking back and forth was ringing in Emily's ears.

Ethan He picked up the knife and bagel as Emily stood there frozen, feeling the blood pooling in her ears. He motioned to the cream cheese with the knife while looking in Emily's direction with a raised eyebrow. She nodded as if saying *yes*. Ethan took the knife and spread the topping over the sourdough bread, moving it back and forth circling the top.

Christ, could he do that any slower or sexier? He's totally eye-fucking the shit out of me. Oh, Mr. Carlson you do not play fair.

When he finished, the knife was gently placed back on the serving tray, and he took his left hand as if presenting the bagel to Emily like a prize. Still frozen, Emily felt her heart pounding rapidly in her chest, and the deep ache between her thighs was pure torture. Seconds later, which felt like minutes, she finally reached both of her hands up removing the bagel from Ethan's grasp.

Ethan moved from standing in front of her to standing behind her and whispered in her ear,

"You look beautiful today, Em." Ethan stopped to tangle his fingers through a few of Emily's loose curls that hung just below her shoulder. "Good enough to eat," Ethan hissed seductively. "So delicious in fact, I'd love nothing more than to spread you out on this table and fuck you until you beg me to stop."

Emily's mouth curled up as she bit her bottom lip. Walking to the left side of the table, Ethan grabbed an apple out of the basket and lightly tossed it up in the air with his right hand. The apple came back down and Ethan grasped it, pulling it up to his mouth and taking a bite. He looked back giving Emily a wink, and with that he walked out of the room.

All the air expelled from Emily's chest as her palms hit the flat surface of the table causing the bagel to roll a few inches towards the edge. *Fuck me! Did he just say that?*

Desperately trying to compose herself, Emily stood there thinking about the previous evening with Ethan. Knowing the super-charged heated attraction was still rippling between them today sent shockwaves coursing through Emily's entire body. Emily couldn't help but grin wickedly as she walked back to her office. It was going to be a good day.

After work, Emily had entirely too much energy. She headed straight to the gym and ran nearly six and half miles on the treadmill. Standing at the water cooler she came face to face with Libby Westin and a twinge of anxiety and a flash of guilt crashed through Emily.

"Hi Emily," Libby gleefully hummed. "How are you?"

"Libby, so nice to see you again," Emily replied. "I'm doing okay. What's new with you?"

She studied the soft lines on Libby's face noticing the delicate splash of freckles under her vibrant blue eyes. Libby was an attractive woman; she had a naturally slim build with a narrow waist and pale pink lips that pressed into a full pout.

"I could be better. Ethan and I broke up, and that's been hard to deal with," she said, while pinning her dark red mane of hair up into a swinging ponytail.

Emily's spine stiffened when she noticed the glint of pain flash in Libby's eyes. What could Emily say to Libby, without sounding the least bit overjoyed? Emily did what all women do, she faked it.

"I'm sorry to hear that Libby," Emily offered giving her a sympathetic smile.

Libby kept talking about how much she missed Ethan. Emily knew she was in dangerous territory, listening to her go on and on about how still loved Ethan and was hopeful he reconsider the break-up was heart-wrenching. Barely concentrating on Libby's words, Emily replayed the hot and heavy kissing session she and Ethan participated in the night before. The sound of a gruff male voice pulled Emily from her lustful thoughts.

"Hey, Emily, it's good to see you here working out," Andy snorted.

Knowing she needed to get away from Libby, Emily apprehensively asked Andy to show her a few core exercises. He happily said he would, allowing Emily to say goodbye to Libby, while offering a comforting touch to the arm followed by a "hang in there" sentiment.

The pair walked over to the mats and began with some light stretching. Once Emily saw Libby comfortably situated on the bike in spin class, she thanked Andy and said, "I'm sorry, I have to be leaving. I have a friend coming over for dinner."

Andy frowned, replying, "I hate to see you go, but I love to watch you walk away."

A repulsive shiver curled through Emily. *Gross. He's such a douchebag meathead.*

"Andy," Emily huffed. "Do you really think that line sounds remotely sexy?"

Caught off guard by her snide tone, he replied, "Worked on you once, babe."

"Actually, Andy that wasn't the line you used on me. And for the record, it wasn't that great," Emily snapped.

Andy's mouth hung open as if the words she uttered were completely foreign to his self-inflated ego. She turned on her heel and started to walk away, but Andy pulled her into his solid frame. Her sweaty back clung against his rippled chest, he was completely stiff.

"Let me go, Andy," she warned.

Andy panted a few deep breaths. Emily cringed as his warm breath drifted across the back of her neck over her ear. Curling his heavy arm around her waist, she felt the complete weight of him. Andy's body was a fortress of stone and dominant alpha maleness.

"Don't cause a scene, Emily," he whispered, as he pressed his palm against her flat stomach then told her to raise her hands above her head.

"Spread your legs," he grinned. Now squat," he commanded.

She did as she was told, and he backed away. Andy made Emily do ten squats all the while muttering sexual innuendos through low groaning noises.

Disgusting pig.

Although to everyone else in the gym, it just looked like a typical scene—a trainer helping a fellow gym member, but for *Emily* she knew Andy was trying to make her as uncomfortable as possible.

When she finished her set, Emily shot him an icy glare and grabbed her water bottle.

"Bitch," he scowled after her. Emily ignored him and walked briskly to the ladies locker room.

After that unpleasantness, Emily decided to change gyms immediately.

Chapter Eleven
Ashleigh

"Good Afternoon, Miss Preston," Ashleigh heard a familiar voice say as she crossed the lobby of her building.

"Good Afternoon, Thomas," she cheerfully greeted the man with slicked back dark red hair. "How are things at the River House today?"

Thomas was one of four security guards that worked at the building complex. He was a nice older man, about fifty-five if Ashleigh had to guess, with a short and stalky build and bright blue eyes. Ashleigh frequently brought a postcard from the cities she travelled to for Thomas to hang in his office. He was determined to collect post-cards from all the fifty states and as many exotic locales as possible, Thomas had the travel bug, bad. Unfortunately, she didn't have one for him today since she traveled to London so frequently. Behind his desk, Thomas kept a binder of all of Ashleigh's articles, often experimenting with recipes from the food she described in her features. She thought it was sweet.

Helping Ashleigh to the elevator with her second bag he said, "Things are good here. How was your trip to London?"

"Honestly, it was too short, but I'm glad to be back home, if only for a short while anyway."

"Oh, where are you off to next Miss Preston?" Thomas asked, giving her a wide-eyed look.

"I'll be off to New York City next month for an entire week."

"The Big Apple. I've always wanted to visit the city that never sleeps, Miss Preston. Never had the chance to though. Maybe someday I will," he said giving her a wink. "Have a nice rest of your afternoon."

"I bet you make it there Thomas. You do the same."

Ashleigh lived on the 30th floor of the River House in a posh three-bedroom penthouse that had floor to ceiling windows with three terraces that offered panoramic views of the city, one of which over looked the Grand River. Ashleigh loved her penthouse, it was quite the investment, but thanks to her hard work and a guardian angel she was able to afford an incredible lifestyle. Her home was filled with light quartz countertops, rich dark custom cabinets and white ceramic floor tile throughout, aside from the bedrooms and living room where plush carpet covered the floors.

She took her suitcases to her bedroom which was her private retreat—her personal sanctuary. A color scheme of silver pink, dark grey and silver chalice accented the space from accent rugs and pillows to picture frames and décor. Ashleigh had a separate seating area in the master suite with two dove-grey club chairs and a Venetian style mirrored coffee table near the fireplace that faced three large windows with a view of the river. Her most prized possession was the custom California king sized bed that sat upon a dove-grey tailor made tweed frame adorned with studded pewter-finish nail heads featuring a matching winged headboard. It's a pity that Ashleigh has never *properly* broken in her gorgeous bed. Maybe, someday she would.

After she had unpacked and put some of her laundry in the wash she went to the kitchen to grab a bottle of water. Upon inspection of her fridge and pantry she realized she would need to hit up the market. Taking a chicken breast out of the freezer, she put it in a plastic bag and covered it with some marinade before placing it back in the refrigerator.

She began to make a grocery list: bananas, milk, yogurt, bread, lettuce, San Pellegrino.

Finishing her inventory, Ashleigh grabbed her keys, the faint sound of thunder rumbled in the distance. An eerie shiver washed over her body, and she placed the keys back on the counter. Picking up the phone she decided to have her groceries delivered instead.

Chapter Twelve
Ashleigh and Emily

"Emily! I'm here," Ashleigh called as she shut the front door behind her with her foot. The smell of vanilla made Ashleigh's mouth water. She made her way from the foyer down the hallway and past her guest bathroom to find Emily was baking in the kitchen. Ashleigh grinned, noticing that Emily was whipping up a Blueberry Buckle. *Is it odd that someone who hates cooking with a passion loves to bake?*

"Should I pour some wine for us?" Ashleigh inquired.

"Of course," Emily said while scooping the mixture into a large cake pan. "You know where the glasses and the bottle opener are. Go for it."

Ashleigh opened the wine and the smell of crisp gooseberries and melon cascaded out. Pouring two glasses, she handed one to Emily.

"So, how's Liam?" Emily inquired after she took a sip of the wine.

"Liam is good."

Emily looked at Ashleigh sideways and smiled. "Is that all you have to say? Just that Liam is good?"

With a laugh she ignored Emily's question and just smiled. While Emily finished cleaning up her kitchen, Ashleigh padded to the living room and noticed several photographs scattered on the coffee table.

"Emily, what is all of this on your coffee table? Are you getting ready to start scrap-booking like my Aunt Gloria?" she joked. Ashleigh began fumbling through the photos, noticing a very young Emily in most of the pictures.

"Oh that. No, but close. I want to scan them in to my computer, and then I am going to place the originals in a photo album."

Even though Emily was still going on about the pictures, Ashleigh's ears turned off when she came across a photo of Emily standing next to a guy wearing a white button down shirt and khaki shorts. Carefully examining the picture she noticed something familiar about him. Emily sat next to Ashleigh on the couch and picked up a few photos placing them back in the box.

"Emily, this is Craig right?" she inquired while holding up the photo in front of Emily's face.

"Yes," she replied with a deep sigh.

Craig Walker had vanished from the face of the Earth and out of Emily's life. Five years ago, Emily had gone home to Marquette for Thanksgiving. When she returned to their apartment in Chicago, Craig was gone. No note, no goodbye, nothing.

The situation was puzzling because Emily had talked to Craig several times over the few days she was at her parents' house. Things seemed normal. Nothing alerted her that there was trouble. When Emily tried to call his cell phone to let him know she was on her way to Chicago, she received a message saying the number had been disconnected. She tried a few more times thinking it was a technological error, but Emily kept getting the same message. When Emily walked into the apartment she found his closet empty. Craig took nothing else, just his personal effects. None of Craig's friends knew anything about where he had gone, either, and no one at the CME Group seemed to want to return Emily's calls. Both of Craig's parents had died when he was in college, and he wasn't close with any other relatives, leaving her with no leads.

Over the next several months Emily would get together with Craig's best friends, Jared and Scott, once a week to talk about Craig and try to solve the puzzle that was his disappearance. Talking with them helped Emily deal with her emotional heartbreak and slight depression. As the frigid winter dragged on, their meetings became less regular. Jared had gotten engaged; Scott was promoted at work and moved to Austin.

Determined not to let Craig's sudden vanishing act affect her life, Emily began to see a therapist so she wouldn't become an emotional wreck for her friends and co-workers. However, being in Chicago and living in the condo they once shared kept her from moving on. All Emily could do was leave the city and try to come to terms with the fact that Craig Walker had vanished and was determined not to be found. When summer came she landed a job at Cooper Bentley and made a fresh start in Grand Rapids.

"Emily," she paused for a moment. "Don't freak out, but I think I saw Craig in London."

The blood drained from her cheeks. "What?" Emily said in a tight voice as she turned to face Ashleigh.

"Listen, when I was at Heathrow coming home, there was a guy who was standing outside the coffee shop in my terminal. I kept trying to place him because he looked so familiar, but I had only seen Craig's photo a few times. I wasn't sure until this moment, but seeing those steely blue eyes I'm sure it was him—so certain I'd bet my last paycheck on it."

Emily could barely hear Ashleigh talking over the thundering beat of her heart. She was dizzy, not knowing if she was going to throw up or pass out.

"Emily, are you okay?"

Collecting her thoughts and looking directly at Ashleigh, Emily shook her head in slight disbelief and said, "Wait...so... you're telling me that you think the guy you saw in London is Craig?"

"Emily, I swear it's the same guy. I should have taken a photo of him with my phone. He walked past me as a little kid knocked over my suitcase, and Craig picked it up for me. He had an American accent, and he looks almost the same, a little older—hot as sin."

Emily took another drink of wine, and then another, finishing her glass. The timer for the oven buzzed, startling her. Outside, the rain was beginning to pour again, and the thunder was so loud Emily felt as if it was right on top of her house.

"Hello, Earth to Emily?"

"Yeah, I'm fine," she lied. "It's weird to think that after all this time Craig would suddenly resurface."

Could it really be him? For a second Emily thought about booking a ticket to London and going on a quest to find him, but what would she say to him after all this time? What the fuck happened to you? That question would be at the top of the list. Along with a slap to the face followed by a deep passionate kiss to his generous full lips.

Emily was snapped from her daydream that reunited her with Craig when Ashleigh spoke. "True. I wonder if he actually lives in London."

Shaking her head Emily replied, "I'm not sure I'll ever know."

Emily had tried to search for him on the internet and even on Facebook, but the search always comes up with the same three Craig Bennett Walker's, and none of their pictures resemble his likeness.

"Well enough about Craig. I want to know more about your night with Ethan."

Handing Ashleigh a slice of cake, a smile returned to Emily's face as the bewildered look that had just been there evaporated.

"Honestly, I cannot believe it happened. Ashleigh. The electricity that sparked when he kissed me ignited instantly, like he set my blood on fire."

"Wow…" Ashleigh swallowed hard. "That's intense. And he told you that he and Libby ended their relationship?"

Nodding, Emily replied, "I can hardly believe it, but I'm definitely not sad about it."

"So, did anything else happen?"

"Well nothing as exciting as what you're conjuring in your dirty mind, I assure you of that, Ash. However, it wasn't for his lack of trying to fuck me right there in his office. Believe me he tried—*relentlessly*. I probably would have let him, but my stupid brain kept telling me to make him work a little harder for it," Emily said with an aching groan. "Ash," Emily wailed, "It took *everything* in me not to give in to Ethan's expert hands as they skimmed over my body. I mean *Jesus*. The man has amazingly strong hands *and* long fingers." Emily's eyebrow arched as she shot Ashleigh a sly smile.

Fanning a hand across her face, Ashleigh swallowed the last bite of cake and said, "So let me get this straight, the man who drives you insane now wants to drive you out of your mind with pleasure?"

Emily shrugged and smiled.

"This is truly quite the turn of events. Sounds to me like things are going your way, Em. I wouldn't give Craig another fucking thought. Just move forward with your life."

Raising an eyebrow, Emily said, "I could advise you of the same where Liam is concerned, Ash. I know you're still dealing with your feelings for Nick, but don't you want to get married and start a family?"

"Not all of us women want the white picket fence, the 2.5 kids and the shuffling back and forth between swim lessons and soccer games." Her tone was laced with sarcasm.

"I understand that suburban domestication is not everyone's cup of tea," Emily said while clearing the plates. The storm, now in full force, caused Emily's lights to flicker. "Hell, I'm not even sure it's mine."

Emily went back and forth on the issue of marriage. Some days she wanted to be married; others she shared Ashleigh's sentiments. When Emily was with Craig she imagined their future together many times. None of the men in her life since Craig have sparked the same kind of romantic visions.

While it wasn't so apparent to Emily, Ashleigh knew that her friend still carried a torch for her long lost love. Emily needed closure to move on. Ashleigh, on the other hand, had a love life that was a bit more complex than just obtaining closure. Her emotional scars ran as deep as the Grand Canyon.

"Besides, Liam lives half-way across the world, Em," she said dryly. "I don't see how a relationship is possible. Plus, he thinks of me only as a friend. He tells everyone we are *just* friends."

"London is not *that* far away." Emily scoffed. "I don't know Ashleigh. There's no way a powerful man like Liam Frost remains single unless he's got his eye on one woman whom he's crazy in love with." Emily lifted an eyebrow at Ashleigh.

Ashleigh didn't think of Liam as a powerful business mogul. She only knew him to be the thoughtful, charming gentleman who showers her with affection and passionately makes love to her without demanding a commitment.

"What's not to love about Liam? He's witty, smart, successful and rich. I read the latest article on his personal wealth. It's astounding. Have *you* read it?"

Ashleigh grazed her teeth over her bottom lip and recalled the article regarding Liam's personal financial portfolio. He's everything a woman would want on paper and in person. Liam had invested in a small startup which ended up turning an enormous profit. Liam's investment quadrupled. Along with his already hefty base salary, quarterly bonuses and now the startup, Liam has accrued a small fortune over the last year.

"I think you're insane, Ash. Just the purr of his accent alone would be all the reason I would need to shamelessly flop on my back and let him fuck me senseless. Christ, I'll marry him. He's fucking gorgeous."

She had to chuckle. Once Emily gets a few glasses of wine in her system her language would make even a sailor blush.

"Let's call him now. Maybe I can set the two of you up." Ashleigh grabbed her phone and pretended to bring up Liam's number.

"No, don't you dare. Ashleigh, put your phone down," Emily wailed. "Whether you want to hear it or not, you two *are* practically a couple. You've been sleeping with him regularly for two years. There have been no other men in your life, Ash. You need to think about that. Don't you love Liam?"

Emily's words were coming out fast and furious, jarring on Ashleigh's soul. Ashleigh hadn't thought about whether or not she loved him. There were feelings of love she had for him, but to be in love was another story. Having a relationship with Liam was just not possible.

"Emily, I appreciate what you're saying. I really do, but I'm meant to be alone. I have my career, my family and friends. Face it. I'm just not fucking marriage material."

"I wish you felt differently. Have you...," Emily's voice broke. "Have you considered therapy? You know, to talk about what happened with..."

Ashleigh's eyebrows shot up at the mere thought of going to some crack pot therapist's office to talk about her feelings of love and loss. Emily could see by the expression on Ashleigh's face that she was pushing her friend to revisit a dark part of her life. Re-hashing the Nick situation is just too much for Ashleigh to handle. Maybe it's best just to leave it buried in the past.

"Emily, I do not believe I need a man to have fulfillment in my life."

As if on cue, lightning crackled, thunder clapped and the lights in Emily's house flickered twice and went out.

"Ashleigh, I think someone out there has a different opinion on your love life."

The lights quickly came back on in the house. Emily shot Ashleigh a look as if to say, told you so. Ashleigh scoffed and took a sip of wine.

Chapter Thirteen
Amanda

Amanda and Vince arrived in New Jersey at 7:48 P.M. at a private airport in Teterboro. From there they took a town car to an elegant and upscale French restaurant, La Bonne, on Manhattan's Upper East Side. Amanda had already looked up the website and menu after Vince told her on the plane where they would be dining. This was the first time since Brandon had taken her Christmas shopping a few years ago that she had been back to Manhattan. The city had changed so much since then, but somehow felt the same—vital and energetic. There's really nothing quite like winter in New York City, it's magical, but this gorgeous May night was shaping up to be pretty spectacular.

As they drove down The FDR Amanda looked out the window of the town car towards the East River, which was pitch black except for the lights that illuminated the bridges above. They turned onto York Avenue passing charming outdoor cafés, lovely boutique shops with fabulous summer themed window displays and old neighborhood corner bars offering happy hour drink specials.

The car ride from the airport to the restaurant was mostly silent except for the two phone calls that Vince took in the span of ten minutes. One call was regarding a warehouse problem at one of their base hubs, the other was someone inquiring how the flight experience was to New York City. Vince remarked, telling the person on the other end of the phone, about the performance of the pilot, the two flight attendants, the extremely comfortable seats and their excellent choice in carpeting. She noticed that Vince was a serious man, very particular with details and a man of few words, or at least tonight he was.

Amanda had managed to strike up a conversation with Vince on the flight. She learned that he had two kids, a son, Logan, who was ten and a thirteen year-old daughter, Addie, short for Adeline, both from his first marriage. Apparently Addie was into music, which was the reason he was at the boutique the day they met. Vince was looking for vintage records because he had purchased her a turntable for her upcoming birthday. With all of today's modern technology, this girl wanted a record player to spin the tunes.

Amanda desperately wanted to have children of her own. She loved kids, especially her nephew Conner who would turn four this year Amanda and her sister, Julie, had always been close and would meet secretly about every six weeks to check-in on each other. However, the sisters couldn't seem to get their schedules to work over the last few months and Amanda hadn't seen Conner since February. When the news of Amanda's cheating scandal broke, Julie felt like the only one who tried to help Amanda put her life back together.

Amanda's public indiscretion had caused all kinds of problems for the family. From what Julie told Amanda, their father, Jack, was losing business deals left and right. Their mom, Donna, was asked to resign from several boards and committees. Julie tried to keep the family together, but she could only do so much.

After her husband Brandon threw her out of their home she had no place to go. Amanda's parents wouldn't even talk to her , so Julie sent Amanda on a month long

South Pacific vacation assuring her that when she returned everything would be back to normal.

When Amanda arrived back in Bloomfield Hills, Julie informed her that their father had forbidden any kind of contact with Amanda. Jack made it clear to Julie that if he found out she was in contact with her sister he would cut off Julie's trust fund. This meant Conner's too and any other children they might have with her doctor husband, David. His job made for a nice lifestyle, but having the trust fund provided extra security for their family. Luckily, Julie managed to convince their father to let Amanda keep the remaining funds in her trust to live on. Her sister also told her to strap in because Brandon was serving her with divorce papers immediately.

When Amanda's trust fund had completely run out last September Julie had loaned her $5,000. However, Amanda blew through that money quickly which is why she finally had to break down and get a mall job last November.

The private jet Vince chartered for them this evening was very roomy and bright, far more spacious than Brandon's family's G200, which only seated nine. Upon entering the plane there were two sections for passengers to sit on either side of the aisle. To the left there was a white couch, with white, grey and black throw pillows on each end. Walking down the aisle on the right stood a large black marble dining table with four oversized white chairs. To the left of the table across the aisle sat another long white couch with grey and black throw pillows and a cozy grey blanket gently placed over the armrest. There was a wet bar at the back, behind the dining area with all kinds of alcohol, bottled water and pop. The carpeting was a chevron print of charcoal grey and black, except for a few glossy black and chrome interior finishes, much of the cabin interior was a crisp white.

"We're almost to the restaurant, Mr. Everett," the driver announced.

"Very good, James. I will call you when we are ready to be picked up."

"As you wish, Mr. Everett."

The car pulled up to the front of La Bonne where there were a few limos, elegant sedans and sleek sports cars waiting to be parked by the valet service. James parked in the front near the valet stand and came around to open Vince's door. Exiting the car Amanda felt like a celebrity. She remembered this feeling, and she needed tonight to go well. This was the life she was meant to have. Without saying a word, Vince offered Amanda his right arm, and she graciously wrapped her arm around his as they walked to the door.

Monday morning came way too early for Amanda, who was still reeling from her weekend trip to New York City. She and Vince had returned late Sunday afternoon, and while Amanda had plenty of sleep she couldn't seem to motivate herself for work. Maybe because today was Memorial Day and she would rather be going to a party on the lake or a barbeque with friends. Traipsing to the bathroom and rubbing her eyes, she turned on the shower letting the steam from the hot water quickly fill her bathroom. As the mirror began to fog up, she stepped into the shower as the hot water cascaded over her shoulders.

She tilted her head up to the streaming water and it gently sprayed her face. Now she was awake.

"Knock, knock," Daniel said as he entered the bathroom. "Hey sweetie, I got you a vanilla latte from Starbucks."

"Oh thanks Daniel. That was awfully nice of you. So you finally made it home this morning, huh?"

Amanda was rinsing the shampoo out of her hair while Daniel yammered on about meeting the perfect man while he was out clubbing Saturday evening. Amanda could not remember the last time she talked to Daniel. He was not at their condo when she arrived home. She had gone to bed early but had woken up in the middle of the night for a drink of water and Daniel was not in his bedroom.

"Girl, so you know my weekend was pretty fun. How was yours?"

"It was nice. I went out with a friend Saturday night, and we had dinner and drinks. I ended up staying the night."

Amanda decided she was not ready to share anything too personal about Vince with Daniel yet.

"What time do you have to be at work Amanda?"

"I'm opening today, so I've got to be there before eight. I have to prep and check the payroll numbers."

Amanda started to shave, allowing the conditioner in her hair to stay for three minutes before rinsing it out.

"I worked yesterday and then went to my parent's house for dinner. My sister was there, and we ended up talking and drinking on the deck until about one in the morning. I was so tired. She insisted I stay the night, so I did."

"Sounds like a relaxing evening."

"It was, definitely. Well, I will let you get ready. Have a good day, girl."

Daniel exited the bathroom. Amanda pulled back the shower curtain grabbing her towel and gently patting her arms and legs dry. After taking a drink of her coffee, she let out a huge sigh and wrapped her hair neatly in the towel. Crossing to her room she opened the dresser, pulled on her panties and then her bra. A text from Vince popped up on her phone: GOOD MORNING GORGEOUS. I LOOK FORWARD TO SEEING YOU THURSDAY EVENING. MY

DRIVER WILL PICK YOU UP PROMPTLY AT 7:00 P.M. WE HAVE DINNER RESERVATIONS AT 8:00 P.M. AT CYGNUS 27. DO NOT GO TO THE TROUBLE OF FINDING SOMETHING TO WEAR, YOUR ATTIRE WILL BE WAITING FOR YOU IN OUR SUITE.

Wow! He was taking her to the Amway Grand Plaza, one of the best hotels in Grand Rapids. Her stomach did backflips, front handsprings and a few round-offs upon reading the message. Reaching for the happy pills in her medicine cabinet, she thought about taking one and washing it down with her latte. She withdrew her grip from the bottle muttering, "Not today, Amanda. You don't need the pills today."

Chapter Fourteen
Emily

The month of June was whizzing by. Emily sat at her desk checking email when she noticed she had to be at a meeting in fifteen minutes. This was not a daily or weekly scheduled meeting, Emily was anxious to know what it was about, especially when she saw Ethan was going to be there as well.

Emily and Ethan had been quietly dating for a few weeks. No one at the office seemed to have a clue about their relationship, even though they had a hard time keeping their hands off each other at work. Stealing kisses in the break room, rounding third base in the supply closet where they nearly were discovered by Susan. Then there was the heated make out session on Ethan's leather sofa in his office last Friday during lunch, which left her in a sexually frustrated haze for the remainder of the day. Thankfully for Emily, Ethan was able to relieve her of her frustrations later that evening.

Emily's office phone rang sweeping her back to reality. She hit speaker phone, "Hello, this is Emily Greene." There was no answer, and Emily said hello again. Still, there was no answer from the other end of the phone. Emily tried once more to say hello when she heard a click. *Must have been a poor connection, they'll call back.*

Gathering her items she headed for the bank of elevators. Today's meeting was in the Executive Conference room upstairs. Her cellphone began to buzz. It was one of the printing companies she had contacted for a price quote regarding the sales brochures.

"Hello, this is Emily Greene."

Emily walked slowly up the stairs to the conference room instead of taking the elevator, listening intently to Frank from Cambria Printing give her details regarding the order. Ending her call as she entered the conference room, Emily stood silently for a moment staring out the window, admiring the white fluffy clouds against the bright blue late afternoon sky.

Suddenly, Emily felt the air shift. She turned around and noticed Ethan standing behind her, his mouth twisted into a devilish grin. He looked completely delicious in his grey suit and silk blue tie.

"Ethan, nice to see you today," she said sweetly while nodding at him. "What are you smiling about?" Emily asked as she tried to move past him but was stopped immediately. The touch of Ethan's grip on her narrow waist caused Emily's body to tingle all over.

"The sight of you in this black skirt with red pumps is provoking enticing thoughts," he said slyly reaching for her hair and sweeping one of her long tendrils off her cheek. Ethan slowly walked backwards and hit the button on the wall which instantly changed the glass windows that overlooked the alcove from transparent to opaque. Emily swallowed the lump in her throat as she heard the door lock—panic swept through her.

"Ethan…what are you doing? We have a meeting in five minutes," she managed to croak out.

Ethan stood in front of Emily replying, "You and I have a meeting in here for the next thirty minutes, and then the rest of the executives will be in. I told Clark that you and I needed some time to bang out a few issues…with the Northwest Territory sales infographics."

Emily nearly lost her balance hearing the words tumble from Ethan's lips. His hand slid down the curve of her hip to the hemline of her skirt just above her knee, pushing it up slightly to reveal the top of her stockings. Emily was unable to move. She was frozen.

"Garters, Emily?" he groaned. "You're killing me."

Ethan trailed soft kisses from the base of her neck to the curve of her jaw. Emily felt a surge of electricity hit her stomach. That spark jolted her body, whizzing her back to life. Moving her hands up to his neck, Emily wrapped her arms around Ethan as her fingers fisted his hair. Ethan proceeded to graze his fingertips over her bare flesh. Covering her mouth with his, Emily's lips parted, and Ethan brushed his tongue to hers moving his hand to the swell of her bottom, cupping it firmly. Gripping Emily tightly, he lifted her gently onto the conference table. Ethan shrugged out of his jacket and rolled up the sleeves of his white shirt as Emily loosened his tie.

Ethan traced his thumb over the top of Emily's garters. Carefully he unclipped each one, allowing him to slide her panties down her legs and over her heels. Emily's breathing escalated as she wondered what Ethan had planned for her. She tried to close her legs but Ethan stopped her, holding her knees apart with one hand. He gently clipped her garters back to the top of her stockings.

"Now," he said firmly while holding her green silk panties in front of her face. "These now belong to me, Miss Greene. You can have them back at the end of the day if you do as I say. Do you understand?"

"I see, Mr. Carlson," she replied in a low voice. "So, you like to play games?"

Ethan nodded and replied, "We're going to play lots of games, Miss Greene, and I promise you will like it too. Please continue to address me as Mr. Carlson for the remainder of the day."

Emily swallowed hard at the realization that Ethan Carlson was a little kinky. Reaching into his jacket pocket, Ethan produced a black silk bag which contained two silver balls the size of marbles. *What the fuck are these things?*

"Miss Greene, these are Ben Wa Balls. Do you know what they are used for?"

Emily shook her head, replying softly, "No."

"Put them in your hands and feel them," he instructed.

Emily did as she was told, feeling the cool glass on her palms and noting their weight.

"Stand up, Miss Greene," he ordered as he dropped to his knees in front of her.

Emily's breathing became labored as she felt Ethan's hot breath on her thighs. He traced his fingers on the backs of her knees and up and down her long sculpted legs. Her heart pounded in her chest. Sweat began to bead at the back of her neck. Emily knew the door was securely locked, but nervous excitement curled through her body thinking they might be caught.

"These are simply meant to increase sexual desire by tightening your keigel muscles making your vagina feel smaller and tighter," Ethan said while circling Emily's sensitive flesh with the pad of his thumb. Letting out a low gasp, every nerve ending in her body rocketed straight to her core as Ethan plunged into her with his index finger.

Teasing her mercilessly, Emily's hips bucked forward as Ethan palmed her sex, driving her wild with his slow and steady movements.

Ethan gently eased both elegant glass balls inside giving her strict instructions not to cough or sneeze. If Emily kept the delicate balls in for the remainder of the workday, she could have her panties back. Emily quickly became aware of the sensitivity of her body. The smooth movement inside her caused her breasts to swell and her thighs to quiver.

Shifting on her heels Emily asked softly, "Eth...Mr. Carlson, how am I supposed to get any work done the remainder of the day?"

Grinning wickedly at her, Ethan began to walk backwards. Puzzled as to why he kept moving farther away, Emily slowly inched closer to him. Her unsteady and wobbly motions reminded her of a newborn deer trying to walk for the first time. With each stride her body became more aroused. Now she understood, and thank God there was only an hour of the workday left. She found herself standing directly in front of Ethan now. Drawing his arm around her to the small of her back, Emily felt her knees buckle.

"Try, Miss Greene," he whispered and closed his mouth over hers. Ethan began rolling his tongue with hers slowly while gently caressing her breast causing Emily to experience the most sensational orgasm. All she could do was bite her lip to keep from moaning for the entire reception area to hear. Ethan cradled her against his sturdy frame, keeping her from crumbling to the floor.

Still clutching Ethan while leaning into his body, she panted, "*Jesus*...Ethan."

"Miss Greene...you called me Ethan." His tone was stern.

Crap! Emily quickly shuffled to an upright position looking Ethan directly in face and said, "Sorry, Mr. Carlson." How was it possible that this demanding, stern and sinfully playful side made Ethan even sexier?

Looking at his watch Ethan smiled, "Now, Miss Greene you have exactly eight minutes to tidy yourself together before the meeting. I suggest you visit the ladies room."

Emily felt her skin dance with heat as the blood pooled in her stomach. Walking to the bathroom, she was a bundle of nerves certain everyone was going to sense something was off. Mustering all her strength Emily managed to control her breathing, allowing her to walk gracefully to the ladies room. She returned moments later to find Ethan sitting at the table as if nothing had happened. Giving her a warm smile he gestured to the seat across from him. She nodded and took her seat.

Just then Clark, Susan and a few others entered the conference room. Emily shifted in her chair as Ethan just sat there smiling looking calm and collected. He was the cool guy, the guy that adapted to any situation, never letting anyone see him sweat.

"Good afternoon everyone," Clark began. "We have some very exciting news to share. Ethan here is very close to signing the contract with LA Business Design; he worked all day to make this deal happen. The paperwork should arrive this afternoon."

Without looking too obvious, Emily shot Ethan a quick smile. She then reached for her phone and sent him a text message: "WAY TO BE AN OVERACHIEVER WORKING ON A SUNDAY. SERIOUSLY, THAT'S AWESOME." Emily saw Ethan look down at his phone and smile seeing the text from her. She saw him fiddling with the phone. He must be sending a reply, she thought. Emily's screen lit up with a message: "THANK YOU. CAN I TAKE YOU OUT FOR DINNER TO CELEBRATE?"

Emily was having a difficult time concentrating. She was careful not to shift in her chair because every movement sent electric pulses radiating to her vagina. A few minutes into the meeting she made the mistake of crossing her legs which had her gripping the curve of her chair tightly. Ethan caught her movements and grazed his tongue over his bottom lip. Emily had no idea what Clark was saying. The deep ache between her legs was unnerving. Ethan would have to fill her in later. Emily cursed him under her breath for putting her in this horny as hell haze. As Clark continued the speech, Emily managed to find some way to compose herself allowing the blood to drain from her ears.

"Now, for the second part of the good news," Clark announced. "We will be collaborating with LA Business Design on a special marketing campaign with TV, radio and print advertising. Emily you will be travelling to Los Angeles to work with them and their advertising team to come up with the right campaign that mutually benefits both of our companies."

Emily had a look of utter shock and amazement on her face. Ethan smirked. She caught his gaze, returning an icy, yet playful "fuck you" glare. She was the Director of Marketing, but this was huge for her career. Emily had participated in helping formulate advertising spots for radio and print for Cooper Bentley in local markets, but this was a much larger scale.

"Emily, be ready to pack your bags. You and Ethan leave next Monday for Los Angeles," Clark said with a smile.

If the news of her helping to direct an international ad campaign wasn't enough to send her into a somewhat state of shock, this bit of information would certainly be the lynch pin. She was going on a business trip alone with

Ethan. Her mind raced, but she very calmly said, "Not a problem, Clark. I'll be ready."

She was careful not to show emotion or even look in Ethan's direction. Emily could feel Ethan's gaze on her—if she met his stare in that moment she thought it might send her body into a total sexual frenzy. A text from Ethan caused a smile to cross Emily's lips: SO, ABOUT THAT CELEBRATORY DINNER. SHALL I PICK YOU UP AT 7:00?

She happily replied, "YES."

Chapter Fifteen
Ashleigh

It was a beautiful summer day in Manhattan. The warm, late afternoon sunlight was pouring through the windows of Ashleigh's town car as it made its way down FDR heading south to 63rd street. Traffic was surprisingly light, but then again, no one was headed out of town quite yet for the weekend. Ashleigh was glad she decided to come to the city on a Thursday rather than Friday. Her phone began to ring, a sly smile lite up her face as she realized it was Liam.

"Hello Liam."

"Hello my darling, Ashleigh. Where are you?"

There's that gritty sexy accent, she loved hearing so much. Ashleigh was looking forward to spending some much needed quality time with Liam.

"I'm in the town car you sent for me, and we are almost to Fifth Avenue. I should arrive at the hotel shortly."

"Very good, I cannot wait to see you."

"Same here Liam." She beamed asking, "Where are we going for dinner?"

"I have booked us a table at Asiate for 7:30."

"Wonderful, I have heard many good things about the new chef, not to mention the views of the city are sensational."

"I have the Taipan Suite if you'd like to stay with me. There's plenty of room."

"Thank you Liam, but I've paid for my room already. I think you'll be tired of me after the weekend anyway."

"Nonsense my dear, I relish our times together."

"Well, I should be there very soon. We just turned onto Central Park South."

"See you in a bit, Ashleigh."

Ashleigh placed her phone back in her purse as the town car came to a complete stop. Looking out the window all she could see were stopped cars and people hurriedly crossing the street.

"Sorry Miss Preston, looks to be some kind of traffic jam or construction. We might be delayed for a short time."

"Typical Manhattan traffic, I'm used to it. What can you do?" she shrugged. "And Phillip, please, you can call me Ashleigh."

"Yes, as you wish *Ashleigh*," Phillip replied smiling in the rearview mirror.

Closing her eyes, she leaned her head back and her mind drifted to her conversation with Emily. Was she being too closed off to the idea of a relationship with Liam? He did just offer her to stay in his hotel suite. It's almost as if they are a long-distance couple. They see each other nearly every six weeks or so. *Could this relationship work?* Suddenly her mind shifted gears. Ashleigh remembered that unusually warm mid-September day. The sky began to darken, then lightning flashed and the thunder began to rumble. The pop-up thunderstorm was beautiful with rain falling gently over Lake Erie in grey misting curtains. She heard cheers coming from the TV as the Wolverines had just scored another touchdown against the Notre Dame Fighting Irish. The University of Michigan fight song was blaring.

Hail! To the victors valiant Hail! To the conqu'ring heroes Hail! Hail! To Michigan the leaders and best...

Nick was elated. Jumping out of his chair and pointing at the TV shouting, "Did you see that Ash? Did you see that play?!" She was looking at his handsome face. Her sweet Nick was standing there, smiling at her, looking gorgeous wearing his University of Michigan long-sleeve tee-shirt. Then he was gone.

Beep…Beeeeppp, "Come on man. Move your truck!" Phillip was shouting at the driver in the left lane.

"Sorry Ashleigh. This guy will not move," he said, slightly frustrated.

"It's okay Phillip, I'll text Liam and let him know we are stuck in traffic."

"Don't bother, here we go… *finally* moving." Phillip said.

Moments later, they arrived that the hotel. Phillip had already opened her door and unloaded her bags onto a luggage cart. She dug her phone out of her purse and checked into The Mandarin Oriental Hotel on Foursquare.

"Thank you Phillip. It was so nice to see you again. Tell your mother I said, hello."

"Will do, Ashleigh. I'm sure I will see you again while you are in the city. Mr. Frost hired me for the entire week."

Check-in was a breeze and she headed up the elevator to her room. Upon entering her hotel room, Ashleigh noticed a large vase filled with pale pink roses on the table with a note attached. "FOR MY DARLING, ASHLEIGH. I LOOK FORWARD TO A WONDERFUL WEEK IN THE BIG APPLE WITH YOU. YOURS, LIAM"

Ashleigh's heart swelled and sank. She swallowed hard and inhaled the sweet aroma of the gorgeous long stemmed flowers.

The Lobby Bar was completely full, not a seat anywhere. But, on a Friday night, that was to be expected in Manhattan. Liam was upstairs on the phone and told Ashleigh to wait for him in the bar. She finally found a table near the window and ordered a scotch and soda.

"Ashleigh? Ashleigh Preston?" a male voice inquired.

Ashleigh looked up through her long lashes and saw Jake Heatherton standing at her table.

"Oh my goodness, Jake! What are you doing in New York City?" She jumped up and threw her arms around his neck. Jake worked with Nick back in Troy, where they were both Financial Analysts. Jake was handsome, but not in an obvious way. He was about ten pounds heavier, his blonde hair was ashen, but his blue eyes glimmered with youthful vitality. The lines on his face were more pronounced and his skin was pale and dry. Jake had charisma, but you could tell years of the corporate grind were beginning to take their toll.

"Hi. I'm still with The Newborne Group, I'm a Vice President with the company now. I live in Manhattan with my wife and our two kids."

Motioning to the empty seat at her table, Ashleigh said, "Please have a seat, Jake. Did you end up marrying Brandy?"

Taking the seat across the table from Ashleigh he motioned to the server and ordered a bourbon on the rocks.

"No, Brandy and I broke up, and then I met Hannah, my wife just a few months later. We've been married for six years. We had our first child, a boy, Trent, he's four and we just had our second, a girl, Taylor in February." He said with a beaming grin and took out his Blackberry, showing her the photos of each of the kids and his wife. They were the model family. There was even a family portrait with the four of them and their Golden Retriever.

"What are you up to these days? Are you still writing and taking pictures?"

Ashleigh took a sip of her drink and smiled. "Well certainly nothing as exciting as you, Jake. Married, kids and a big career move. You have a lovely family."

"Well, thank you very much. I feel like the luckiest guy in the world."

"Still writing, but I'm a freelancer now. I live in Grand Rapids, but I'm lucky because I get to travel all over the world."

"Is that what you're doing in New York?"

"Yep, I am attending the grand opening of the Refinery Hotel next week, but right now I am spending the weekend here with a friend."

Jake lifted one of his blonde eyebrows, inquiring, "A male friend?"

"Very perceptive Jake, but we *are* just friends."

"So has there been anyone since Nick for you Ashleigh?"

"A few guys, but nothing serious."

"You know Nick would want you to be happy, Ashleigh," Jake said as he put his hand on top of hers. "I miss him too. There's not a day that goes by that I do not think about my friend."

Ashleigh peered out the window and felt her throat tighten. She could feel the tears coming on, but she pushed them back as hard as she could. She quickly changed the subject.

"Well, what are you doing here at the Mandarin, Jake?

Jake removed his hand from hers and sat back in the chair, "We just wrapped up our corporate planning meeting— budget analysis, financial outlook and things of that nature."

She only half heard what he actually said, replying, "That's wonderful to hear Jake," she smiled affectionately at him.

Jake took the final sip of his drink. "Ashleigh, it was great seeing you." He pushed to his feet. Ashleigh stood to join him and he kissed her cheek. "If you ever need anything at all, do not hesitate to call me," Jake offered while handing her his card.

"Thank you Jake. You're very kind," she replied softly. "It was lovely to see you. Please take care."

Jake walked away and when he was out of her view, the tears began to well up in her eyes. Feeling waves of heat wash over her skin, she began to chew her lip. The tears streamed down Ashleigh's face, and she quickly turned to the window so no one in the bar could visibly see her crying. She desperately tried to choke back the tears. Looking at her phone she saw it was nearly eight, but she had no message from Liam. She wondered what was keeping him. The crowd seemed to have filtered out, and there Liam stood at the bar in a well-tailored ink-blue Dior Homme suit with contrasting red polka-dot tie. She picked up her napkin and dabbed under eyes, but it was too late. Liam had walked over and saw her mascara had been ruined.

"Ashleigh what is the matter? Why are you crying, my dear?" Placing his drink on the table he moved the empty chair closer to Ashleigh.

"I just saw an old friend and he reminded me of someone special I knew a very long time ago."

"I see. Do you want to talk about it?"

"Actually Liam, I think I *need* to talk about it. I want to tell you, but it's a tale of woe and it's really personal. Not the most inviting dinner conversation."

Liam placed his hand on hers and smiled. "You can tell me anything. Would you like to put on some comfortable clothes, drink lots of wine and order room service?"

Ashleigh wiped her nose and gently brushed the tears from her cheeks. "That sounds like a very good idea."

"Come with me and I'll escort you to your room so you can change."

Liam picked up his phone cancelling the reservation he made for the two of them, apologizing and rescheduling for Saturday evening for the same time. Walking to the bank of elevators Liam put his arm around her trim waist, whispering comfortingly, "Everything will be alright

Ashleigh. This is what friends are for, to help pick you up when you're feeling down."

He noticed her lips and cheeks were bright red, as if she was trying not to break down in front of him.

"*Breathe*, Ashleigh," he whispered clutching her hand.

All of the air that she hand been holding in quickly expelled from her lungs. They stepped into the empty elevator car, and Ashleigh nuzzled herself into his towering frame. He gently put his arm around her shoulders pulling her in close and tight.

Chapter Sixteen
Amanda

Amanda woke up dazed. Sweat was running down the back of her neck and chest. There was an empty vodka bottle on the nightstand. Sunlight filled the room. *Why the hell are the goddamn blinds open?* She never slept with the blinds open. Amanda looked at the clock. It was nearly one in the afternoon. Her eyes widened, and she reached for her phone which had three missed calls, all from The Bath Shop. Trying to sit up she was dizzy and her head ached. She fell back onto the pillow and closed her eyes.

The long black cocktail dress was crumpled on the floor. The diamond earrings Vince gifted her with were still in her ears. They were heavy and stinging her earlobes. She tried to open her eyes and focus. Looking around the room she noticed she was not at home, not in her bed and not feeling well. Staring at the ceiling, she felt her insides churning. Her heart was pounding, and her thighs and abs hurt. *What the hell was going on?* Amanda was totally confused and sick to her stomach. Mustering enough strength she darted to what she thought could be the bathroom. Lucky for her she was correct. Flipping up the lid to the toilet she began vomiting. When she was finished she collapsed onto the floor. The cold tile felt so good against her warm skin.

Amanda heard voices and tried to open her eyes, but all she saw was dark shadows. Her skin felt warm again, and she could feel the soft fabric under her fingers. Something was poking her hand, and then it stung. Something cold was on her forehead, it felt so good. Her tongue felt fuzzy, and so did her teeth.

"Do you think she will be alright?" a male voice said.

"Yes, she should be totally fine in a few days, but after this she will be feeling much better and her fever should break," a woman replied in a soft comforting tone.

"I want you to call me as soon as her fever breaks and let me know if anything changes. I will be back before I leave for New York to check on her again," the gruff, strong male demanded.

"Will do boss," the first male voice replied.

The voices were getting softer and softer, and her hand felt numb. Her mind drifted.

It was completely dark aside from the table lamp across the room when Amanda awoke. Somehow, she managed to make it back into the bed. Fluttering her eyes open to focus, she managed to roll up out of bed and turn on the second lamp. Her face felt clean, and her jewelry was placed neatly on a silver tray on the nightstand. The black dress, which she had been wearing, was hanging up on the closet door in a clear garment bag that was labeled DRY CLEAN ONLY. She was wearing some silky pajama bottoms and a lace tank top. Her body felt heavy, but she mustered enough strength to ease out of bed. The top of her right hand itched a little bit and she noticed a Band-Aid and cotton ball were there.

Studying her surroundings she realized she was in a very posh apartment with floor to ceiling windows overlooking the city. *This has to be Vince's place.*

She stepped out of what she believed was the master suite and looked to the left. Passing through the great room and the formal dining room she arrived in the kitchen. The kitchen was gorgeous with white cabinets and stainless steel high-end appliances. Opening the door to the refrigerator, Amanda found it was completely stocked with some of her favorite things to eat and drink including: coconut water, Greek yogurt, fresh blueberries, carrots, romaine leaf lettuce and bottled Perrier. There were also a few bottles of Gatorade in several different flavors. Amanda grabbed a bottle of Perrier, stood in the dimly lit kitchen and drank the entire thing. She felt much better than she did earlier. She looked at the microwave which read 8:21.

Walking back into the bedroom and opening the closet doors she noticed all of her clothes were hanging in the closet as well as her shoes and handbags. Across the room near the windows there was a large dresser. Opening all the drawers one by one she saw all of her personal items were neatly folded. Her picture frames and books were on her bookcase and there was a writing desk in front of the window, where her laptop was stationed.

Entering the bathroom it was the same thing with the medicine cabinet. All of her toiletries were there, her toothbrush and electric razor. Swiftly walking, nearly running back into the great room, Amanda drew back the curtains and saw a very large terrace with a view of the river. She knew this layout and she knew this view—it was the River House.

Amanda walked down the hallway to Vince's home office. Alex was there lying on the leather couch watching ESPN. He was either Vince's personal bodyguard or right-hand guy, Amanda couldn't quite figure out what exactly his job title was, but she suspected Vince was a lot more than just a successful businessman. Alex was a nice guy, a retired US Army Ranger, early-thirties, dark brown hair and gorgeous hazel eyes that were thickly lashed. He was, as you can imagine, in top physical condition. He wasn't one of those meathead guys with tons of tattoos and biceps that could strangle a small child, rather Alex was muscular but with a trim build.

Knock…knock.

Alex quickly sat up and straightened his shirt and tie. Clearing his throat he said, "Miss Amanda, how are you feeling?"

"Hi Alex, I feel much better than I did earlier," she said while leaning against the door frame.

"What happened to me Alex?"

Alex explained to Amanda that she had a nasty case of food poisoning. He told her that he found her curled up on the bathroom floor just after one in the afternoon. When he noticed her temperature had spiked, he immediately called Dr. Sherman. Dr. Sherman had to administer two bags of saline, because she was so dehydrated. Amanda didn't know who Dr. Sherman was, but she was going to be sure to thank her for her improved physical state.

"Do you need anything? Are you hungry?"

"I think I could handle some chicken soup or light broth."

Alex stood up grabbed his phone off the coffee table and said, "I'll see if Vince's housekeeper, Mrs. Young stocked the pantry with any soup or broth. I am pretty sure there are a few cans in there."

Walking down the long corridor Amanda still felt shaky, desperately hoping she would not be sick again.

"Miss Amanda, I am sure you have figured it out by now, but Vince asked us to move you out of your condo. Your roommate, Daniel was given the remainder of your half of the rent through the end of the year. I think you should call him because he was very confused as to what was happening."

A ghost of a smile crossed her face. Amanda could only imagine what Daniel was thinking. She had only informed him about Vince and the fact they had been dating for a short time just last week. Daniel's head must have spun around like Linda Blair's in *The Exorcist*. No matter, Amanda was relieved to be out of the condo with Daniel.

"Okay yeah, that is good idea." She paused for a moment, "Alex, can you do me a favor?"

The light flipped on in the pantry and Alex began moving things around, when he looked back and said, "Sure anything, Miss Amanda."

"Can you just call me Amanda, please?"

"I can absolutely do that," he said looking at her and smiling. "Hey! I found some chicken broth and saltine crackers." He was holding them up in her direction. She nodded and took a seat at the breakfast bar.

"I cannot believe I got food poisoning. That is totally embarrassing. Did I throw up a lot in front of Vince?"

"Not in front of Vince, just me," he said winking at her.

"Oh God, I am so sorry," she said burying her face in her hands. "I'm so completely embarrassed."

Grabbing the can opener and the sauce pan he looked at Amanda and said, "I'm not sure if you know this about me, but I have seen far worse in combat."

"Yes, I suppose that is true."

Amanda propped her arm up on the bar and rested her chin in her right hand. She watched Alex carefully pouring the broth into the saucepan and then stirring it. He took a

147

glass from the cupboard on the left side of the refrigerator and poured some Gatorade.

"Dr. Sherman said you were to rest and if you experience any more symptoms, we were to get you some over the counter meds."

"Fabulous, thanks for looking out for me, Alex," she replied.

The smell of broth filled the kitchen. Alex placed a few saltines in front of Amanda with the glass of Gatorade. Looking at her and smiling with both hands firmly placed on the counter, he said, "That is not a problem. I am just glad you are feeling better. Now, take a small bite of the cracker and a few sips of Gatorade. We will have you feeling better in no time."

"Oh shit! I need to call work. Oh no. No. No. No!" Amanda jumped up from the bar and was frantically looking for her phone. She remembered it was in the bedroom on the nightstand.

"Amanda. I called your work and spoke to a gal who said her name was Katie. She was informed that you were ill and that is why you were unable to go to work today. She didn't believe me," he said with a deep sigh placing the bowl of broth in front of her.

"Yeah, she's kind of a bitch. So that doesn't surprise me."

"You know," he paused in a dramatic like fashion, "I used to listen to your radio show all the time, back in the day."

Amanda looked up from her bowl and stared at Alex. She was noticeably startled. Swallowing hard, she said, "You…you know who I am? How did you listen if you were in Afghanistan?"

"Amanda, there's no need to worry. Vince had me look into your past, but it seems your past is nothing that the public doesn't know already." Smiling sweetly at her, he continued, "Besides, I was in Kosovo and only in Afghanistan for one tour. I retired from the Army over seven years ago."

"Yeah, I guess I don't have the best track record," Amanda huffed. "So are you from Michigan originally then?"

"We all have things in our past that we aren't super thrilled about, but that is precisely why they are in the past. We learn from our mistakes and move on. Yep, born and raised in Detroit."

"You sound like someone speaking from experience," she said eyeing him intensely.

"Like I said, I've seen war and it is ugly. But, I would go again…" his gaze shifted downward.

Amanda smiled sweetly. She had a question on the tip of her tongue and she felt comfortable enough to ask Alex.

"Alex, have you…have *you* killed anyone?" she asked with a bit of fear in her voice knowing what the answer could be.

Alex was standing at the sink rinsing his bowl and spoon. He turned around and gave her a half smile saying, "What do you think Amanda?"

She paused for a few seconds and replied, "I think you have."

Alex's phone began to ring. "Excuse me Amanda, but I need to take this." He turned and walked out of the kitchen. "Hey boss. Yes, everything is good here."

Amanda could no longer hear what Alex was saying, he was already down the corridor past the wet bar. Amanda checked her phone, there was a message saying she had twenty percent battery remaining. Hopping out of the chair she took her bowl to the sink and began rinsing it out.

A few moments later Alex returned and said, "Vince has to stay in New York this weekend. He'll be calling you once he reaches his apartment."

A frown appeared on Amanda's face upon the delivery of that news, another lonely weekend without Vince. She padded back to the bedroom and flopped down on the bed. A half an hour later her phone rang, it was Vince. They stayed on the phone talking and laughing for over an hour. Calmness swept over her body as she drifted peacefully to sleep.

Chapter Seventeen
Emily

The California breeze tousled Emily's long brown hair as she attempted to tame it by putting it back in a low ponytail. From the passenger seat of the silver BMW 328i convertible, she peered through the grey tinted lenses of her sunglasses at Ethan, who was driving them over the Richmond San Rafael Bridge towards Sonoma. Ethan had managed to convince Clark to give him and Emily that Friday off. Ethan had plans for them to spend a romantic weekend together before they needed to be in Los Angeles the coming Monday.

Enchanted by the idea of spending time with Ethan in Wine Country she agreed to the plan without hesitation. Emily had only been to California once, and all she saw then was LAX, before departing for Hawaii. So she was overjoyed at the opportunity to be able to view the stunning countryside and the rugged Pacific coastline, especially with her tour guide being a handsome native of the Golden State.

Emily's phone began to buzz. It was a number she did not know, but she decided to answer in case it was work related.

"Hello, this is Emily Greene." The wind was so loud. It kept her from hearing clearly who was on the other end of the line. No sooner did she end the call than her phone began to ring yet again. It was another number she did not recognize.

"Miss popular today, aren't you?" Ethan said smiling. Emily gave Ethan a half smile and shrugged as if to say *sorry*.

"Hello, this is Emily Greene."

"Emmmilllyyy. Are *yooouuuu* going somewhere ttthhiiisss weekend?" a strange raspy voice groaned. "Are *you* with *Ethan*? Why didn't you tell me *you* were leaving? I thought *WE* were friends, Emily," the voice on the other end was snarling and laughing. Emily did not respond and immediately ended the call. Someone was trying to rattle her, but why?

"Hey Em, are you hungry?"

"I'm starving, Ethan," she replied with a flirtatious smile.

"How does sushi sound?"

"I think having sushi in California is pretty much a top priority."

"Great. I know the best place in San Rafael," he said placing his right hand on her left knee.

Ethan and Emily arrived at Charlemagne Winery just before five in the evening, a beautiful hilltop property with breathtaking views of rolling vineyards, landscaped gardens, picnic areas and natural wetlands. Inspired by Mediterranean design influences and architecture, the estate displayed ornate tiles, covered walkways, roundabouts and a long winding driveway that went up to the property upon passing through the main gate. Gorgeous water fountains and trellises covered in ivy and flowers spanned the grounds. The building that housed the tasting room, marketplace and several large banquet halls was a stunning stucco façade with a clay tile roof.

The tasting room was packed with tourists and wine enthusiasts trying award winning Italian and California/French varietals. Ethan and Emily walked up to the bar and a young blonde woman wearing a white polo style top with the logo of the winery on it asked, "Which wines would you like to sample today?"

"We would like to try some of the California Varietals, the Chardonnay, Sauvignon Blanc and the Pinot Noir please."

"Which one would you like to try first?"

"Let's go with the Sauvignon Blanc. It's best to try whites then reds and the sweet wines should always be first," Emily said.

Ethan looked at Emily and then towards the young blonde and just smiled.

"Very good, that is correct," the young woman said.

Ethan smiled at Emily, whispering in her ear, "You look insanely beautiful today. Have I told you that?"

Emily blushed and replied, "Thank you Ethan."

The young woman returned with the drinks and said, "Now you will notice the…"

Ethan casually leaned into the bar and slowly waved his hand in the air in her direction. "I'm Ethan Carlson. Do you know if my parents, Tom and Jillian, are here?"

Both Emily and the young girl exchanged looks of shock. She seemed to be mesmerized by Ethan, and after several seconds she snapped out of her trance, replying to him, "Uh…huh…yes, Mr. Carlson they are in the office upstairs."

"Kami is it? Call me Ethan, please, Mr. Carlson is my father."

She nodded her head and replied, "Yes, my name is Kami. I am so sorry *Ethan*."

"No need to apologize, Kami," he assured her after taking a drink.

Emily set her glass on the corner of the bar. She turned to Ethan and said, "What the fuck Ethan? Are you crazy or something? Why didn't you tell me *this* was your family winery?"

Ethan only smiled and winked at her. He was quite possibly fucking with her. Emily knew that Ethan's family owned a winery, but she had no idea he was planning to introduce her to them and as what, his girlfriend?

"Ethan, don't you think it's a little too soon? I...I ...mean what will they think?"

He reached out, took her hand and delivered a light kiss to her palm saying, "Emily, it's only dinner. Please don't worry. They *will* love you."

"Ethan, I don't like surprises, and this quite frankly *is* a surprise."

As they finished the last sip of their Pinot Noir, Ethan took his money clip out and handed a fifty dollar bill to Kami. She smiled and said, "Mr. er...*Ethan* this is too much, you are too kind."

"I insist you keep it, Kami, and thank you very much for the drinks."

Taking Emily's hand, Ethan led the way as they turned and walked away from the bar. Threading in and out of the crowd they came upon a grand tile staircase with wrought iron railings. They made their way upstairs, and Emily suddenly became quite nervous.

Is he taking me to meet his parents now?

She wanted to pull away and run to the bathroom to check her makeup and pop a breath mint. Emily's phone began to buzz again. She grabbed it out of her purse and saw it was the same number from earlier and hit ignore.

"Who keeps calling you?" Ethan inquired.

"It's a wrong number," Emily replied, her voice was tight. "I am sure when they hear my voicemail message they will realize they have the wrong person."

They reached the top of the stairs, and Ethan clutched Emily's hand, pulling her in close to him. Moving his hands to her waist, Emily looked up at Ethan. He lowered his chin and his lips met hers.

"Come," Ethan purred with a devious grin. "I want to show you something."

Ethan led Emily down the backstairs. He stopped in his father's office and grabbed a key. Thank God, the office was dark and Emily didn't get a formal introduction right there on the spot. She wished Ethan had prepared her to meet his family, this was a bit unfair. She could curse him for forcing her into this awkward situation.

As they continued down the hallway they stopped in front of a door that unlocked a circular room. The outside was covered in Field ledge stone, and the door was solid wood with a rounded top. CARLSON EST. 1970 was branded precisely in the middle. Ethan flicked on the light. Emily's mouth gaped at the sight of all the bottles that surrounded the space. Not only was there a full bar, but there were two high-top tables that sat four people comfortably. To the right there was a plush seating area with a brown leather couch that could easily seat eight. Wood beams crisscrossed the ceiling. Gorgeous wrought iron sconces lined the walls along with vintage photos in black textured frames featuring the winery and the people through the years.

"This is one of our four private tasting rooms." Ethan grinned, and Emily could see the gold flecks around his iris' gleaming. He looked like a kid in a candy store.

"Ethan, this room," she paused. "This place, it's spectacular." She ran her hands over the stone, traced the lines of grout and the bottles, magnificent in color. People go into old libraries and run their hands over shelves lined with first editions inhaling the scent of warm leather, rich mahogany and aged notepaper. This was Emily's library, new and vintage wines with the lingering scent of oak barrels and cork soaked with the luscious fruit of the vines.

"Em, what would you like to try first?"

Stunned and overwhelmed by the amount of choices, Emily shook her head and said, "I can't decide, you pick."

Ethan selected last year's Pinot Noir and poured two glasses for them. Emily situated herself on the couch. Soft music came began to pour throughout the room. A smile slid across Ethan's lips as he joined Emily in the seating area.

"A toast to you Miss Greene, oh how you've tamed the wild beast within me," he offered with a devious smile. Emily giggled and took a sip of the wine that made her cheeks pucker and taste buds tingle.

"Yeah, you were kind of a jerk before you got involved with me," she teased.

Ethan moved his lips up the base of Emily's throat to her jawline where he began fluttering feather light kisses.

Emily's body radiated with tingling heat, and she felt a low hum in her belly. The hum was all Ethan's doing. He stirred emotions in her body and feelings she never knew were there.

His touch—expert and gentle when he needed it to be; other times it was raw and merciless. Emily didn't care how Ethan possessed her or claimed her body. He owned her, and Emily was all too happy to be owned. The object of one person's desires and affections—it was thrilling.

Ethan took Emily's mouth, covering her soft lips with his, kissing her jolted sparks causing her skin to prick with heat. Emily placed her wine glass on the table in front of her and pushed to her feet. She reached under her skirt and slowly removed her panties handing them to Ethan. Ethan's eyebrows shot up at her sudden silent suggestion. Emily climbed on top of Ethan.

He stopped her and said, "Not here."

Confused she knitted her brows together giving him disappointed expression. Embarrassment washed over her, and she quickly reached for her panties feeling rejected by Ethan. Grabbing her by the wrists before she could push to her feet, Ethan pulled Emily into his frame. Hurt and confused she tried to wriggle free.

"Miss Greene, when I said "not here" I meant not on the couch."

"Oh," she hummed. Her breathing escalated when Ethan picked her up and carried her over to the bar.

"Stand here, face forward, press your palms flat to the table and put your feet on this brass bar," he instructed calmly.

Emily did as she was told. She was a few inches off the floor standing on the brass railing. She heard the buckle of his belt followed by the sound of his zipper. She tried to sneak a look over her shoulder, but Ethan cleared his throat saying, "Eyes forward Miss Greene."

Her stomach tightened and her thighs began to quiver. Ethan wasn't even touching Emily and she was excited with anticipation. She thought she might come undone at the mere grip of his arm around her waist. He brushed his lips to the back of her neck. Emily felt his warm breath hit her earlobe sending a rippling vibration down her spine. Lifting her skirt with the other hand, he said, "Arch your back and guide me in, Miss Greene."

Emily gasped when she felt Ethan's erection on the swell of her bottom.

"Take me," he growled. "You're the driver, baby."

Emily leaned her body forward and widened her stance. Pushing off the curve of the bar with her hands, she rolled her hips to meet Ethan, easing down until she covered the hard length of him. She winced at the pain still tender from their early morning tryst, or rather multiple trysts. Once she began her slow rhythmic movements, Ethan cupped her swelling breasts. Skin tingling, stomach fluttering, her body had now become accustomed to instantly responding to his touch. Emily's pace quickened as she became more aroused. Her palms glistened with dampness as she broke out in a light sweat.

Emily was losing her grip, on the bar and she let out a whimpering cry. Her core trembled as she clenched around Ethan in desperation. Noticing Emily's struggle to maintain her balance, Ethan gripped her hips tightly allowing her to regain control.

163

"Ethan… oh *please*," she moaned.

Emily felt her body climbing higher and higher until she could no longer stand it. She was on the edge. With one more thrust to her core Emily would be sent spiraling over.

"Now… Em… Come for me *now*," he commanded in a low voice.

Ethan's words unraveled Emily, and she unleashed herself feeling her body pulsating over and over.

"*Ah*," Ethan groaned. "Fuck, baby, I love it when you come around me."

Ethan was still thrusting inside, her driving her body back to the dizzying euphoric state. Feeling like she would implode, unable to endure the onslaught of electrifying shocks, she begged, "Ethan, it's so good, but…I can't take it."

He responded with a few sharp thrusts, a final exhilarating invasion to her body that left Emily completely listless and grasping for breath. Emily collapsed, her flushed cheek hit the cool bar, its surface fogging over and evaporating with every exhausted breath she took.

"God, Emily you…you are sensational," he groaned.

"I…I have no words for you Ethan, except…*wow*…just wow."

Chapter Eighteen
Ashleigh

Liam was changing into his pajamas in the bedroom of his hotel suite while Ashleigh finished her meal from room service. She managed to eat some soup and half of a turkey sandwich. By now the tears had subsided, but she had an awful headache. How was she going to tell Liam about Nick? Where would she begin? Liam emerged from the bedroom and walked to the bar pouring two glasses of scotch. He handed a glass to Ashleigh, and she immediately took two long sips. Liam brought the bottle over to the couch and refilled her glass.

"How are you feeling, Ashleigh?"

"I'm better than I was before but still feeling a bit blue. I don't know where to begin with my story, Liam."

"Why not start at the beginning," Liam said after taking a sip of his drink.

That statement made Ashleigh laugh for some reason. She replied, "Seems so simple doesn't it?"

Liam nodded at Ashleigh.

She took a drink and sighed, "Just before I started my job at *Maison Bleue* I worked at the Dior beauty counter at Saks Fifth Avenue. One day this gorgeous man walked in, and I noticed him right away. He was wearing a three piece slate grey suit with a black tie. He had dark hair and blue eyes. He was tall and lean with an athletic build, kind of like you, Liam," she said warmly, her wet eyes gleaming. Liam let out a soft chuckle.

Ashleigh walked over to the window and stared out at the city. After a long pause she turned back around and continued, "He was at the Kiehl's counter which was directly across the way from where I was working. No one ever seemed to be working at that counter, so I walked over to see if I could help him."

"Providing good customer service of course," Liam said with a smile.

"Something like that, but really I just wanted to meet him. Anyway, I helped him pick out a few gifts for his sister. He was shopping for her birthday. Apparently she was a bit of a Kiehl's fan because he purchased nearly $200.00 worth of beauty products," she laughed. "The attraction was mutual. He asked me out on a date right then and there. We talked for what seemed like forever. I found out he was quite a bit older than me.

Liam raised an eyebrow, "How much older?"

Ashleigh padded back and sat on the couch crossing her arms over her knees.

"Well, let's see. I was twenty-four when I met him, so he was thirty-three."

Liam shot her a look of surprise upon hearing that tidbit of information.

"Yes, that's right, a nine year age difference. Oh, don't look so shocked. I *like* older men," she said looking intensely at him.

"Oh, so, now you *like* me?" he teased using finger quotes while saying the word like.

"You know what I am saying," she replied while laughing and throwing a pillow at him which he managed to skillfully catch in between his legs.

"Not too old I hope, Ashleigh."

"Don't be gross, Liam."

"I'm sorry, please forgive the terrible joke and continue."

"And so we ended up really hitting it off on our first date. The age difference didn't really seem to matter. We had so much in common. Same taste in music, movies and even sports teams. We were both huge University of Michigan football fans."

"And by football you are not talking about soccer?" Liam hummed.

Ashleigh got up and grabbed the bottle of scotch and refilled their glasses. "Uhm, no, not soccer."

"So, then what happened? How long were you together?"

"We were together about three years." Ashleigh took a drink and swallowed hard. Her throat tightened. The glimmer in her hazel eyes turned off like a light.

"Liam, Nick died. He was killed in a car accident. He went out for some ice cream and he never came back. It was raining heavily, and a teenage girl had crossed the center line of the road in her car, hitting him head on. She couldn't see the lines in the road because the rain was coming down so hard. She only had her license for about two weeks. During pop-up thunderstorms in Michigan the downpours can be heavy, the weather can just be so unpredictable, especially near the lake."

Ashleigh paused for a moment to collect her thoughts. Clearing her throat she said, "Nick was rushed to the hospital where he later died from massive internal injuries. And as if the story wasn't sad enough, I had just told him I was pregnant, and he was completely overjoyed. He wanted to celebrate the good news, and that's why he went out for ice cream. I was scared, but Nick, Nick was over the moon, and he said everything was going to be alright before heading out the door. If I had only waited until the storm passed to tell him the news.

Liam was staring at Ashleigh, his face said everything. He was in complete shock. Liam ran his hand over the curve of his jaw. He let out a deep sigh, and his face fell.

"Ashleigh, I don't know what to say," his voice was brittle. "I am incredibly sorry for your loss. I cannot imagine what you went through." Liam moved from the chair to the couch as tears were running down Ashleigh's face. Thoughtfully, Liam had placed a box of tissues on the coffee table earlier anticipating she might begin to cry again. He handed her a tissue and put his arms around her, bringing her head into his chest. He kissed her on top of her head. "Shhhhh, you're Okay, Ash."

"I...I...obviously did not have the baby. I had a miscarriage which is common in women who are Rh-negative. I'm fine now, and I will be able to have children in the future if I want."

Ashleigh wiped her eyes with a tissue and took a sip of her scotch. "After Nick died, I found out he had changed his life insurance policy and his will after we had been together a year. He left his entire estate to me. He had been a Financial Analyst with The Newborne Group for seven years where he made good money and had a sizable amount in savings. I knew Nick loved to play the stock market, and I knew he often made investments. What I didn't know is how much he profited from the investments he made from the emerging tech and media markets years ago. He invested any money he earned from summer jobs and used his personal knowledge along with everything he was

171

learning as a Statistics major. Nick had a small fortune stashed away, close to two and a half million dollars. I found out a few months later that he and Jake, who I just saw downstairs earlier this evening, were saving money to start their own financial investment firm. Nick apparently had big plans for the future and was even entertaining the idea of getting into venture capitalism." Ashleigh stood up and walked to the window that overlooked Central Park. "I...I...felt so guilty, only knowing Nick for a few years and the fact that he left all that money to me." She was bawling at that point.

Liam approached Ashleigh placing his hands on her shoulders. "Ashleigh, I hope you know that you don't need to feel guilty. It sounds like Nick loved you very much, and he wanted you to be taken care of if anything should have happened to him."

Ashleigh turned to face Liam, she hugged him tightly and said, "I know you're right Liam. Thank you for listening to me."

"Of course, darling. I cannot believe you were holding onto this for so long."

"I actually feel like a weight has been lifted off of me by telling you, Liam," Ashleigh said. "Besides my family, Emily is the only one who knows I was ever pregnant, and now you know."

Ashleigh sat the remainder of her drink on the coffee table and curled up on the couch. She began to cry, sobbing so hard she fell asleep. Liam grabbed a blanket from the closet and placed it over her. He sat back in the club chair across from the couch sipping his scotch and peering out the window at the bright lights of the Manhattan skyline. Once he finished his drink, he scooped Ashleigh up from the couch and took her into the bedroom. Liam slipped off her shoes and tucked her into bed.

Ashleigh moved slightly causing her hair to sweep across her face and let out a soft moan.

He brushed her long brown tresses away from her face and kissed her on the cheek, "Goodnight my darling, Ashleigh. I hope you feel better in the morning."

Ashleigh was suddenly jolted from her deep sleep. She rolled up from beneath the covers discovering that she was in Liam's guest suite. Padding across the living room, she found Liam sleeping peacefully in the master bedroom. Ashleigh gently lifted the covers and slid into bed next to him. The sounds of her body stirring beneath the cool sheets woke Liam.

"Ashleigh, are you okay?" Liam asked as he shifted towards her.

"I'm fine, Liam," she lied.

Ashleigh was not fine. In fact she was feeling lonely, wanting nothing more than for Liam to make love to her so she could feel something other than sadness. She shifted her body, pressing close to Liam. His arms instantly wrapped around her slender frame. Feeling his warm body against her cheek, the soft, light dusting of hair spread across his broad chest tickled her nose. Looking up through her long lashes, she grazed her teeth over her bottom lip. That was her tell –Ashleigh wanted to be kissed. Liam was all too familiar, as he had seen that glint in her eyes and look on her face many times over the last two years.

"Kiss me, Liam," Ashleigh begged softly.

Sweeping her long wavy tresses over her shoulder he obliged her request. Capturing her mouth with his, he delivered slow lush licks. Ashleigh rolled her hips closer to Liam's body and climbed on top of him. Slowing pulling her shirt over her head, Ashleigh tossed it to the floor. Admiring her soft and lightly bronzed skin, Liam ran his hands over her body, cupping her firm breasts in his hands. Liam rolled up, encircling his arms around her back while kissing her soft lips over and over. Ashleigh's breathing escalated as Liam began nipping her jawline while his fingertips strummed against her smooth skin. Feeling Liam's touch, his hands expertly roaming over her body, she began to build.

The anticipation, this heated dance they did, twisting their bodies with one another, pulling apart and coming together, it was electric and sensual. The perfect combination of wanton need and passionate feelings weaving together created the most beautiful intimate moments between them.

Liam flipped Ashleigh to her back, grinding his hips into her and flexing fingers around the curve of her hip. Her heart pounded in her chest, and a whimper escaped her lips. He steadied himself over her, as she removed his pajama bottoms down his long legs. A delicious smile crossed her lips when Ashleigh heard the bundle of cotton fabric drop to the floor. Staring into Liam's dark eyes, she saw the lustful desire sharpen. He hitched his finger under the waistband of her lace panties and pulled them from her body.

Ashleigh inhaled sharply as she felt the weight of Liam ease into her, and they began to move in rhythm with each other.

"Liam," she breathed.

Liam only smiled, giving her exactly what she wanted and needed. He took pleasure in knowing he drove her body to writhe in ecstasy. Liam began kissing her, engulfing her mouth with fevered twists of his tongue. Ashleigh returned those kisses as her hips bucked wildly against his hardened frame.

Every moan, every whimper, every gasp and heart pounding climax—Liam knew how to work her body to trigger the release at the exact moment she desired.

Ashleigh dug her nails into Liam's biceps, and the orgasm flooded through her body sending radiating waves straight to her core. Her cheeks were red, her lips were swollen and her body trembled uncontrollably at the rush of the release.

"I love watching you unravel beneath me," he growled.

Liam thrust deeply, his hips working relentlessly, driving into her core. His orgasm riveted through Ashleigh causing her to spill out a severe pleasure filled, breathless cry.

Warmth spread through Ashleigh. Liam held her in his arms until the early morning light peeked through the white curtains. Pulling on her clothes, she quietly exited his hotel suite, returning to her own.

Liam's eyes fluttered open, at the sound of the heavy door catching and locking into the frame. A deep sigh escaped him as he lay, staring at the ceiling.

Chapter Nineteen
Emily

The evening at the Carlson's was coming to an end. Ethan's family was so welcoming to Emily, making her feel at ease immediately. Evan and his wife had just said goodnight and were on their way upstairs to their living quarters. Ethan's sister Lauren and her fiancé were helping Ethan's parents clear the remainder of the dishes from the table on the veranda. Dinner was fantastic, Marisol, the Carlson's housekeeper, and Jillian made Margherita pizza in the wood burning oven. For appetizers they had fresh guacamole made from California avocados and shrimp and avocado spring rolls served with rice noodles. After everyone devoured the tasty appetizers, Marisol brought out the California Cherry Walnut salad. Dessert was a mixed berry coffee cake, which reminded Emily a lot of her blueberry buckle. Drinks, of course, consisted mostly of wine and champagne, but the bar was fully stocked with multiple kinds of liquor and beer.

Only one word could describe The Carlson's estate — palatial. Just a few miles away from the winery itself, it sat on ten acres of land. Emily immediately noticed the romantic sprawling rose garden that surrounded a sparking plunge pool. It was picture perfect.

The house itself had ten bedrooms all with en-suites. On the main floor was the master suite with a private courtyard and a large fountain. Down the hallway was a guest wing that hosted two suites with private entrances. There was also a movie theater, wine cellar, formal living and dining rooms with ceilings that soared sixteen feet high and a gourmet kitchen. The remainder of the bedrooms were upstairs along with a great room featuring a full bar. In other words it was immaculate, an ultra-chic California wine country home. And it also made Emily realize just how wealthy Ethan's family was.

After everyone had said their goodnights, Emily and Ethan positioned themselves comfortably on two lounge chairs in front of the large stone outdoor fireplace that overlooked the saltwater pool.

Once they were alone, Emily turned to Ethan and asked, "Why didn't you go into the family business of wine making?"

"I intended to, but I was recruited by this high-end specialty retailer, Golden Gate Home Furnishings, for an internship the summer before my senior year at San Diego State, and I found out that I really liked the business. My boss offered me a permanent position after I finished school. I was there for about eight years. A few years ago I met Clark, and he recruited me to join the team at Cooper Bentley."

Emily remembered Ethan's first day at Cooper Bentley as if it was only yesterday. Standing at the reception desk wearing a sleek indigo suit paired with a crimson tie, she noticed Ethan right away. Breezing past him confidently, Emily felt his dark eyes bore into her as she met his gaze. When Clark introduced them later that morning, Ethan shook Emily's hand, sending a wave of electricity up her spine. She knew immediately she was in trouble—instant attraction. But, he soon became involved with Libby, and

Emily just pushed romantic thoughts of Ethan out of her mind.

Smiling at Emily, he said, "I wasn't sure about moving to the Midwest and dealing with cold weather, but it's not so bad." He sat up swiftly swinging his legs off the lounge chair and stood up. Ethan grasped Emily's hands pulling her to her feet. She inched towards him, closing the space between them. Ethan lowered his head so his lips brushed hers. He moved his hands to her face and kissed her.

"Come on, let's grab a bottle of wine and take it upstairs," he said softly as he took some loose strands of her hair and gently tucked them behind her ear. Ethan took a bottle of Pinot Grigio out of the wine cooler. Showing her the label, Emily nodded in agreement.

Ethan's room was as grand as a posh five star hotel suite, with a hand carved four poster king bed, a fireplace, and a separate living room area complete with a media center. Ethan had some amazing photographs featuring iconic images from Hollywood scattered around the lush room; there was a beautiful black and white photo of the Hollywood sign, a picture of an old movie studio, a few stills from various classic movies and one of a director standing behind a Panavision camera. They were all in shiny antique zinc frames with ivory matting. Emily especially liked the photo of a Hollywood actress standing on the red carpet facing all the photographers, but you could only see her from the back.

A minibar sat in the corner near the double doors that opened to a private terrace. The etched crystal glass and barware was the exact same design Ethan had in his office. The bathroom had marble topped dual sinks, a walk in rain shower with gorgeous navy blue and white glass tile and the largest oval shaped, free standing whirlpool bathtub Emily had ever seen.

Emily kicked off her sandals and sat down in one of the plush square framed, charcoal colored chairs in the living area.

"Emily, I've shared my 'how I got to where I am now story'. I think it's only fair you indulge me with yours," Ethan hummed, and then took a sip of wine.

Replying sweetly, "My story is not half as interesting as yours, Ethan." Emily shifted her legs underneath her and carefully observed Ethan as he began to light a few of the candles staggered throughout the room.

Ethan's voice is light with laughter as he says, "I am sure that is not true, but what brought you to Grand Rapids? I know you were in Chicago before you came to Cooper Bentley."

Emily pondered his question. She could basically say that Chicago was filled with too many memories of her ex-boyfriend Craig, who pulled a Houdini. That would prompt Ethan to ask why someone would up and leave Emily, sneaking out in the middle of the night like the Baltimore Colts did in 1984. It was too much, Emily wasn't sure she was ready for that intense conversation with Ethan quite yet. Admittedly she stuck around those few months after he disappeared hoping if she stayed in one place Craig would find his way back to her. *Pathetic.*

"That's an even longer story, and I will share it with you someday," she replied coolly. She wet her throat with a sip of wine then worked up enough courage to broach the topic she'd been dying to discuss with Ethan.

"Actually, Ethan, I'd like to discuss a far more interesting topic with you."

Lifting one of his thick eyebrows, "Oh," he says. "And what interesting subject does the curious and sexy Miss Greene want to discuss?"

A flirtatious smile crossed Emily's lips, "*Your* sexual activity…preferences, I guess is what you might call them." She felt her cheeks warm as the words tumbled out of her mouth.

"Ah, I see, and what about my preferences exactly would you like to discuss?" he inquired as his eyes widened.

Emily felt her skin grow hot and prickly all over.

"I guess the simplest question is why?"

Ethan's dark eyes narrowed. "You want to know why I enjoy a bit of kink?"

Emily nodded and mumbled, "How did you know it was something you wanted?"

"I didn't know until someone introduced me to it."

Shock washed over Emily's face. She replied, "Someone introduced you to it? So, someone controlled you with sex?"

"No, it wasn't like that, and I hope you don't feel that way Emily—controlled I mean."

Emily swallowed hard, "No," she paused to take another drink and continued.
"Surprised...intrigued...stimulated, but not controlled."

"Good," Ethan replied his voice was tight. Pushing to his feet he walked to the bar and refilled his empty glass.

"Having fun and pleasing my partner is all it's ever been about for me personally, Emily. You become much more aware of your body and the level of pain, pleasure and sensitivity you can endure."

"How did you, know that day in the conference room, that I would submit to your terms so favorably, Mr. Carlson?"

A devious smile crossed Ethan's lips. He replied, "I didn't. Honestly, I was a bit nervous, but I'm glad you didn't slap me or worse." He let out soft chuckle. "I sort of felt that you might be open to exploring your physical desires."

Emily blinked at Ethan feeling the muscles in her vagina clench, "Oh," she paused for a moment then asked, "And what drew you to that conclusion?"

"It was the way your body responded to my touch. You were…expressive …and greedy," Ethan replied smoothly.

"So, because I muttered a few dirty comments and commands in your ear you decided to entice me into your wicked sex games?" Emily replied, as she stood up and padded to the double, French doors that opened to the terrace.

"Of course," he chuckled and took a sip of his drink.

Emily looked over her shoulder glancing in Ethan's direction and slowly pushed the doors open. The scent of lavender rushed over her, and she inhaled deeply. She closed her eyes while folding her arms over her chest and smiled.

Ethan followed her onto the terrace. Encircling his arms around her from behind, he began kissing her neck. "I don't want to play games tonight, though, Miss Greene."

Emily turned around so that she was facing Ethan, replying, "Oh, so does this mean you're not going to spank me, Mr. Carlson?"

Taking her gently by the hand, Ethan led her back into the room, stopping only to pick her up and carry her to the bed. Emily's heart was pounding. She felt nervous and excited at the same time. Ethan smiled as he playfully tossed Emily onto the bed and kicked off his shoes. She could feel her skin growing warmer as Ethan's hands glided over her body.

"Not tonight, Miss Greene." He brushed his lips over the curve of her mouth, kissing her chastely. "Tonight, I have much more intimate plans for you."

Emily wrapped her trembling hands around the back of Ethan's neck as he began softly kissing her throat. The earlier playfulness retreated from the air, replaced by sensual desire and quiet desperation.

"Tonight, I want to memorize your body." He paused for a moment as he began to unbutton her blouse, pushing the delicate fabric over her shoulders. "All the angles, contours and curves every… *kiss*…single…*kiss*… inch."

A shuddering wave of pleasure ran over Emily as she opened her eyes catching the light grey sheer curtains that were hanging over the large windows dancing in the background. The breeze had blown out a few of the many candles Ethan had lit earlier.

Lifting her chin up, he brushed his lips against hers kissing her deeply. Ethan skimmed the tips of his fingers over her thigh, running his hand under the small of her back returning his lips to her neck. Emily took a deep breath. Ethan raised his head, and their eyes met.

"Ethan, I…" she breathed.

"Shhh… I'm going to make love to you now Emily," he whispered.

The smell of lavender filled the room. Emily inhaled deeply. Closing her eyes, she surrendered her body, feeling Ethan's hot mouth work an erotic magic over her bare flesh.

Chapter Twenty
Amanda

Amanda was stretched out on a bright orange lounge chair on the terrace of her new apartment, enjoying a cup of coffee and reading a magazine. She was glad to have her weekends free again, quitting her job at the mall was liberating. Vince would be returning from his trip later that Saturday afternoon, and Amanda couldn't wait to see him. She didn't want to spend another minute alone this weekend without him. Taking a sip of her coffee she noticed it was cold. Amanda went into the kitchen for a refresher.

Amanda was certainly feeling refreshed these days. She hadn't felt sad, anxious or depressed in weeks. In fact she was feeling so good these days she made an appointment with her Doctor to see if she could lower the dosage of her happy pills. She even quit drinking in the morning.

Stepping back onto the terrace, she felt the wind beginning to pick up and heard thunder rumbling in the distance. Knowing the rains could start at any moment, she started to gather her things from the coffee table when she heard her phone buzz, Vince was calling.

"Good Morning, Vince."

"Hi gorgeous, Are you feeling better today?"

"Still a little nauseous. However, I feel much better than I did yesterday."

"I'm glad to hear it, and I'm sorry I wasn't there to take care of you."

"That's okay Vince, Alex made sure I was well cared for in your absence."

"Alex is a good man. I'm calling because, my flight has been delayed. There is a storm that just won't let up, and it's keeping us from taking off. I am not sure when I will be back."

Amanda frowned and let out a deep sigh, "Hurry back Vince. I miss you."

"I miss you terribly. I'm not happy about the delay either," frustration seeped through his tone. "Alex, will be dropping off a credit card and some other items for you later this morning."

"A credit card?" she inquired. "What is the credit card for, Vince?"

"You will have a personal expense account and a weekly allowance. I want you to enjoy yourself, go shopping or even pamper yourself. It's my treat."

Amanda could not believe what she was hearing. This was all too surreal. A smile crossed her lips, "Vince, you are being so incredibly kind to me. Why?"

"Amanda, you're very special to me, and you will be treated as such. I hope to be back early this evening. I'm sorry the weather is keeping me away from you this weekend," he sighed. "I have something incredible planned for us tomorrow."

Hearing that Vince had planned something perked her right up, pulling her from her sullen mood.

Amanda ended the call and returned to the kitchen, taking a few sips of her coffee. All of this was like a dream, she had only known Vince a few short weeks. In that time he had moved her into his apartment, was showering her with lavish gifts and now was giving her a weekly allowance. If Amanda didn't know better she could have sworn she was a paid companion. However, she had yet to sleep with Vince. He hadn't really even tried to have sex with her since they had been together, although she had kissed him plenty. She thought about having sex with Vince many times, often wondering if it would be mind-blowing or boring. Maybe the sex was bad and that is what ended his marriage?

"Amanda, are you here? It's Alex."

"Hey Alex, I'm in the kitchen."

Alex entered the kitchen carrying a few garment and shopping bags from Louis Vuitton, Gucci and Jimmy Choo.

"Alex, what is all this?" Amanda asked in a surprised voice.

"Well, Vince had me pick up a few items he thought you might like," he replied while placing all the bags across the breakfast bar.

"Alex, did *you* pick out all of this stuff? Who knew you had such feminine and classic taste?" she teased as she began to open one of the garment bags.

"Girl please, *you* know I love a lacy dress and killer pair of heels," Alex joked.

Amanda laughed and rolled her eyes, "This stuff is so beautiful. It's all exactly my taste. How did this happen?" she said holding up the emerald green Gucci dress.

"I am not sure. I think Vince's assistant called up a few stores and gave the Personal Shopper's your sizes."

Amanda was mesmerized as she ran her fingers over the soft fabrics. The best surprise was the four boxes in the Jimmy Choo bag. She read the labels: THE ANOUK PUMP IN BLACK, THE LUNA PUMP IN NUDE, THE VITA PUMP AND A PAIR OF LANCE SANDALS IN SILVER. Her brain screamed with delight.

"Whoa, those are fancy shoes," Alex said pointing to the Lance sandals Amanda was holding in her hands.

Amanda smiled and said, "Yes, *yes* they are."

"Okay Amanda, here is your credit card. It has a $20,000 limit. Your monthly allowance is $5,000. June's gift has already been deposited into your account," he said handing her all the items.

Amanda was overcome. It felt like her birthday, Christmas and all the holidays and special milestone events rolled into one.

"Alex, I'll be right back," she said. She felt like she was having a panic attack. She flung open the medicine cabinet and popped another Zoloft. Taking several deep breaths Amanda returned to a calmer state. She collected herself and returned to the kitchen. Alex had poured himself a cup of coffee and was sitting at the breakfast bar.

"Alex, can I ask you a question?"

"Sure thing Amanda. What's up? Did you want me to put your clothes and shoes in your room?"

"Please Alex, you're not a bellman. Don't be silly." She sat down beside Alex at the bar and said, "Does Vince do this sort of thing a lot?"

"What do you mean?"

"Did he do this for previous girlfriends? You know, giving allowances and clothing." Alex knitted his eyebrows together. "I've worked for Vince for the last two years. There have been no other girlfriends that I am aware of."

Amanda smiled politely as she carefully placed the shoes back in the boxes.

"Now for the best part," Alex said handing her a set of car keys. "These belong to your new car. Vince wants me to sell your old car."

Amanda's mouth hung open as she took the keys from Alex. "What kind of car is it, Alex?"

"Why don't you come down to the parking garage and see for yourself?"

A smile crossed Amanda's face, and she and Alex headed down the elevator to the parking garage. Amanda wondered if it was a sports car or a maybe a roomy SUV that she could pack full with bags from the many shopping trips she was planning to take. No matter she thought to herself, any car is better than the piece of shit Altima she had been driving around the past few months.

"There it is," Alex said pointing to the shiny two-door, grey metallic Mercedes Benz.

"No way! A Mercedes!" Amanda shouted.

"It's an E350 Coupe. Here's the other set of keys."

"Nice, Alex," she said while clutching the keys in her hand. "These have the Mercedes logo on them. You didn't want to give away the surprise, did you?"

He shook his head, "Nope. The look on your face is priceless."

"Alex, let's take it for a spin. What'd you say? Do you have time?" she beamed as she opened the driver's side door and the new car smell rushed over her. The interior was black with burnt walnut wood trim. The tailoring was impressive, it reminded her a little bit of the Lexus that Brandon had bought her as a wedding present. Amanda lost her beautiful luxury automobile in the divorce. She thought Brandon might show her some mercy and let her keep the car, since it was technically a gift. He obviously did not.

"That sounds like fun. Yeah, I can go with you." He opened the passenger side door and climbed in.

"Where to?" Amanda said curling her hands around the sterling wheel.

Alex smiled, suggesting, "How about driving over towards Millennium Park?"

"Sounds fantastic!" She revved the engine as she pulled out of the parking garage and turned onto the highway.

Chapter Twenty-One
Ashleigh

Ashleigh returned home from her week in New York feeling relaxed and refreshed. On Sunday, she drove out to the Hamptons with Liam for lunch and a polo match. Over the course of the week, she and Liam spent their time shopping and walking around the city. During one of their event free evenings, they went to see an Off-Broadway play about two teenage vampires who were in love, but their parents would not allow them to be together because of some lifelong feud among the two families. Ashleigh thought it was all very Hatfield and McCoy's. Liam compared it to Romeo and Juliet, of course he did. Needless to say it was ridiculous, but Ashleigh and Liam got a kick out of making fun of the performance.

After the long week of meetings, cocktail receptions, food and wine tastings and events at The Refinery Hotel, Ashleigh spent her last day in New York at the spa being pampered. She even went to Dream Dry for a blow out and Oribe treatment.

Telling Liam about losing Nick and the baby was painful, but she was glad she confided her secret to him. Besides Emily, Ashleigh considered Liam one of her best friends. Keeping this part of her life from him seemed a bit unfair or like she was hiding something.

Ashleigh began to unpack. She accidently bumped the nightstand with her suitcase and heard something fall to floor. Bending down to see what it was, she spotted the Union Jack keychain Liam had given her. She picked it up and placed it back on her nightstand. Grabbing her phone off the dresser, she pulled up the Skype app to see if Liam was online. He was not. *Where could Liam be?*

He left New York a day before she did. She looked at her watch and realized that it was nearly eight-thirty in the evening in London. Liam was probably having dinner with friends, but she found it odd that he had not checked in with her. Usually he sends her a message to see if she arrived home safely.

She decided to check her email and found there was a message from her Editor. It was the assignment schedule for the next few weeks which included travelling to

California, Seattle and then Montreal after the Fourth of July. After Montreal she would be back in London. Summer was going to go by fast, she thought. She had better make some plans or these remaining weekends would pass her by.

Ashleigh continued to unpack, and she saw a flash of lightning in the distance. She threw some clothes into the washing machine and headed downstairs to retrieve her mail. Crossing the lobby to where the mailboxes she came face to face with Amanda.

"Amanda?!" she inquired, her voice thick with shock.

"Ashleigh!" Amanda shouted excitedly. "Hi. How are you?"

"Amanda, what are you doing here? I haven't seen you in a few months."

"Yeah, I've been busy. I moved out of my apartment, and I live here now," Amanda said grinning from ear to ear.

The first question that came to Ashleigh's mind was, how the fuck could Amanda afford to live at the River House? Then, she wondered what unsuspecting rich man she had taken advantage of to give her such a posh lifestyle, thinking it better not be Mr. Sullivan. The man was a serial husband, he had just finalized his third divorce in five years.

Ashleigh could not hold her tongue, and the words sarcastically fell out of her mouth. "*How* are *you* living here Amanda?"

"The man I'm seeing, his name is Vince, he lives here, and he asked me to move in with him," Amanda replied sharply.

"Oh? I didn't know you were involved with anyone," Ashleigh quipped.

The dislike these two women had for each other was quite obvious. There was an awkward silence—the tension hung in the air around them. Emily had introduced Ashleigh to Amanda a few years ago at a dinner party, Emily naively thought Ashleigh might be able to help Amanda make some connections that could to lead to a job opportunity, since Amanda had just been fired from the radio station. Although, Ashleigh quickly found out that Amanda had no intention of getting a job.

Amanda told Ashleigh she had a plan to win her ex-husband back, and if not him she would find another rich guy. That worked out well for Amanda, as Ashleigh knew she had been working at the mall for the last few months and her only known sexual relationship was with her divorce lawyer. Ashleigh thought Amanda probably traded sex for legal representation.

After Amanda had gone completely broke, she made everyone feel sorry for her to get free drinks and food, always playing the "help me I'm poor" card. Ashleigh never liked Amanda, but she didn't have the heart to tell Emily. After all, Emily was a sucker for helping someone she thought had potential.

Emily saw Amanda in a different light. She knew her back during the *happier* times. According to Emily, Amanda used to be pretty funny. Ashleigh didn't see it, but what exactly did Amanda have to laugh about these past few years? Amanda and Emily had met at a charity event a few years ago, before Amanda lost everything. Now, she was divorced, lost her job, was publicly humiliated by a cheating scandal and her wealthy family disowned her.

"Yes, I have been dating Vince for a while now, and he just bought me a Mercedes. Not to mention, he spoils me like crazy, buying me designer clothes, shoes and fabulous jewels."

Amanda was laying it on pretty thick for Ashleigh. Part of her wondered if Amanda was just lurking in the lobby to see if she could find a man with money, and this was all just a fabrication.

A brittle smile crossed her lips. "Oh, that sounds amazing. I'd love to see your place, Amanda." There was only one way to find out if Amanda was telling the truth or not, and that was to see if she actually had an apartment in the building.

"Sure thing, Ashleigh. I'll take you there now. Do you have the time?" Amanda said with a grin.

"Yeah, just let me grab my mail first," Ashleigh said as she took her key and unloaded her mailbox.

Both women walked in silence to the elevator. Amanda pressed the up arrow, the doors immediately opened. Amanda pressed the button for the 20th floor.

This should be good, Ashleigh thought to herself.

Chapter Twenty-Two
Emily and Ashleigh

Emily's phone rang, it was an unknown number. Not recognizing the area code, thinking it could be someone from LA Business Design, she answered, "Hello, this is Emily Greene."

"Hello Emily. Are you having a good afternoon?" The gruff voice said. "Did you have a nice time in California?"

"Hi. Yes I did have a nice time in California," she said while walking to the kitchen.

"Why are you with *him*, Emily? You know he'll never love you." The voice was now seething with anger.

Emily replied, "I'm sorry, may I ask who this is?"

"You don't get to ask the questions. I do. Do you like games, Emily? What about surprises?"

"Excuse me?" Emily inquired. All she heard was a faded laugh and then a click.

On top of being annoying, these calls were downright harassing. A million things ran through Emily's brain: *Who is calling? Why are they calling? He'll never love me?* She thought about changing her number, but that would be more trouble than it's worth.

Emily grabbed her workout bag and headed for the gym. She needed to blow off some steam.

After her workout she met Ashleigh for coffee at the Bagel Beanery. Despite her best efforts of switching gyms, Emily managed to run into Andy. He explained that he had a few clients he worked with at both locations. Even though he still made her uncomfortable, Emily maintained a polite conversation with Andy. Surprisingly, he didn't pester her or make crude comments today. He actually left Emily alone as she finished the remainder of her workout session.

"Okay, so tell me about Amanda. I want all the gory details, Ash."

Ashleigh explained all she knew about Amanda's current living situation and what little she knew about the man she was cohabitating with at the River House.

"Vince Everett," Emily commented. "Yeah, I've heard of Everett Sterling Airlines. I read a recent article about the company in the *Lakeshore Press*. They're hosting some big event in a few weeks, a dedication for the new Aviation building at Graysen College."

"Amanda seemed pretty happy, Emily," Ashleigh remarked.

"Are you sure it wasn't an act?" Emily's tone was sharp.

"Honestly, for once she didn't seem to be faking the happiness. I saw a real spark in her eye when she talked about this guy. It *could* be love."

Emily remembered when she had first met Amanda at a fundraiser for the Phillip Cooper Foundation, the Cooper of Cooper Bentley. Amanda's then husband Brandon's law firm handled all of Cooper Bentley's legal matters, and they still do to this day. At the fundraiser Emily and Amanda were seated at the same table. Finding themselves a little bored at the event, the two women were able to bond over fashion and travel while sharing a bottle of chardonnay. Emily ran into Amanda at another event for the

Foundation later that summer, and it was apparent they were going to be good friends.

Today, it was like she didn't even know Amanda. Since Amanda lost her job, her husband, her family and her lifestyle she had become a bitter person. For the last several months Amanda's ugliness had festered into a cancer that was draining Emily to the point where she didn't seem to care about Amanda's well-being in the least.

"Can we change the subject please?" Emily wailed.

Ashleigh laughed, agreeing another topic would be much more pleasant. She told Emily about her trip to New York and her time spent with Liam.

"So you told Liam about Nick, had sex with him and then left his bed?" Emily interjected. "That's kind of cold, don't you think?"

Ashleigh looked away from Emily's biting gaze. She swallowed the lump in her throat feeling a twinge of guilt. The guilt was because Ashleigh knew it was shady to have snuck out in the early morning hours, leaving Liam to question why she'd gone back to her room and possibly feeling used. Although he never asked her directly, Ashleigh could only assume those were Liam's thoughts. Also, Ashleigh might have used Liam for sex as an escape that night, like drugs or booze, to dull the stinging pain she was left with upon recounting her memories. That didn't mean that Ashleigh didn't enjoy it, but it probably wasn't the best time for sex.

"We usually sleep together, yes," Ashleigh corrected.

"Sleeping together means you actually sleep next to him and wake up with him after you've had your way with him," Emily scoffed.

She shot her friend an irritated glare, "Are you lecturing me about Liam, Emily?"

Truth of the matter is that Ashleigh has never stayed the night with Liam. She always ends up back in her hotel room. She never invites Liam to her room. It would break her heart to kick him out. Continuing to have sex with Liam might be confusing for him. It's definitely confusing for her. But the rules have been established— they are good friends who have occasional casual sex. But, it's been two years. Suddenly, Emily's haunting words from their previous conversation came screeching back. *Was Liam waiting for her? Was she waiting for him? Why hadn't they engaged in relationships with other people?*

Emily sighed, "I'm sorry Ash. I just think you and Liam could have something really great. I just want you to be happy."

"What makes you think I'm *not* happy?"

Emily felt the tension in her body tightening. She took a sip of her latte and said, "You're right Ashleigh, I have no right to question you or your relationship with Liam." She paused then continued, "It's your life, and it's not fair for me to lecture you."

Ashleigh leaned back in her chair and crossed her arms. She was defensive because she knew there was a hint of truth to Emily's words.

Ashleigh bowed her head, sighing, "No, Emily, you bring up some good points. I need to talk to Liam or better yet just stop having sex with him."

Emily shifted the conversation asking, "So where are you off to next?"

"California, Big Sur actually," Ashleigh replied then took a sip of her tea. "Speaking of California, why don't you fill me on your time with Ethan and your big campaign?"

Emily explained how she and the rest of the advertising team were able to come up with some creative strategies for the impending campaign. Ethan even sat in on a couple of the brainstorming sessions and offered some helpful suggestions for promotion. She and Ethan will need to return to Los Angeles when they begin shooting the commercials, but that is still a few weeks away.

"We had a wonderful time. Ethan introduced me to his family and took me to their winery."

Ashleigh's eyebrows lifted, "Really? Seems kind of soon."

"Tell me about it. I was pretty ticked with him at first, but it was very casual. His family made me feel right at home like I'd known them forever. We stayed the night on Friday then Ethan took me to this amazing resort and spa in Santa Barbara. We drank wine, ate delicious food, and Ethan booked me a spa treatment. I had the most amazing seaweed facial and deep tissue massage."

Emily's phone began to buzz, the caller ID said private. She answered, but there was no one there. A few seconds later a text message then appeared: WHAT'S YOUR FAVORITE GAME? MINE'S WATCHING YOU, EMILY.

Knots twisted in Emily's stomach. Her heart began to race, and she just stared at her phone. Emily slowly scanned her surroundings. She didn't notice anyone suspicious. All the message did was leave her feeling freaked out.

"Emily, you okay?" Ashleigh asked. "You're as white as a sheet."

Emily passed her phone to Ashleigh so she could view the message. Emily began to tell her about all the strange phone calls she'd been receiving. A shiver moved through Ashleigh.

"Are you going to talk to Ethan about these creepy messages and phone calls?"

"Things are going so well between us, I'm not sure our relationship is ready for this kind of drama."

Ashleigh scoffed and said, "That's ridiculous, Emily."

Emily shot Ashleigh an irritated look.

Ashleigh strummed her fingers on the side of her cup, then said, "Hey…what about that former Assistant of yours, could she be involved?"

"That's an interesting thought," Emily pondered. "This is exactly the kind of shit she'd pull. Next time the phone rings, Morgan's getting a piece of my mind."

"If you engage her though, she will know it bothers you. It's probably best to just ignore every unknown call and force it to voicemail. She will eventually tire out," Ashleigh advised.

Emily felt better knowing that Morgan was most likely the pest behind the calls. Emily recalled time and time again how Morgan tried to capture Ethan's attention in the break room or shamelessly flirt with him at company events. It was entirely possible that Morgan found out that Emily was dating Ethan and it sparked jealously.

Thunder rumbled in the distance. Ashleigh hurriedly grabbed her purse and said, "I gotta go Emily. I don't want to be caught in this rain storm."

Ashleigh gave Emily a quick hug and darted to her car. Emily waved as Ashleigh peeled out of the parking lot. *I hope you get over your fear of storms someday soon Ashleigh.*

Chapter Twenty-Three
Amanda

Amanda found herself feeling restless and bored on a Saturday afternoon. Should she go shopping? Hit the gym for a workout? Vince had been in his study for most of the morning and had scheduled a round of golf at the club that afternoon. He invited Amanda to accompany him to the club where he thought she might want to work on her tennis game or have a spa day, but she declined. Amanda had spent the previous day at the spa and was apprehensive about picking up a tennis racket again. It had been so long that she was sure her game was more than a little rusty.

Amanda's feelings for Vince were growing stronger with each day. However, things with Vince had yet to reach a physical level, and she was beginning to think either he was not attracted to her or that he was impotent. Vince was a hard man to read at times. Through all the gifts, dinners and even the surprise overnight trips she was still unclear of his feelings for her. He had yet to introduce her to his kids, not that she minded, but it did seem odd. The more she thought about it, she wondered if Vince had even seen his kids at all this summer.

Maybe his ex-wife was a bitch, or crazy, or both. Amanda didn't know much about his kids, his ex-wife, what their marriage was like or even why they were divorced. Amanda thought maybe she should be grateful that the wife and kids were not a distraction or worse, a problem. She would welcome the idea of coordinating schedules for school activities, weekends and basically step-parenting business in general, if Vince wanted her too.

Picking up a bottle of lotion, she poured some in her hand and began rubbing it onto her legs. In that moment she wondered how everyone at The Bath Shop was doing, which was weird because Amanda never imagined she would ever think of her former co-workers again. These were a bunch of people who she never much cared about.

Earlier in the week, she had gone to lunch with Daniel and he filled her in on the new guy in his life. The relationship was still blossoming— they had been dating for about two weeks. Stephen was a Pediatric Speech and Language Pathologist. Daniel said work was positively boring since she had left the company, and he had transferred to the Woodfield Mall to take over Amanda's position. It was a shorter commute, for which he expressed his gratefulness many times as he knocked back a few martinis.

Amanda checked her phone for the time and noticed she had missed a few things. She saw Emily had checked in on Foursquare to the Fulton Street Farmer's Market, and Ashleigh had a Facebook status that said she just had a great workout and was ready for her trip tomorrow.

Her boredom, along with thinking about Vince's ex-wife, led her to do something she hadn't done in a long time—social media stalking of her ex-husband, Brandon. But first, she needed some liquid courage. She walked to the bar and poured herself a vodka on the rocks. She was starting to feel quite anxious, so she retrieved two pills from her medicine cabinet and washed them down with a swig of the cocktail.

Amanda had Julie's Facebook login information, which allowed her to look at Brandon's page. Julie was one of the last ties to her old life. If there was anything she needed to know, Julie was the one who kept her in the loop. It was nice to see Julie still maintained a friendship with Brandon despite the divorce. Last update she heard from her sister, Brandon was so busy with his case load at the law firm he had no time for a social life. Although, looking at his Facebook page, Amanda saw a much different story

It looked like Brandon had found a new girlfriend and recently taken a trip to Costa Rica. He and Erica Hamilton spent a lovely vacation at the Four Seasons at Peninsula Papagayo. Erica was very pretty, but quite the opposite of Amanda. Erica had short dark hair, bronzed skin, basically no curves, except for an all too apparent chest enhancement, and brilliant blue eyes. Amanda studied the photos of the two of them. Brandon looked happy, like over the moon elated. She was glad for Brandon. He deserved to be with someone who made him smile so genuinely.

She stumbled upon something else of interest, Andrew Langston's profile. *Why is Jules friends with Andrew Langston?* Amanda couldn't imagine that their father would allow this friendship. Amanda searched Julie's messages for a conversation between the two of them and found nothing. She clicked on Andrew's page. It seems he had graduated from college and was living in Chicago working at Alpha Street Partners, a private equities firm.

Amanda decided to leave Julie a message. It was a code they had worked out when they wanted to see each other. Amanda pulled up the inbox and created a new message to Julie Richards and simply typed "TEST". Julie would see that message, read it and delete it. Then she would get her disposable phone and use it to call Amanda. It could be hours or days, but when Julie had the time she would find a way to contact her sister.

Amanda logged off of Facebook and decided she needed to work up a good sweat. The best way for her to do that was to run, since sex apparently was not an option at this point. If Vince didn't try to fuck her soon, Amanda's BOB was going to have a meltdown from overuse. Amanda heard the door to the apartment open as she was putting her running shoes on.

"Amanda? Are you around?"

"Hey, Alex, I'm getting ready to go to the gym."

"Would you like some company? I'm feeling like a run, too."

Amanda opened the door of her bedroom and saw Alex looking a bit flustered.

"Yes, that would be fun. You okay, Alex?" Amanda approached him gently placing a comforting hand on his shoulder. His entire body became stiff, and Amanda drew in a sharp breath. His gaze caught hers, and she dropped her hand back to her side. *That was weird.*

Alex cleared his throat and said, "I will be. I just had a fight with my sister about our dad's birthday party next weekend. My sister is impossible."

Amanda replied, "I know how you feel Alex. Sisters can be a real pain in the ass. I understand completely."

Alex let out a half-hearted laugh, "Okay Amanda. Let's go run it out. Give me a few to change."

Just then, she heard the front door open again. Walking into the living room she found Vince was home.

"Hey, Vince. How was the golf game?"

"Hi, gorgeous." He greeted her smiling, and then gripped her waist kissing her firmly on the lips. "We had to cut it short. There's been an emergency in New York with one of our clients. I have to fly out tonight and try to smooth some things over and make sure everything gets worked out. I am so sorry to bail on you this evening and abandon our dinner plans. Can you help me pack me a suitcase? I need two suits, two casual outfits and of course my pajamas."

"Oh Vince please, you never have to apologize for your work schedule," she replied calmly trying to not let her disappointment ring in her tone. "Will Alex be joining you?"

"No, he is going to stay there with you. I should be back after work on Monday."

"I'll go pack your things now, and you can get cleaned up."

Amanda was upset that Vince was leaving. He seemed to be gone almost every other weekend.

Why didn't he ever invite me to go with him?

Since Amanda didn't have a job and Vince was practically gone all the time, it left her feeling irritated and lonely, like she felt when she was married to Brandon. She needed to shake things up. You can shop, workout and go to the spa only so much before you turn into a zombie.

"Ready to go hit the gym, Amanda?" Alex asked as he came around the corner in his workout gear.

"You go ahead Alex. I have to pack Vince a suitcase for New York City. He has an emergency with a client."

The expression on Alex's face changed instantly. "Okay," he said quietly. "See you down there."

"Good. We're going to have a chat about this difficult sister of yours."

Alex gave Amanda a sour look and playfully stuck out his tongue as he turned around to close the door.

Amanda walked down the corridor past the bar to the bedroom. She didn't mind that Vince had a personal bedroom all to himself. She liked having her space. Vince spent most nights in his own room because he worked late and did not want to disturb Amanda, who usually went to bed around eleven. Entering Vince's room, Amanda heard the shower running and Vince singing. She smiled. Amanda grabbed his suitcase out of the closet placing it on the chair by the window. Thinking that Vince's head was probably in problem solving mode she took a chance and decided to ask him if she could get a job.

Stepping into the bathroom she took a deep breath and said very sweetly, "Hey Vince, can I ask you something?"

"Sure, anything you need, gorgeous."

"Okay, here it goes. I'm finding myself being a little bored. I didn't think I would ever miss work, and I'm not saying I want to work forty hours a week or anything, but would you object to me getting a part-time job?"

There was silence for a few moments. Finally, Vince replied, "Instead of a part-time job, have you thought about doing volunteer or charity work?"

That idea hadn't even occurred to Amanda. She didn't need money, she just needed an outlet. Working on a charity project or a fundraiser was something she could definitely do. She was on the board of a few notable charities and often helped organize special events when she was married to Brandon.

"Vince!" she shouted. "That's a wonderful idea. Do you have any suggestions? "

221

"I have lots of connections Amanda. I will have my secretary send you a list of the charities and organizations I support and you can take your pick."

"Vince," her voice became shaky. "You don't think any of these organizations will hold my past against me do you?"

"They better not if they'd like to stay in my favorable and generous graces."

Amanda swallowed the fear that had crept in her throat upon hearing Vince's reassuring words.

"I…I…don't want to be a bother for you Vince or wreck any relationships you have built because of my errors in judgment."

The water turned off and Amanda saw Vince reach for his towel. She got a glimpse of his naked body through the fogged glass.

"Amanda," he said very calmly. "In case it's unclear, I always get what I want. People need me, I don't need them. Whatever charity or foundation you decide to put your efforts into, they *will* accept your help without question. I'll make dammed sure of that."

As Amanda finished putting Vince's clothes in his suitcase, she realized the incredible reach of Vince's power. He stepped out of the shower, and Amanda couldn't help but sneak a peek at his chiseled abs and sculpted arms. Vince was incredibly fit. Her hormones kicked into overdrive. He walked into the bedroom and stood directly in front of her. She could feel the heat radiating off his body. Water droplets from his wet hair splashed on Amanda's skin as he kissed her on the cheek.

Amanda couldn't take it anymore. Vince looked totally edible standing there half-naked in front of her. She did something bold—she kissed him and tugged on the towel. Vince pushed her to the bed. She was spread out beneath him, and his firm body molded to hers. Vince yanked the tie out of Amanda's ponytail releasing her blonde hair from its hold. He dipped his head to kiss her. She let out a soft moan, and her knees went weak as Vince slowly removed her clothes from her trim frame.

"Vince...I," she panted breathlessly.

"Hush baby, I got you. No more talking," his deep voice commanded.

Amanda threw her head back, letting out a whimper, as she felt Vince lower his dark head delivering slow licks to the most sensitive part of her body.

Oh, God…this was definitely worth the wait.

Chapter Twenty-Four
Ashleigh

Ashleigh had only been home for a few days. She had just returned from a hotel opening in Seattle and was getting ready to leave for Montreal in the morning. The Le Petit Hotel & Café in Montreal was Ashleigh's first stop on her next assignment regarding the best boutique hotels in North America.

She had convinced her Editor to let her write the piece. Combining all the research Ashleigh had compiled from past trips with the latest online guest comments of the hotels she picked, the article would be a breeze. In addition, Ashleigh had emailed all her contacts at nearly thirty boutique hotels across the continent letting them know about her article, and she immediately had responses back. Hotels wanted to be on that list, badly.

With all the activity of the past few weeks, Ashleigh had been so engrossed with work she realized she had barely talked to Liam. She looked at her phone and quickly calculated what time it was in London, 7:00 P.M. She stopped packing and pulled up Skype to see if Liam was logged on, not sure if she would be able to catch him online on a Saturday night. She looked, just in case, but Liam was not online. Checking his twitter and Facebook feed for any recent activity made Ashleigh feel a little bit like a stalker. His last tweet was about a recent article he read regarding a new hotel opening in Dubai, and that was on Friday. Liam's latest Facebook post was a check in at the Newman Arms Pub on Rathbone Street in London that said, "HAVING A FEW PINTS WITH THE LADS."

Gazing out the window of her penthouse that overlooked the river, she wondered what everyone was up to at that moment. She knew Emily was currently at the Farmer's market with Ethan. Ashleigh had been invited to join them for drinks that afternoon, but she still had packing to do before she left for Montreal early the next morning.

Suddenly feeling very lonely, she contemplated texting Amanda to see if she wanted to hangout. *Why am I feeling so lonely?* She realized that she was really missing Liam, and sent him a quick Facebook message: HI LIAM, HOPE YOU

ARE DOING WELL. I JUST WANTED TO SAY HELLO AND SEE HOW THINGS WERE GOING.

Closing her suitcase she walked to the kitchen and grabbed a bottle of San Pellegrino out of her refrigerator. She came back to her laptop and clicked on the message she had just sent Liam. She knew he had read it because it now displayed: SEEN 12:13 P.M. with a checkmark. Usually Liam responds quickly to her messages, but this time he did not. Then again he was out with friends, but that had never stopped him from getting back to her before. Now Ashleigh was starting to wonder if she had offended Liam in some way. Even worse, maybe he had a different opinion of her now, knowing her past.

Quickly she put those thoughts out of her mind and decided to hit the gym for a quick workout to unwind. Maybe she was just stressed from all the travel and work she had been putting in lately. It does take a toll on the mind and body. Changing into her workout clothes she put her hair up in to a tousled bun and headed off to the gym.

Chapter Twenty-Five
Emily

Emily and Ethan were on their way back to her house from the Fulton Street Farmer's Market. They had picked up lots of fresh veggies, fruit and some wine while they were shopping. Emily was planning to make Caprese salads for lunch and relax on the back patio with a glass of Pinot Grigio. Ethan pulled his black Lexus into the driveway, and they began to unload the groceries.

"Here let me unlock the door, Emily. Hand me your keys." Ethan could see that Emily had undoubtedly picked up one too many bags and was struggling.

"Here you go," she said as she handed him the keys and walked up to the door.

"Emily, did you leave your house unlocked?" Ethan noticed her front door was not locked when he turned the key. He had locked the door instead of unlocking it. Just then Emily heard a loud noise from inside her house.

"Ethan…" Emily whispered.

Ethan replied calmly, "I heard it too. Emily stay here, and I'll go check it out."

Ethan set the wine and the bag of groceries down and slowly opened the door.

When he reached the kitchen he saw Emily's patio doors were open. The noise they heard was the sound of her lamp on the credenza near the stairs crashing onto the wood floor. Pieces were scattered everywhere.

Emily shouted in a low whisper, "Ethan, what's going on?"

He didn't answer. She grabbed the bag of groceries and tapped the door open with her foot. Walking into her house, Emily felt a chill in the air. She felt like crying. Looking around, nothing seemed to be out of order, but the fact that a stranger had been in her home made her feel uneasy. Ethan turned the corner, and Emily let out a shrill scream. He jumped, and Emily dropped the bags.

"Dammit Em, I told you to stay outside," he scolded.

She looked down at the floor and the pile of fresh vegetables that pooled at her feet. The apples bounced and rolled to the kitchen.

A sigh escaped Emily as she asked, "Ethan, did you happen to check upstairs when you were in here?"

"No, I didn't. Stay here and I'll go look." Ethan walked up the stairs in a stealthy manner like Jack Ryan as Emily stood in her kitchen waiting for the news or an all clear from Ethan.

"Ethan, is everything okay up there?"

"Em, I think you should come up here," Ethan replied stopping halfway down the stairs. His face seemed to be drained of all color. Emily became frightened and felt all the muscles in her body tighten upon seeing Ethan's expression.

"Ethan, what is it? You're scaring me," her voice hitched as she gradually followed Ethan up the staircase. Ethan carefully opened Emily's bedroom door. She entered with caution. What she saw hanging on her bedroom mirror and walls stopped Emily in her tracks, paralyzing her with a fear she had never felt. She stood motionless then gripped Ethan's hand.

"Em, call the police, *now*," Ethan instructed. "And you're not staying here tonight. You'll be coming home with me."

"Hello? Someone at this address called the police?" a female voice said.

Emily's heart was pounding as she moved her eyes from one location to the next. Her bedroom was covered with photos of her and Ethan together. Shopping for groceries—together, working out—together, eating at a restaurant—together, and there were even a few pictures of the two of them talking in the parking lot outside of Cooper Bentley. The most frightening photo of all was a picture of the two of them clearly having sex in what appeared to be Ethan's bed. The photo showed Emily from behind with her dark hair cascading down over her shoulders and her back. You couldn't see her face, as she was on top of Ethan, but you could plainly see him.

"How in the hell did someone take *that* picture?" she inquired with anger in her voice while pointing to it on the wall.

Ethan walked over and angrily ripped the photo down. Seeing the same image in another spot, he reached out his hand, but quickly drew back thinking he could be destroying evidence. There was another photo that was at such close range, Emily wondered if the person who took it was in the room with them.

"Anyone home? You called for the police," the female voice inquired again.

"Emily, come on," Ethan said as he tugged her elbow.

"Uhhh…yes…I called the police. We'll be right down." Since there was really no time for Emily to freak out, thanks to the speed of the Grand Rapids police, she tucked her hair behind her ear and walked down the staircase. Ethan followed.

There in her kitchen, stood two officers. The female officer was short with dirty blonde hair that was tucked into a low bun under her hat. She had deep brown eyes and looked to be in her late twenties. The male officer was tall and had a mustache. *Of course he did.* He smelled like aftershave and cigarettes.

Emily reached her hand out to the female officer and said, "Hi, thank you for coming. I'm Emily Greene, and I'm the one who called. This is my friend, Ethan Carlson."

"I'm Officer Scott, and this is Officer Randolph. Can you tell me what happened?" Officer Randolph tipped his cap and nodded towards Emily.

Emily recounted all she could, which was really not all that much. She pointed out the broken lamp and the open patio doors. Officer Scott was diligently taking notes as Officer Randolph scanned the living room and kitchen.

"Is there anything else Miss Greene? Is anything missing?"

Emily bit her lip, and her eyes welled with tears. Ethan noticed she was beginning to break. Gently placing his arms around her, he said, "Officers, you should probably come upstairs and have a look for yourselves."

The senior officer looked at his younger partner and directed, "I'm going to inspect the backyard and the rest of the house, while you attend to the upstairs matter." Officer Scott nodded in agreement.

Emily and the female officer ascended the stairs into her bedroom, where Officer Scott's eyes widened. She looked at Emily and said, "Whoa, this is some freaky stuff, but I have seen worse."

"Oh, you mean like *murder*?" Emily said sharply.

"Sorry, Miss Greene I wasn't trying to offend you," Officer Scott replied softly as she crossed the room and scanned a few of the photos.

"It's okay," Emily said as she looked away from the all too personal photos that clung to her bedroom walls. "I know you meant no harm. My emotions are all over right now. Someone invaded my personal space," Emily said feeling her throat tighten.

She choked back tears because she did not want to cry in front of the female officer who was nearly 10 years her junior, but she was not sure how long she could hold them back.

Officer Scott gave Emily a sympathetic look and said, "I know you're scared. This *is* a total violation of your personal space. I will have to call this in and get a Detective over here."

Officer Scott left the room and proceeded to call the station. Ethan quietly came in and put his hand on Emily's shoulder. Startled, she flinched and turned around to face him. She threw her arms around his neck, and that was her breaking point. Tears ran down her cheeks. Ethan responded by hugging her tighter.

"Emily, hey... look at me." He pulled back gently and met her gaze. "The police and detectives will find this person. If they don't, I will pay for a Private Investigator and handle the matter myself."

"Miss Greene," Officer Randolph interjected. "We found these items sitting on the table on your patio with this note attached. Do you recognize these pictures?"

The experienced officer held up the photos and the box. They were hers. All the photos of Craig by himself or Craig and Emily together had been separated out and bundled together with a rubber band and a note that read: HE'LL NEVER LOVE YOU.

Ethan shot Emily a puzzled look. Just then Emily remembered the cryptic and creepy phone calls she had been receiving over the past few weeks. *Were the phone calls connected somehow? Was the person who was calling her the person who broke into her home? Did it have something to do with Craig?*

Emily was shaken thinking that Morgan might not be the culprit and this situation was far more serious than she originally realized. It was time to tell Ethan about the calls, the texts, and her suspicions of Morgan and about Craig.

"Yes, these belong to me. The note however, does not."

"Very well, Miss Greene we'll submit the note as evidence and have the pictures dusted for prints," Officer Randolph replied.

Once he left the room, Emily, who was trying so hard not to cry again, walked over to her desk and said, "Ethan, I have something I need to talk to you about."

Ethan looked at her curiously. His face went rigid. "This sounds serious."

Emily's skin prickled as if hot pins were jamming into her flesh, and a lump swelled in her throat. "Well, I'm not sure how serious, but given the recent events I feel I should share a few things about my past with you."

Ethan could see the pain in Emily's face. It crushed him to see how worried and scared she was.

Softening his expression, Ethan said, "You can tell me anything Emily, no judgment."

"Excuse me Miss Greene, Mr. Carlson," the female officer said as she re-entered Emily's bedroom. "The detectives are on their way. They will sweep the house in addition to asking you both some questions."

"Thank you Officer Scott," Ethan replied firmly.

"I'll be downstairs waiting for the detectives if you need me," she said giving Emily a warm smile before leaving the room.

"Now, what do you have to tell me?" Ethan said as he walked over to Emily and wrapped his arms around her. Emily sighed and hugged Ethan tightly.

Through her sobs, she managed to croak out, "I'm really scared, Ethan. Can we talk tonight at your house?"

Pulling back from their embrace, he nodded. With the pad of his thumb he brushed the tears away from her reddened cheeks. "Please don't worry, Em." His voice was soft with a soothing tone. "No one will ever hurt you as long as I'm breathing. I'll take care of you."

Chapter Twenty-Six
Ashleigh

Ashleigh arrived in Montreal and set up a workstation near the window at her favorite café in the Little Italy section of Rosemont–La Petite-Patrie. She had her Lavazza coffee, a delicious pastry and had just checked into the café on Foursquare. She opened her laptop and began checking email. A notification on her phone from Liam brought a smile to her face. She immediately pulled up the app and read the message that said:

HI ASHLEIGH, I AM SO SORRY I HAVE NOT BEEN IN TOUCH WITH YOU IN A WHILE LOVE. I HOPE YOU HAVE BEEN WELL. THINGS AT WORK HAVE BEEN ABSOLUTELY MAD. LAST NIGHT I WAS OUT WITH MY MATES HAVING A FEW PINTS AND WATCHING FOOTBALL WHEN I GOT YOUR MESSAGE, WHICH I WAS GLAD TO RECEIVE. I HOPE YOU HAVE A LOVELY TIME IN MONTREAL. I THINK I WILL BE SEEING YOU WHEN YOU TRAVEL TO LONDON IN A FEW WEEKS. LET ME KNOW OF YOUR ARRIVAL AND I WOULD BE HAPPY TO ARRANGE A CAR TO PICK YOU UP AT THE AIRPORT. CHEERS, LIAM

Ashleigh was relieved to hear from Liam, and his message had assured her that things between them were still normal and their friendship remained unshaken. She closed the app and realized she had a string of text messages from Emily.

SOMEONE BROKE INTO MY HOUSE YESTERDAY AFTERNOON. I AM FINE. I WASN'T HOME WHEN IT HAPPENED. NOTHING WAS TAKEN, BUT LONG STORY SHORT, I THINK I HAVE A STALKER...IT'S BIZARRE. I THINK IT COULD HAVE SOMETHING TO DO WITH THE PHONE CALLS I HAVE BEEN RECEIVING. ETHAN HAS BEEN WITH ME THE ENTIRE TIME AND I AM STAYING WITH HIM AT HIS PLACE UNTIL I FEEL COMFORTABLE ENOUGH TO GO BACK TO MY HOUSE. I JUST WANTED TO LET YOU KNOW.

Ashleigh immediately responded to Emily's text message, letting her know she was sorry to hear the news and that she was glad Ethan was able to be there for her. She told Emily if she needed anything or if there were any further developments to please notify her immediately. Ashleigh felt horrible for Emily, but she was glad Ethan was able to be there for her friend.

Staring out the window, she wondered who would be there for her if someone had broken into her home. Her parents, maybe, but they lived in Troy which was just a little over two hours away. Emily definitely would be there for her in a time of crisis, she had always been a great friend to Ashleigh over the years and vice versa.

Ashleigh and Emily met at an Alpha Iota Nu sorority event that the Grand Rapids Alumnae chapter was hosting. Emily had just moved to Grand Rapids from Chicago and since she knew virtually no one in the area, she decided to attend an Alumnae event with the hope of meeting some new people. With this group, she knew they already had one thing in common. The pair became fast friends and got to know each other over sushi and martinis at one of Ashleigh's favorite eateries.

Her thoughts returned to how overjoyed Emily seemed in her new relationship with Ethan. Even Amanda had someone special in her life. Up until recently, Ashleigh thought little of her own romantic life, other than knowing she probably didn't want to be married or have children. However, Emily insisted that Liam and Ashleigh were clearly perfect for each other. What Emily didn't seem to factor in, though, was that Ashleigh and Liam lived on two different continents. If they did get together, how would that even work?

"What's so interesting outside on the street?" a male voice asked. Ashleigh looked up and saw a very handsome man wearing a black V-neck t-shirt and dark denim jeans standing in front of her.

Wow…just…well done Greek Gods of…oh fuck it. Damn!

"Oh, I'm afraid you caught me daydreaming," Ashleigh replied with a smile.

"Ah ha, an American accent, I take it you don't come here too often?"

That made Ashleigh laugh as she answered the handsome stranger's question, "No, I'm afraid I'm not a regular of this lovely café. However, this is my favorite one in Montreal. I come here at least once when I visit. I love their chocolate panforte."

"Good choice. I come here for the cronettos, and of course the coffee," he said taking a sip of his beverage. "I'm Xavier, by the way."

"Nice to meet you Xavier. I'm Ashleigh. Would you care to join me?"

"Well, it looks like you are quite busy. I don't want to interrupt your work."

"Fortunately for you, I'm really just killing time until I have to check in to my hotel. I'm not really working on anything special. I insist, please have a seat."

"Which hotel are you staying at while you are visiting?" Xavier inquired.

"I'm staying over at the Le Petit Hotel & Café. I have been there before, but I'm writing a piece for a lifestyle blog, and it's the first stop on my list."

"That's interesting. A writer, huh?"

Ashleigh politely replied, informing Xavier of her job. She paused for a moment then asked, "So what do you do Xavier?"

Xavier told Ashleigh he was the Director of Marketing for a Sports Management Agency, which was why he was up early on a Sunday morning. Apparently his company was hired to produce a VIP golf outing that day. He had to go into the office, which was one block up the street, and make sure everything was on the up and up for the event. Ashleigh thought she could listen to Xavier talk all day. His French accent was incredibly sexy, but not as sexy as Liam's Welsh brogue. Xavier was just as handsome as Liam was, he had medium brown hair, bright green eyes and sported a bit of facial stubble. Then again, maybe he didn't shave because it was a Sunday morning. Before they realized it, the pair had chatted so long they had each drunk two more cups of coffee.

"Can I get you another cup of coffee, Ashleigh?" Xavier asked.

Ashleigh looked at her phone and realized it was nearly noon. Feeling a bit buzzed from so much caffeine, she really just wanted some more water and to use the ladies room.

"Actually, it's nearly noon. I think I should be leaving to check in to my hotel and grab some lunch. It was so lovely meeting you, and I really enjoyed our conversation."

"I'd be happy to take you to your hotel. My car is parked right down the street at my office. It would be no trouble, and you can save money on cab fare."

Secretly, Ashleigh didn't want their time to be over. She was really enjoying the conversation. Plus, she didn't actually have to start working until tomorrow. She had scored a meeting with the concierge the next morning at nine, which would be followed by her indulging in the continental breakfast. Ashleigh had planned to spend Sunday shopping and then relaxing in her room with a good bottle of wine, but having some company would obviously help her take her mind off this sudden feeling of loneliness she was dealing with.

Ashleigh rolled over in bed and realized she was not alone. She looked at Xavier who was sleeping so peacefully and naked. She giggled to herself as she threw the covers over her head. She had a wicked headache. After sliding quietly out of bed, Ashleigh retrieved some ibuprofen from her purse. She grabbed her phone off the nightstand. It was 6:34 A.M. Looking around the room you would think a couple of rock stars had a party. Two empty bottles of red wine and a few minis of vodka and whiskey lined the desk. Opening the door to the mini-bar she took out a bottle of Evian and went to the bathroom. She swallowed the ibuprofen, took a few sips of water and decided to brush her teeth. When she was done Ashleigh climbed back into bed and Xavier rolled over.

"Good Morning, Mademoiselle," he greeted her with a raspy French accent.

"Morning," she said gazing at Xavier with a lazy smile. "It appears we had some fun last night."

"Hmm…that we did. I'd like to have some more fun right now," he said as he began to kiss her shoulder.

Ashleigh's body came alive as Xavier brushed his lips against her skin. She felt his hands gently roaming her body, exploring each angle and curve. His lips met hers as she encircled her arms around his neck. He kissed her with such passion, over and over. Xavier was a take charge kind of guy. Ashleigh could see it in his eyes, they were demanding and full of power. He moved his hand along her thigh, underneath her silk slip and found that she was more than ready for him. He gently eased one of his long fingers into

her, causing her to let out a soft moan, "Oh Liam."
Ashleigh opened her eyes and realized what she had said.
Xavier was staring at her with a perplexed look.

"Oh my God, Xavier. I'm completely horrified. I'm
so…so sorry." Ashleigh sat up in the bed and thought her
heart might explode out of her chest. Then she heard
Xavier laughing. Now *she* was looking at *him* with a puzzled
look.

"Ashleigh, this isn't the first time a woman has cried
out another man's name when they were with me." Xavier
rolled over to his side of the bed where he began laughing
again.

Ashleigh couldn't help but laugh, "Please tell me this is
only the second time it's happened?" she inquired.

"Would you believe it's the *third* time?"

Shaking her head, she fell back and pulled the covers
over her face. "I cannot believe I called you, Liam." Her
voice was muffled by the sheet, but Xavier heard exactly
what she said.

"So this Liam is he an ex-boyfriend, husband, ex-
husband or lover?" Xavier asked.

"No, I'm not married. More like friends with benefits, but much more complicated."

Xavier kissed Ashleigh on the cheek. While climbing out of bed he said, "You'll figure it out gorgeous. Love, relationships, even friendships all come with complications."

He pulled his jeans on and lifted his shirt from the back of the office chair slipping it over his head. Ashleigh watched him intently as he dressed. He *was*, without question, dangerously good-looking. His eyes dazzled for being so early in the morning. *No wonder I fell into bed with him so willingly. Those eyes, goddamn they're hypnotic.*

"Ashleigh, here is my card. If you find you have free time in your schedule while you're here, call me. I would love to read your article when it's finished. What publication will it be in again?"

"*The Business Traveler's Wife*," she replied sweetly. Ashleigh climbed out of bed and retrieved one of her business cards from her laptop bag. "Here's my card, Xavier."

Xavier reached out and took her card, "Thank you, Mademoiselle, Ashleigh. Ashleigh *Preston*." He purred her name, his voice was sultry. "I have to go home and shower and change for work, but this has been fun, *really* fun."

The glint in his green eyes was mesmerizing. Ashleigh's breath hitched as his soft lips gently brushed hers. As they hugged goodbye, Ashleigh lingered a bit, but that could have been a slow reaction due to her immense hangover. He smelled like pine needles and cedarwood. She inhaled his masculine scent and felt like she was taking a stroll in the woods.

He walked to the door, warmly nodded and said, "Bye gorgeous."

Blushing slightly she raised her left hand, "Bye Xavier."

As Ashleigh stood there feeling cold and alone. Despite the circumstances, the reality was that Xavier had given her a huge gift. For the first time in years, Ashleigh realized her feelings for Liam were more than that of friendship and casual sex. *Now, what am I going to do?*

First things first, shower and get some coffee.

Chapter Twenty-Seven
Amanda

Amanda sat quietly sipping champagne at the table. A sigh escaped her mouth as she looked to the empty seat that sat to her left, the seat that was supposed to be occupied by Vince. He had been delayed yet again at a meeting in Manhattan. This was the second weekend in a row that Amanda attended an event alone. She didn't even know why she bothered attending this dedication for the Graysen College Aviation School. She was hopeful he would make it in time for dessert.

Amanda finally heard from her sister, Julie, and they set a date to meet for coffee. She was anxious to hear how Conner was doing and tell Jules about Vince. Despite the fact that Amanda was currently miffed at him, she found herself falling hard. Instead of sulking she decided to play the role of the dutiful CEO's girlfriend and put on a happy face, taking the opportunity to represent Vince instead of resenting his absence. She had a feeling he would be arriving any moment.

Amanda briefly chatted with Emma Sterling whose husband Grant was Vince's business partner. The pair exchanged pleasantries regarding the Phillip Cooper Foundation gala, which was coming up near the end of August. Amanda was in charge of securing items from companies for the silent auction. Emma, who had volunteered multiple times for the event, made a few suggestions and gave Amanda some sage advice on how to approach potential donors.

It was nearly eight in the evening, and dinner was about to be served. Amanda's phone began to buzz. It was a text from Vince: I'M SORRY, AMANDA I HAVE TO STAY OVERNIGHT. PLEASE FORGIVE ME. I'LL CALL YOU LATER.

Amanda scooped up her clutch and politely excused herself from the table. She retrieved a hundred dollar bill and presented it to the bartender who then popped a bottle of champagne and handed it to Amanda. Lifting the bottle to her lips she took a long sip. She made her way to the back of the room and quietly slipped out through the heavy wood doors. Walking down the long curved hallway she began looking at the bronze and metal sculptures that lined the walls. She noticed a gold and black plaque on the wall outside a rather large room that said: EVERETT STERLING LECTURE HALL A GIFT FROM VINCENT L. EVERETT & GRANT M. STERLING underneath their names was the date of the dedication. She rolled her eyes and pushed through the glass doors.

Making her way outside, she turned towards the newly constructed airplane hangars. Her blood was boiling, she was seething with anger. Seeing the plaque with his name only fueled her temper.

Vince was always gone, and Amanda was left alone most nights and weekends. All of this was familiar territory, though Amanda understood that with money and power sometimes came personal sacrifice. Amanda could handle a lot of things when it came to being involved with men whose time was demanded by so many people. But, loneliness, more specific repeated loneliness was something with which she had difficulty.

Amanda took a few more sips from the bottle. She was beginning to feel the effects of all the alcohol she consumed. Her body felt slightly heavy as her belly was warmed by the intoxicating crisp bubbles.

"Amanda!" a voice shouted from behind her. She peered around and saw Alex standing there in a black tux. His hair was slicked back, and he was clean shaven.

A smile slid across her vibrant red pout, "What…what are you doing here Alex?"

"Vince called me and told me to join you at this event. He…he didn't want you to be alone tonight," he replied softly.

Alex inched closer to her, closing the space between them. They were now standing face to face. Amanda reached out and ran her hands over the smooth lapels of his jacket. He gripped the bottle from her hands, lifted it to his lips and took a long drink.

The moonlight bounced off Amanda's diamond earrings as her blonde hair swirled around her neck from the light breeze. Amanda turned on her heels and walked towards the Jet that sat inside the hangar. The door was open, and she began to climb the stairs. Curiosity got the better of Alex, and he followed. He found Amanda inside making herself a cocktail at the bar.

"Would *you* like something, Alex?" Amanda inquired, her voice light with laughter.

His eyebrows arched. He nodded his head, saying, "One drink, and then we need to get back inside for dessert."

The cabin was bright and airy, almost the exact same color palette as the jet she and Vince took to New York on their first date. The carpeting in this jet was an indigo blue with soft grey accents in the chevron print. Amanda handed Alex his drink and sat beside him on the white couch. The leather felt cool against her warm flesh.

"Alex, do you have a girlfriend?" she hummed, her voice hanging on the last word.

Letting out a soft chuckle, Alex replied, "No, Amanda I don't. Can you believe it?"

Amanda shook her head and said, "No, I can't." She paused and took a sip of her drink, "Why?"

"*Why?*" Alex repeated and sighed before taking another sip. "I had a fiancé, but we ended things. We were young and she wanted to stay in Detroit, I did not."

Amanda let out a hiccupped giggle, "Who *would?*" she scoffed.

A grin slid across Alex's mouth, and he let out another throaty chuckle. "You're a bit giddy tonight. How much have you had to drink, Amanda?"

Amanda felt her body sliding down the soft leather cushion. She pulled herself up and turned to face Alex. Amanda noticed the glimmer of blue in Alex's eyes and the greying hairs around his temples. The lines on his face were deep, and his skin had slight sun damage. Amanda thought it was more than likely from being under the hot desert sun. None of it took away from the fact that he was incredibly handsome.

"What are you the booze police, Alex?" she teased before pushing to her feet. Walking slowly towards the bar, she stopped and kicked off her heels. She nearly fell over as she tried to steady on one foot, but Alex hopped up and gripped her arm. Stumbling forwards she accidentally crashed into him. Her head fell and bumped his chest, and she almost fell over. Alex managed to cradle her in his strong frame. A shuddering wave of electricity passed through Amanda and went straight to her stomach. She looked up pushing back her thick bangs that fell across her cheek and met Alex's gaze.

He was still holding her in his arms, and Amanda molded her body to his. Fire burned through Amanda as she felt Alex's heart thumping in his chest. His breathing was ragged, and his teeth grazed over his bottom lip.

Amanda's breathing escalated. "Alex," his name came out in a shaky whisper.

She shifted her head tilting slightly left. Alex leaned down brushing his lips to hers. Amanda parted her lips and Alex's tongue dipped inside her mouth with soft rolling licks. A whimper escaped.

"Amanda," Alex whispered. "I want *you*."

Amanda pushed Alex to the couch and straddled his sturdy thighs. His hands hiked the soft silk of her strapless ivory gown over her hips. He dipped his finger inside the waistband of her lace thong and tugged it gently. The barely stitched together delicate fabric withered from her body. Amanda shoved her fingers through Alex's hair and kissed him. His hands slid over her bare back and she felt his erection against the inside of her thigh. Amanda deepened her kiss as she lowered her arms, running her hands over Alex's thick shoulders.

His hands fell from the firm grip he had on her waist, and Amanda heard the zipper of Alex's trousers release. Her heart began to thump wildly in her chest as Alex's finger traced the slickness of her sex. Every muscle in her body convulsed causing her to let out a low moan into his mouth. Sweat began to form at the base of her neck and in between her breasts.

He pulled back from their kiss and said, "Lift to your knees, Amanda."

She gripped the back of the couch for balance and hovered over Alex allowing him to lift his pants to push them down farther. The soft fabric of his pants brushed the swell of her bottom, and Amanda felt the tip of his cock against her clit. Alex's eyes met hers, she felt exposed sensing he could see how vulnerable and fragile she was.

The feeling was frightening yet comforting at the same time. They were face to face in this intimate moment, and merely inches away from a wide open door to the world for anyone to interrupt at any given second. The need she had to desperately wash away the aching loneliness was raw and biting.

"Jesus, *Amanda*," he gasped as she lowered onto him. Alex was rock hard, velvety steel. His hands flexed underneath her, and Amanda clenched her jaw. He began to roll his hips and Amanda had to move from side to side to allow him to plunge deeper. He was too big for her. The stretching was almost unbearable, and she didn't notice that she had stopped breathing. Amanda was holding on tightly to the tension in her stiff body. The pressure was too much. It was building inside her, and she was in agony, not from discomfort, no more from the shock.

"Amanda, you need to breathe, baby," Alex said through strained breaths. He cupped her face in his hands and looked into her eyes, "I'm here Amanda, and I need you here with me."

Alex leaned into her, taking her mouth with his, delivering gentle kisses. Suddenly the tightness in her chest began to loosen, the knot in her stomach began to unravel and her shoulders slumped in relief. Warmth ran over Amanda's body, and she felt a single tear escape her eye. She drew in a breath and let go. Finally, aching hurt was released from her body and floated away.

Alex felt her body relax. He whispered in her ear, "Good girl."

She smiled at him, wrapping her arms around his neck and nipping his earlobe with her teeth. He lifted Amanda and flipped her back onto the couch. She let out a soft moan as he pushed smoothly, deep inside her. His breath was warm against her neck, and she gripped his firm shoulders as he buried his face in her hair.

"You feel so good, Alex," she moaned hoarsely.

He picked up his thrusts and Amanda came unhinged, crying out his name. When her body clenched around him, Alex came forcefully inside her, his entire body shaking. Panting breathlessly he eased out of her as Amanda gasped in pleasure.

Upon the buttery soft leather, she lay there helpless, unable to move. The shocks were vibrating her core. Her body was limp, and her skin was misty. Alex moved to his feet adjusting his pants and smoothing his shirt. He picked up her thong and shoved it into his jacket pocket.

Amanda's eyes opened, and she saw Alex standing there looking at her, eyes wide. His mouth was twisted up on one side, and he ran his hand through his glossy brown hair.

"Amanda," he said in a low voice.

Amanda pushed to her feet quickly and balled up her fists. She hurried to get her pumps that she had kicked off and looked around frantically for her clutch.

"No, oh no, what have I done," she mumbled.

Amanda scanned the jet for her purse and found it lying on the bar. Tears welled in her eyes, and she couldn't stop from crying. Alex stepped in front of her, "Hey, slow down. What's wrong?"

"Don't you see Alex, this…*this* was wrong," she sobbed. "Vince is going to find out what we've done and hate us both." She rushed to the open door and slid on her heel.

"Amanda, please don't leave," Alex protested. "Let me take you home."

"I'm sorry Alex, I...I need to be alone. I'm sorry if I hurt you," she said, giving him a warm half-smile. Descending the staircase of the jet, she turned around to Alex, who had caught up with her and said, "Alex, I'm trouble."

Pivoting on her heel she started to walk briskly to the parking lot. Alex gripped her arm and spun her around to face him.

"No, I don't accept this," he huffed.

"It's best if you stay away from me, Alex. I'll bring nothing, but chaos to your life," she warned waving her clutch in the air. She wriggled out of his grip and made her way to the valet stand. Alex watched her get into the limo. Shoving his hands into his pockets a deep sigh escaped him.

Chapter Twenty-Eight
Emily

Two weeks had gone by since Emily's house was broken into, and the police had no leads. A few days after the break-in Emily learned that there were no fingerprints on anything in her home. The police weren't able to pull a single print from the note or any of the pictures that were splashed all over Emily's walls. The perpetrator was careful in everything they touched, almost methodical, which made Emily uneasy.

Emily told Ethan about the phone calls she had been receiving, what was said and how she speculated at first that it could be Morgan. He was pissed that she never made any mention to him that she was being harassed. As much as it pained her, she divulged her entire past with Craig to Ethan.

Ethan wanted to hire a private investigator, but Emily hadn't received a phone call or any creepy text messages since the break-in happened. Not a peep from the stalker. Every time her phone would ring, her thoughts immediately drifted to the eerie voice that could potentially be waiting for her on the other end. Thank goodness for caller ID. Admittedly, Emily *was* frightened, knowing someone was out there possibly watching her every move. If the stalker's main objective was just to scare Emily— goal achieved.

The downside to all of this madness was that something had changed between Emily and Ethan. There was a definite tension between them, or at least it felt that way to Emily. Ethan had not said much to Emily in recent days, she thought he seemed annoyed or miffed at the drama encircling their lives. She desperately wanted to talk to Ethan and ask him what was bothering him, but the first two times she tried, he said everything was fine. When Emily broached the subject earlier today, Ethan demanded sharply that she stop asking him what was wrong.

Emily arrived at Cooper Bentley and pressed her keycard in the panel to disarm the security system. She left Ethan's house without saying a word to him, not even goodbye. Inside, she felt helpless and emotionally wrecked and that Ethan was slipping away. The only logical to thing to focus on now was work, with hopes it might take her mind off of everything, at least for a while, but being at Cooper Bentley right now only reminded her of him. Presently, she was in a lose/lose situation with her emotions.

Emily stood up and walked to the break room. She thought about calling Ashleigh, but realized she was working at a wine tasting event in Chicago. Instead, she made some tea and headed back to her office where she was nearly scared half to death by the sight of Ethan sitting in the corner of the room at the work table Emily used for small meetings.

"Ethan... Jesus you scared me."

"Sorry Emily that was not my intent," he replied apologetically.

"How did you find me?" she inquired while taking a seat at her desk.

Ethan pushed to his feet and began to walk towards her. "If you don't want to be found you probably shouldn't use Foursquare," he advised with a smirk.

"I'll keep that in mind next time," her tone was laced with sarcasm.

Ethan stood directly in front of her. He was brooding. His eyes were narrowed, and his jaw was rigid. Emily sensed something heavy was weighing on his mind.

"Can we talk, Em?" Ethan inquired as he took a seat in the chair in front of her desk.

The blood pooled in Emily's ears as her heart pounded rapidly in her chest upon hearing those words. He sounded serious which made Emily nervous and a bit on edge. She really wished she had something stronger than tea to drink.

"Not if you're going to bite my head off, Mr. Carlson," she joked trying to lighten the mood.

Lifting his eyebrow he replied softly, "I suppose I deserve that, Miss Greene."

Emily stood up and walked around the front of her desk and sat next to Ethan. Sitting at the desk across from him made the situation feel too formal and business like. They were involved in a romantic relationship, and Emily wanted to be close to him, even if he was about to drop a bomb on her.

"Emily, I have been thinking, and honestly this past week has made me realize a few things. First, I need to

265

apologize to you. I've been a real jerk. Pushing you away when you needed me the most was not acceptable."

Relief at the soothing tone and warm words washed over her. "I can't disagree with you on that Ethan," she teased offering a warm smile.

Ethan stood up and walked to the window. He ran his hands through his brown hair and sighed deeply. Leaning against the wall he said, "Em, I'm going to admit something to you that I don't normally say out loud."

Emily knitted her eyebrows together and gave him a puzzled look.

"The truth is I *am* a man who needs to be in control of certain matters in my life."

Emily's jaw dropped, but secretly she understood Ethan's need for control. Emily liked to be in control of things, too, especially when it came to her job. She guessed she was probably less obsessive about it than Ethan, however. Still a bit apprehensive of what was to come next, Emily stood up and padded towards where Ethan was standing.

"Can you explain exactly what you mean, Ethan?"

"All of the chaos that happened with the break-in, the photographs and your confession to me about the weird phone calls shook me off my axis. I guess you could say it threw me for a loop. There was nothing I could do to help you. It was tearing me up inside and pissing me off. In turn, my oversized male ego got the better of my emotions," he admitted.

Emily swallowed the lump that had crept into her throat and was finally able to settle her heart rate.

"Then there was the matter of your ex-boyfriend who disappeared. Now, that really did a number on me emotionally."

Emily was even more confused, wondering if Ethan had been drinking before he came to the office. *Was Ethan Carlson jealous? No, there's no way.*

"What do you mean? Why did it do a number on you?"

He turned to face Emily and replied smoothly, "Because I love you."

Emily thought her heart was going to burst out of her chest. "You *love* me?" she asked feeling her eyes beginning to well up.

Emily had done more crying in the last two weeks that she had all year, especially taking into consideration that crying during movies and commercials didn't count. Ethan placed both hands on the side of her face and kissed her. Emily was overjoyed and relieved at the same time. The anxiousness she had been feeling evaporated. Something *had* changed between them—he loved her and she loved him.

"Yes, I love you. I might have known for a while. I don't want to lose you, and I especially don't want anyone to hurt you," Ethan said as he gently brushed Emily's hair off the side of her face. "I guess some part of me thought you might still be in love with your ex. After talking with my brother, I realized those thoughts were utterly ridiculous."

Emily put her hands in his. Looking him straight in his deep brown eyes she said, "I don't love Craig. He left me, but if I get the chance to have closure from that part of my life, I *will* talk to him. I hope you can understand that, Ethan."

268

Ethan pulled Emily in close and replied, "Yes. I can certainly understand that. Evan made me realize that I cannot control the past, and that I should be more supportive. I think in a way I was spooked by the possibility of getting hurt." He let out a deep sigh, "I haven't mentioned this, but Libby cheated on me once, and it wrecked me. I forgave her, but that was a turning point in our relationship."

"I'm sorry Libby hurt you, but your brother gives excellent advice," Emily said with a wink. "Oh, and in case you're wondering, I love you too, Ethan."

A smile crossed Ethan's lips, and he leaned in and gently pressed his lips to hers.

Breaking their kiss, Ethan said, "Get your things, Miss Greene. *We* have some celebrating to do, and it involves me taking you to bed and gifting you with repeated orgasms."

"That's quite the promise, Mr. Carlson. I hope you can make good on that," Emily replied while giving him a playful smirk.

He smacked her bottom as Emily began to gather her things. The warm July air was heavy and thick. The scent of fresh mulch and lavender filled the air, with the lavender reminding Emily their time together in California. She smiled, placing her keycard back in the security pad she set the alarm. Emily gripped the door tight, and locked it.

"I'll meet you at my house," Ethan called as he approached his car.

Just as Emily was about to step off the curve of the sidewalk she heard the screeching of tires. Swinging her head to the left she noticed a white Cadillac barreling at a high rate of speed through the parking lot.

Emily screamed, "Ethan! Get out of the way! Ethan!"

Emily panicked as she saw the blinding light from the car's headlamps heading towards Ethan. Turning tightly after nearly swiping his Lexus, the car sped out of the parking lot. Fear spread through Emily's body. Frantically, Emily ran towards Ethan. He was lying on the ground moaning in pain.

"*Ethan*, oh my God, Ethan," she bellowed through tight sobs.

"I'm okay Emily," he said a bit winded. "I dove out of the way and landed right on my knee. I'll be fine."

"Ethan your arm is bleeding. You must have scraped it."

Ethan looked at his arm and turned back at Emily. "Em, are *you* okay?"

Nodding her head, she replied, "I'm fine, just shaken. Do you need me to take you to the hospital, Ethan?"

"No, but did you get a good look at that car?" he asked panting through deep breaths. Ethan began to stand up. "License plate? Anything?"

"I think so." Her voice was a bit shaky. "I can see the license plate number in my head. I'm going to take down everything I remember right now."

Pulling out her phone she began to take notes typing fast and muttering to herself. Looking up she noticed Ethan was on his phone.

"Hey buddy, it's Ethan Carlson. You got time to do me a favor?" he inquired. There was a long pause. "I'll pay you double the fee if it will get my name to the top of your list." Ethan winced as he let out a low chuckle. "Great, thanks. Can you meet me at my house tomorrow morning before you leave for Chicago?"

Ethan turned back to Emily. "My buddy is a Private Investigator. Actually, he's a little more than that, but that's all I can say."

Emily gave Ethan a perplexed look, but realized that if he needed to keep a secret she wouldn't push the issue.

"He's going to find this asshole who is stalking us. I know that fucking car meant to do one or both of us harm."

Her insides began to churn. Desperately trying not to think that this event was related to the break-in and the calls, Emily offered a sympathetic smile and said, "Okay, I understand. Are you sure you can drive Ethan?"

"Yeah, just follow me okay, Em?"

Emily nodded, and they drove out of the parking lot. *Hopefully this will all be over soon and Ethan's friend can help us find out who is messing with our lives. Who could want to hurt us?* The initial shock wore off, leaving Emily completely terrified. Tears started running down her face, and she realized the very dangerous turn the situation had taken.

Chapter Twenty-Nine
Ashleigh

It had been three weeks since Ashleigh had returned from Montreal. Three weeks had gone by since her 'Liam Epiphany'. That is what she was calling her revelation, realizing she did in fact have strong feelings for him. Three weeks had gone by, and Ashleigh had done nothing about it. Ultimately she wanted to tell Liam in person, and this trip to London was just the right moment.

Over the last few weeks she had thought endlessly about precisely how she would tell Liam she loved him. The moment had to be perfect. It was almost as if she was planning a proposal or something. Ashleigh had done a lot of self-reflection over the past few weeks, but there was no way she was ready for that to happen. Or was she?

I've got to let go of this need I have to control my life. Love, loss, pain, sadness, fear and anger, I want to experience all the emotions. Not the ones I allow myself.

She couldn't stop thinking about Liam as she looked out the window of the plane staring at the clouds below. In a few short hours she would see him, and they would probably spend the entire weekend in bed together. Before boarding she had stopped by the gift shop at the airport and picked up a "Pure Michigan" ink pen for Liam. She was going to give the pen to him along with a card when she told him how much she loved him and was ready to begin her life with him. She knew that Liam would appreciate the thoughtfulness of her gift, just as she adored the Union Jack keychain he had given her. Placing her headphones in her ears she leaned her chair back and drifted off to sleep.

Liam's driver had picked Ashleigh up from Heathrow and was taking her to the Corinthia Hotel, the hotel where she and Liam met for the first time. Ashleigh would be meeting him there in a couple of hours for dinner. She made reservations for two at The Northall and would suggest after dinner drinks at The Lobby Lounge. For the final touch of her plan she had booked The Hamilton Penthouse, just for one evening though. Ashleigh hoped the weather would be nice so that they could sit under the stars on the terrace like they did all those years ago drinking champagne and talking all night. She checked into the hotel on Foursquare and sent Liam a Facebook message letting him know she had arrived.

The smell of fresh flowers rushed over Ashleigh as she opened the door. The penthouse was breathtaking, and it looked just as she remembered. Her favorite room was the bathroom in the upstairs master suite, which hosted a separate walk in shower and a freestanding Apaiser stone bath. Her phone buzzed as she was hanging her clothes in the wardrobe room of the upstairs master suite. It was a Facebook message from Liam saying he could not wait to spend the evening with her.

After a quick nap Ashleigh began getting ready. She had purchased a silver, floor-sweeping Jenny Packham gown for dinner that had a sexy slit in the front. For the special night, she had purchased a few pieces of very sexy lingerie from Chantelle, including a nude Demi-Cup bra and matching thong that she was wearing for the evening. Styling her hair straight, she pulled her tresses back in a low ponytail and swept her bangs to the side before adding the final touches to her makeup. A few strokes of black Diorshow mascara thickened up Ashleigh's long lashes and a slick gloss of red painted her full pout.

Looking in the mirror Ashleigh smiles, "Damn, not bad Ashleigh. Eat your heart out, Liam."

Ashleigh grabbed her gift for Liam that was sitting on the table in the entry way. She had placed the pen and card in small gift bag with tissue paper and tied a white ribbon on the handles. The white ribbon symbolized hope for their future together, and inside the card she wrote: MY DEAREST LIAM, SOMEHOW I ALWAYS KNEW IT WAS YOU. YOU ARE MY LOVE, MY FUTURE. I AM HOME WHEN I AM WITH YOU.

She also included a quote from Maya Angelou, "LOVE RECOGNIZES NO BARRIERS. IT JUMPS HURDLES, LEAPS FENCES, PENETRATES WALLS TO ARRIVE AT ITS DESTINATION FULL OF HOPE."

One last check in the mirror and Ashleigh made her way downstairs for dinner. She was slightly nervous, but confident.

She noticed Liam right away. There he stood at the end of the bar sipping a martini, he was wearing a sleek navy suit with a light blue shirt underneath paired with a slate blue tie. Ashleigh stood at the hostess station for a moment just staring at him. He spotted her, and she walked over to him where he was motioning to the bartender.

"Hey love," he said kissing her on both cheeks. "What are you drinking?"

Ashleigh felt as if her insides were melting like butter, replying sweetly, "I'll have a glass of the Macon Blanc white wine please."

Liam couldn't take his eyes off Ashleigh, taking note of how especially beautiful she looked that night. Although for Liam, she was always the most breathtaking creature on any given day. Ashleigh caught his gaze. She turned away to yawn. She was tired, but her adrenaline was keeping her going.

"Ashleigh my dear, you look positively breathtaking this evening. How was your flight?"

"You're looking quite dapper yourself, Liam. The flight was good, I was able to have a row all to myself in business class, and I managed to sleep a bit, too."

"So you're staying in The Hamilton Penthouse tonight? I did not take you for such a lavish spender," Liam teased as he took a sip of his martini.

Ashleigh giggled and said, "I just wanted to do something special. I rarely treat myself, so I thought I would indulge a bit."

Closing the gap between them, Liam whispered, "Special night? I do love those. What do you have planned?" He brushed Ashleigh's hand with his, and she felt his breath on her cheek. The blood sizzled in her veins merely at his brief touch.

Before she could answer, and not that she was going to admit anything yet, a man in a black jacket approached saying, "Miss Preston, your table is ready. Please follow me."

Liam had already ordered another drink for himself and for Ashleigh. Seeing the couple was being seated, the bartender stated that he would have the drinks delivered to their table.

The smell of roasted garlic and grilled peppers stirred Ashleigh's senses as they crossed the restaurant passing by several tables. As they were seated, Ashleigh noticed the couple beside them was enjoying a chocolate and hazelnut dessert, which made her mouth water. Placing the gift she had for Liam on the seat next to her, she reached for her menu. The server came over, introduced himself and told them about the specials.

"So how have you been Ashleigh? How is summer in the States treating you?"

"The summer has been interesting. I've traveled a bit, and I've managed to keep my social calendar filled on the weekends I'm home."

She went on to tell Liam about some of the things happening at work. She told him about how she, Emily, Ethan and a few others spent a wonderful weekend at Ethan's lake house, while also giving an update about Emily's unfortunate stalker situation.

"How about you, Liam? What have you been up to this summer?" Ashleigh inquired.

The server arrived at the table with their second round of drinks just as Liam was about to answer her question and asked if they were ready to order. Liam said he was ready, but Ashleigh had been concentrating on their conversation, not looking at menu choices. Quickly, she decided on the Goosnargh Chicken with braised celery, bacon and shallots.

After she took a sip of wine Ashleigh returned to the conversation with Liam, asking, "So what's new with you?"

"Work has been going very well, and I too have been able to keep a busy social schedule this summer."

Ashleigh was curious. Liam was always social. He rarely had a night home where he just sat around watching television. He often worked late, had meetings to attend or was out with friends. That is why it was so hard to catch him online. It seemed as though he was never home.

"Oh yeah? What's been keeping you so busy?" Ashleigh inquired while flashing him a sweet smile.

Liam cleared his throat and said, "Well, I've met someone, and we've been dating for about a month. She's quite charming. Her name is Lydia, and I think you would like her very much."

Ashleigh blanched, feeling like all the air had been sucked out of her lungs. The smile slid from her glossy lips as she felt her mouth go dry. Suddenly her ears were buzzing. *What did he just say?* Reaching for her wine glass she took a drink, a very large drink. She swallowed hard, and her eyes met Liam's. Hoping Liam didn't realize she was in total shock, she tried to open her mouth, but there were no words. Her mind was racing. Time was going by, and she'd said nothing. *Come on, Ashleigh. Say something!*

"You've... met someone?" she managed to croak out. "That is...that's so nice to hear, Liam." Ashleigh was mustering all the strength she could to keep from crying in front of him. "Liam, will you excuse me? I need to use the ladies room."

Liam stood up as Ashleigh left the table.

She pushed through the crowd and threw open the door to the bathroom. She tossed her clutch on the makeup vanity. Glancing at her reflection in the mirror, she noticed her chest was splotchy red. *How could he be dating someone?* A million thoughts came to mind. After years of keeping him at a distance, Liam had probably realized things with her weren't going to happen, so he stopped waiting. Maybe Liam just happened to have met Lydia innocently and they had an instant attraction? Worse, what if it was love at first sight? Ashleigh grasped the notion that she may have missed her window for a relationship with Liam and quite possibly her second chance for happiness.

Ashleigh's heart sank. *What should I do? Fight for him? Declare my feelings and see if he picks me? What if he doesn't pick me?* Gathering her composure, she realized she had to remain calm and make it through their evening together.

As she returned to the table she saw her dinner had arrived.

"Ah, there you are, darling. I was about to send a search party to look for you," Liam said with a laugh.

"Oh, sorry. I got caught up chatting with one of the ladies in the bathroom. She was asking me about my dress," Ashleigh lied.

Staring at her food, Ashleigh felt nauseous. She was starving, but how could she eat at a time like this. Noticing the breadbasket on the table she reached for a small roll, gently tearing off a corner and popping it in her mouth.

"It is a lovely dress. I can certainly understand why she would make an inquiry," Liam said as he cut into his sirloin drizzled with a sharp peppered sauce.

Ashleigh needed more information about this Lydia character. What did she look like? What did she do for a living? She wasn't quite sure she could stomach listening to Liam boast about the other woman, who was now her competition. Suddenly it occurred to Ashleigh, that she totally had the upper hand in this situation. History, they shared history and a deep friendship. No random British Chippy could compete with history.

"So Liam, tell me more about Lydia? How long have you known her? Where is she from?"

After about twenty minutes of conversation, she learned Lydia James was thirty-six years old, originally from Bermondsey, a district in south London. Liam described her as being humorous with a good head for business. Physically she was about five foot eight with beautiful honey-blonde hair and blue eyes. He reached for his iPhone and showed Ashleigh a picture. He was right, she was beautiful. In the photo she had on a short, sparkling little black dress. Her hair was blowing in the wind, and she looked like a model. Lydia was tall, thin and stunningly gorgeous. In that moment she thought of Xavier and how he and Lydia would be a perfect match. Maybe she should set those two up. Ashleigh laughed to herself at the idea.

Lydia was an Advertising Executive at a firm in London. A few of her clients were interested in placing advertisements in *Wanderlust,* and because there were several brands and businesses involved, Liam and a few of the other senior leaders of the company were asked to attend the meeting. Liam and Lydia began talking after the meeting, and she asked him out for coffee so he went. He said he liked her quite a lot and asked if she would have dinner with him the following night. Of course she said yes.

After hearing about the fascinating Lydia, Ashleigh thought she might actually hurl. It was unlike Ashleigh to be jealous of a woman she had never met. Liam was a good judge of character, though, so Lydia probably was as lovely as he described her being. Her thoughts were interrupted as the server cleared their plates from the table.

He glanced at his watch and said, "Well this has been a wonderful evening. I unfortunately must go. I have an early meeting." He motioned to the server for the check.

Her face fell as coldness seeped into her body. "A meeting? On a Saturday morning?" her tone was questioning. She wondered if Liam was going to meet Lydia, and now she was experiencing an emotion she hadn't felt in a long time—jealously.

"Unfortunately, I do. When the boss asks you to come in on a Saturday, you do it."

"Sounds serious."

"No, nothing to worry about I am sure."

The server approached with the bill, and Liam placed his credit card on the tray. Ashleigh tried to reach for the bill before Liam, but he lightly batted her hand away. Liam stood up and kissed Ashleigh on the lips, which was weird since he just talked about his new lady friend for nearly a half an hour. Ashleigh wondered if maybe she still had an effect on him.

"May I walk you back to the penthouse?" Liam asked.

As much as she wanted Liam to take her upstairs in the hopes she could seduce him, Ashleigh just couldn't. He looked happy, and Ashleigh wasn't about to interfere with something that could be wonderful for him. All she wanted to do right now was go upstairs, drown herself in alcohol and take a bubble bath, like normal people do when they are hit with soul crushing news. Even though she felt awkward, a little irritated, mostly with herself, not with Liam and overwhelmingly sad, it was good to feel something other than pain and emptiness.

"No, that's okay Liam. I know you have things to do. I think I will order a bottle of champagne and sit on the terrace. It's a nice evening."

"That sounds lovely. Enjoy your evening Ashleigh. I'll ring you tomorrow."

And just like that Liam walked out of the hotel leaving Ashleigh feeling cold and alone. This was becoming a trend. After stopping to order the champagne at the bar, Ashleigh arrived at the penthouse. Upon entering the room she stopped and looked at her reflection in the mirror. Sighing deeply she kicked off her heels. She walked up the staircase and began taking off her jewelry. Halfway up the stairs the doorbell rang. *Must be the champagne.* Turning back around, she walked down the stairs and opened the door to find

Liam standing there. He brushed past her, and Ashleigh could see he was upset.

"Liam…hey…I thought you were on your way home?" Liam held up an envelope that had his name on it. Ashleigh was frozen. *Oh no, the card!*

Chapter Thirty
Amanda

Amanda walked up to the coffee shop, where she would be meeting Julie shortly, when she noticed a young couple across the street from the café holding hands and kissing outside an ice cream shop.

She thought about Vince and how they spent the most romantic weekend together on the yacht. Vince had told her he loved her, and as a token of his affection he had given her a pair of pear-shaped yellow diamond drop earrings, which she decided she would be wearing to the gala. Vince's beautiful words twisted inside her, wrecking her with guilt and filling her with joy. The night with Alex was still fresh in her mind, she couldn't stop thinking about him. Admittedly, she found her heart being tugged in opposite directions, torn between two men.

"Hey, sorry I'm late, sis." Amanda's thoughts were interrupted by Julie's voice. Amanda turned around to see her sister and got a bit of a surprise.

"You're pregnant!? Oh my God, Jules!" Amanda was utterly shocked and gave her sister a huge hug.

Conner wasn't with Julie, and she explained that last time she saw Amanda, Conner told David that Mommy saw her sister today. Julie said she did the best job she could to explain that what Conner meant was that Mommy had run into a sorority sister.

"Did David buy that story?" Amanda inquired.

"I had to be extra persuasive, because he wouldn't let it go. You can see by my physical condition the measures I had to take," she teased Amanda.

"Oh stop it," Amanda said with a laugh "Do you know if you are having a boy or a girl?"

"I'm having a girl, and I'm due in November," she said with a smile.

"What wonderful news. I am so happy for you. Can I get you a tea or something, sis?"

"That would be nice. Yes, an Earl Grey, please."

Amanda told Julie she would be right back with her tea and walked inside the café. A few moments later she returned and found her sister on the phone. She couldn't tell what Julie was saying because she was whispering in a soft tone. Julie sighed and ended the call.

"Everything okay Jules?" Amanda asked, hoping her sister would open up to her.

"Yes everything is fine. I was talking to Mom. She's in the middle of planning the Labor Day celebration at the club, and she asked if I could help her out with some things. So, between prepping for the baby, working at Dad's doing accounting and financials and now helping Mom, I'm feeling exhausted."

"I'm glad to hear Mom is back to doing events for the club. I know that really must have hurt her to be asked to leave...you know after I brought so much shame to the family." Amanda hung her head and sighed.

Julie took notice of her sister's polished appearance. Amanda looked more put together than she did the last time they met. Today, she was wearing a pretty floral print blouse paired with white capri pants and a pair of bright yellow, strappy, patent leather sandals. Sunlight reflected off her gorgeous diamond and lemon quartz drop earrings. Her skin was luminous, and her hair was freshly highlighted with warm blonde pieces.

"Well dear, that is all in the past. However, Amanda you're looking quite well these days, how are things going at the mall?"

"Actually Julie, I am living at The River House now with the new man in my life— Vince. It seems my former life is being restored to me. I have new car, I get a weekly allowance, and Vince showers me with designer clothes and jewels regularly. Isn't that fabulous?"

Julie swallowed her tea and started to cough. She accidently spilled some of it on her blouse.

"Are you okay?"

"Yes, I'm so clumsy these days. Excuse me sis while I go clean myself off."

When Julie walked into the ladies room, Amanda picked up her phone and immediately started checking for any communication between her and Andrew Langston. She scrolled down scanning all the names and conversations. There it was— a conversation between her and Andrew from a few months ago. All it said was: FINAL

PAYMENT DEPOSITED. THANK YOU AGAIN FOR ALL
YOU'VE DONE.

She took a screen shot then texted the message to her
phone. In order to not get caught, she deleted the text and
the image from Julie's phone. Amanda saw her sister exiting
the bathroom and she immediately put Julie's phone back,
pretending to be writing something in her day planner.

"Did you get the stain out of your blouse?"

"Yes, luckily I carry one of these handy stain pens
wherever I go." She paused for a moment, took a sip of her
tea and said, "I'm so glad you reached out to me, Amanda.
I was glad to get your message."

Amanda saw the perfect opportunity to bring up her
former lover. "Speaking of Facebook messages, I used your
login information to stalk Brandon the other day, and I saw
you were friends with Andrew Langston, what is that all
about?"

Julie glanced at Amanda with a puzzled look and asked,
"Who's Andrew Langston?"

Right, like she didn't know who he was. Amanda knew
that tone. Clearly her sister was hiding something. Amanda

knew there was a puzzle to piece together, but how would she go about solving it? Remembering Alex had mentioned once that Vince used him to look into her past, she wondered if he could help her with this project. If there was a connection between Julie and Andrew she was going to find it. Amanda was just going to have to push through the awkwardness that existed between the two of them and try to regain the friendship she had with Alex.

After her spin class, Amanda sat outside the Bagel Beanery soaking up the warm August sunshine and sipping a passion fruit smoothie. Exercise didn't manage to take her mind off the Julie and Andrew situation. Vince was in New York and wouldn't be back until the following evening. She sent a text message to Alex asking him to meet her at the apartment saying she needed to talk to him. He had yet to respond.

A tall woman with blonde hair caught Amanda's attention as she closed the door of her black Mercedes

Benz, that was coincidentally the same make model as Amanda's. She looked to be in her early thirties and was dressed in her tennis whites that showed off her perfectly tanned skin. Two kids hopped out of the backseat, the girl looked about twelve and the boy about ten. The young girl had the most beautiful green eyes and wavy toffee blonde hair that was pulled up in a tousled ponytail. She was wearing a Ramones t-shirt with a pair of jean shorts that had a rip on the front left leg and black Converse shoes.

The boy, who opened the book he was carrying, had extreme ash blonde hair like his mom and brown eyes. He was wearing a Detroit Tigers t-shirt and black shorts. The mom, or she could be the nanny, or maybe a step-mom, stood holding the door open for the kids. The little boy was walking hesitantly to the door as if he didn't want to be there.

"Hurry up. Your dad will be here any moment," she said motioning for the young boy to get inside.

Amanda looked up and saw a silver Mercedes approaching. It slowed down and parked right behind the other Mercedes. *Must be the kids' dad.* The driver emerged from the car, and Amanda nearly fell out of her chair—it was Vince! Her heart was pounding. She turned away from the door so he would not notice her sitting there. She slowly turned back around. Through the window she saw the woman greet Vince with a kiss, and he kissed her back. *A kiss!* Amanda waited for them to approach the counter to order their drinks before going to her car and retrieving a magazine. She slyly walked into the Bagel Beanery and took a seat in a corner booth. She was bound and determined to know what was happening. *Was Vince still married? Was he just friendly with his ex? Why would he lie to her about the trip?* Amanda's mind was scattered with questions.

The four of them cozily slid into a booth about three away from where Amanda was sitting. There were only a few patrons in the coffee place, so it was easy to hear the conversation. The kids were excitedly talking about what they had been doing all day, and the woman said she had won both her tennis matches at the club. Vince, who was seated on the outside of the table facing Amanda asked the kids what they wanted for supper. They both replied, hamburgers on the grill, and the young girl asked if she could have cheese and pickles on her burger.

The mom laughed and said, "I am sure your dad will make you a burger just to your liking."

Vince smiled and said, "I sure will."

The young boy stepped away from his chair and wrapped his arms around Vince's neck saying happily, "I'm so glad you're home dad. Can you come to my football game Thursday night?"

"I told you, Logan, that I have to go out of town this weekend, but I will try to make it to the next one buddy." Vince took his left hand and tapped him on the head, mussing the boy's hair. That's when Amanda saw his platinum wedding band. After seeing the ring and listening to the conversation, Amanda could only conclude one thing—Vince was a lying cheater. *I'm his mistress!*

Chapter Thirty-One
Ashleigh

"You *love* me? Ashleigh....I...I've wanted to be with *you* and only you for what feels like an eternity. Please help me to understand, after all this time of telling me you don't want a relationship, you suddenly have this desire to be involved with me romantically." Liam was speaking vehemently as he held the card in his hands. He then began wildly waving the card around and shaking his head. Ashleigh had never seen Liam so frenzied.

"Liam please calm down. I'm sorry about this. I guess I got sidetracked when you told me you were dating someone." She paused taking in a deep breath, "Yes it's true I love you. I won't apologize for that. I think I have always known, and I was just being selfish. I didn't want to give you my heart because that meant that I was opening myself up for the possibility of being hurt."

Liam stared at Ashleigh, his demeanor became more relaxed and his eyes narrowed. He walked closer to her, clutching her hands in his. It suddenly occurred to Ashleigh that she never actually gave the card to Liam.

"Wait…how did you get the bag?"

Liam explained that he came back into the hotel because he thought he'd misplaced his credit card. The server handed him the bag and said that he found it on the chair, that's when Liam saw his name on the card and opened it.

"Ashleigh, I have been in love with you from the first moment I saw you, or at least it feels like that for me. My heart has ached every day, longing to hold only you, kiss only you and love only you. All I have wanted is to give you the world and show you how much I adore you."

His words were beautiful as they poured from his gorgeous lips. Excited relief washed over her entire body and the mood in the room shifted slightly. Ashleigh's heart was beating rapidly as Liam released her hands. He walked to the bar and poured a glass of scotch. A flash of confusion swept over Ashleigh as she watched Liam slowly sipping the beverage eyeing her intently.

"Liam, I love you. If you love me then we can be together." Her words were a plea of emotional desperation, "Can't we? I am sorry it took me so long to realize this."

Before Liam had a chance to answer, the doorbell rang. Ashleigh turned to open it and this time, it *was* the champagne.

"Where would you like the champagne, Miss Preston?"

"In the dining room would be wonderful. Thank you very much."

Closing the door, she turned around to find Liam standing behind her, looking at her, his dark eyes intense. He clenched his jaw and loosened his tie. Ashleigh stood motionless. *Is Liam mad? Is he upset it took me this long to realize?* His body language was confusing her more by the second.

"Liam please…please talk…"

Suddenly Liam's lips were fiercely placed upon Ashleigh's. Their mouths collided passionately— it was reckless, almost savage. Liam's hand moved up her thigh where the slit of her dress exposed her skin ever so slightly. Ashleigh grabbed Liam's suit jacket and forcefully pulled it from his body. Their hands roamed over each other's bodies feverishly as Liam pinned Ashleigh against one of the mirrored panels causing her to release a low moan. She felt a twinge of pain on her back from the edge of the panel grinding into her. Ashleigh was sure there would be a bruise, but she didn't care. Liam began to move his fingers over Ashleigh's silk thong, and with one forceful tug they dropped to the floor in a tiny crumpled heap.

Breathless, Ashleigh teased, "I just bought those." A smile crossed her lips as she moved her hands from his shoulders to his tie, where she began to untie the already loosened double Windsor knot.

He smirked and whispered in her ear, "I'll buy you a new pair."

She grasped the back of Liam's dark hair, tugging and pulling hard as he moved his hands to her waist. Gliding his fingers gently to the back of her gown he slowly moved the zipper down as the fabric fell over her body exposing more of her lightly bronzed skin. Waves of heat crashed over Ashleigh's body as Liam's hands skimmed the lace fabric on her bra.

Ashleigh's mind raced at the sound of Liam's metal zipper unhinging as he spun her around and pinned her against the wall. She watched Liam in the mirror as he gripped the curve of her hip pushing the dress over the swell of her ass fisting the excess fabric between his hands. She cried out in pleasure as he plunged into her letting out a guttural moan that reverberated through Ashleigh making her thighs quiver. Ashleigh's knee's knocked together as he began fucking her with long slow strides, pushing his cock in and out of her with tremendous force. When it was possible, she corrected her stance allowing Liam better access. Watching him thrusting into her, their eyes met, and it was singly one of the most erotic things Ashleigh had ever experienced.

Hot and wet, Ashleigh was already beginning to lose her mind as Liam stroked her faster, each thrust more powerful than the one before. Ashleigh loved every minute of Liam's heated need to fuck her hard and fast. She wasn't quite sure if this was an anger bang or an "I'm so happy you finally figured your emotional shit out" quick and dirty fuck. Either way, she didn't care. It was brutally exciting and reminded her of the first time they'd been intimate together. As proper as they were in public and business settings, there should be no mistake that Ashleigh and Liam were ardent lovers. Liam is a gentleman by all accounts, but even a gentleman takes his lady to pound town every now and again.

She heard Liam gasp when she clenched her walls tightly around him. Widening her stance Ashleigh drew him in deeper watching his eyes grow darker with each vigorous movement.

"Christ… Liam, fuck me harder… *please*," Ashleigh begged shamelessly. Moans and garbled curses flowed from her lips echoing around the room.

His fingers flexed and dug into her warm flesh, the pain was stimulating, sending electric sparks to each and every nerve ending in her body. Her heart thumped so wildly she felt in her throat.

"I'm so hard for you baby," Liam managed to say through panting deep breaths.

Ashleigh's breathing became ragged, and she licked her bottom lip when Liam buried his face in her neck trailing kisses across her shoulder. Ashleigh's breasts swelled and her abs tightened at the sensation of Liam pounding into her.

"Liam," she cried out. "I'm so close."

"Ashleigh, *fuck*, you feel so good, so goddamn good," he snarled.

Ashleigh bent over further at the waist placing her palms flat against the mirrored panels. Liam covered her hand with his giving a few final thrusts to her core driving them both to euphoric release at the same time. The orgasm ripped through Ashleigh. Her vision blurred, seeing only black then white stars in her eyes, before her body went slightly lax. Liam slipped his arm around Ashleigh's waist to keep her from falling as he poured his orgasm into her. A few moments later, after they've ridden out the wave of ecstasy together, Liam eased out of her causing Ashleigh to whimper at the loss.

Liam gripped Ashleigh's wrist and spun her around to face him. Lifting her chin with his index finger, their eyes met, and Ashleigh pulled Liam's hand leading him up the stairwell.

God he looks sexy. Freshly fucked hair—check. His masculine scent on me, everywhere—check. His breathing, low and ragged—double check. Liam smirks at me, and I want to crumble at his feet and give him the best blow job he's ever experienced. Oh wait, new plan.

"I'm not done with you yet, Mr. Bond," Ashleigh purred.

Grinning wickedly, Liam clutched his hand in a fist over his chest and let out a low growl. "Oh, we're definitely doing *that* again, Mrs. Kensington," Liam replied. With each step her gown fell from her body over her hips, down her legs and finally onto the marble steps of the staircase. Liam bent down to pick it up for her, always the gentleman.

Looking up at Ashleigh, Liam paused in the middle of the stairwell and reached for her, pulling her mouth to his. "In case there was any doubt, Ashleigh, you should know I'm *madly* in love with you," Liam confessed tracing his thumb over her bottom lip.

Her hazel eyes pricked with tears, "I love you, Liam, so much. I'm sorry it took me so long to realize I was *in love* with you. If I'm being honest— I was terrified to fall in love again, but I realized being closed off was no way to live my life, at least not anymore."

She leaned into Liam's strong frame, molding her body to his as their lips met with a deep kiss that left Ashleigh breathless.

"Darling, I promise I will never intentionally hurt you, ever. I promise we'll have more good times than bad," his voice was filled with hope. It's only you Ashleigh. you're the only woman for me."

The empty feeling she had was now filled with Liam's returned love and affection. Ashleigh's heart swelled. She knew Liam was her destiny—her true love. Ashleigh had intensity with Nick, but not like the chemical connection she did with Liam. With Liam it was different, and the realization of just how much she needed him physically and emotionally had finally sunk in.

As they reached the top of the stairs Ashleigh heard a familiar sound hitting the double-doors off the master suite. The calm tapping of rain against the glass reminded Ashleigh of just how soothing it was being with the man she loved. Liam was the man who released her from her fears, unlocking the chains she had wrapped herself up in all these years. It was Liam who showed Ashleigh it was okay to open up the doors and walk into the rain once again. But now, when she felt sad or anxious, Liam would be her shelter from the storm.

His lips began to softly kiss her neck and her shoulders. Ashleigh started unbuttoning Liam's shirt, gently brushing her lips against the newly exposed area of his chest. Carefully sliding his shirt over his toned arms, she tossed it over the chaise at the end of the bed.

Liam took Ashleigh in his arms kissing her intently. Tingles fluttered up her spine. He gently pushed her onto the bed, and she fell back as the softness of the pillows surrounded her. She exhaled and closed her eyes as Liam lowered his dark head between her thighs.

Okay nix my plan, this is fucking heaven.

Ashleigh awoke the next morning to find it was nearly ten o'clock. Liam was sitting on the terrace reading *The*

Times and sipping tea in a grey pair of pants with a matching vest and white shirt. It was clear he went home to change, but Ashleigh was thankful he came back. The table next to him was filled with pastries and fresh fruit that she couldn't wait to taste. The evening's activities had left her ravished, in more than one way.

Ashleigh went to the bathroom, brushed her teeth and combed her hair, pinning it up into a bun. She slipped her silk pajamas off and stepped into the shower. The warm spray washed over her body, and her thoughts returned to the night before. Thinking about how happy she was, a smile crossed her face. Turning off the water Ashleigh reached for her towel and found Liam standing in the doorway.

"Good morning, darling." He walked towards her and kissed her on the lips.

"Good morning, handsome." She turned and began to towel off. "Did you sleep well?"

Ashleigh turned back around to find Liam on one knee, holding a Harry Winston box that contained the most brilliant oval diamond ring surrounded by micropave diamonds in a platinum setting. Looking at the diamond Ashleigh observed it had to have been at least 2 carats… it was 2.25 to be precise.

"Ashleigh Marie Preston, my love, I do not want to go on one more day without you. Will you do me the great honor of becoming my wife?"

She stood there in the bathroom wrapped in nothing but a fluffy white towel with her mouth hanging open. Overcome with emotion, she somehow managed to blurt out with excitement, "Yes! I will absolutely marry you Liam Oliver Frost."

Chapter Thirty-Two
Amanda

The door of Amanda's apartment slammed behind her as she threw her keys across the room. Pacing frantically, she tried to push what she had just witnessed out of her mind. Pouring herself a drink from the bar, she proceeded to Vince's office. She wanted to snoop, but she didn't know what she was looking for or where to start.

"Amanda? Are you home?" Alex called.

"Yeah, I'm here," she answered coldly. Amanda walked to the living room and began muttering. Her tone was thick with anger. "I cannot believe what a goddamn liar he is."

"He, who?"

"Vince!" she snapped. "Who else do you think I'm talking about?"

Alex shot her a look of confusion, "What did Vince lie about?"

"I don't wanna talk about it."

Before Amanda knew it, she was wrapped up in Alex's arms kissing him. She needed him to chase away the loneliness and the hurt she was feeling. She'd been gutted about sleeping with Alex and betraying Vince, all the while Vince was keeping Amanda distracted from what was really going on, holed up in this ivory tower while he fucked his wife and had backyard barbecues with his family. How could she be so blind? Of course Vince hadn't introduced his children to her. Amanda was the other woman.

Alex gripped Amanda's hips lifting her up allowing her to encircle her legs around his trim waist. She fisted her fingers through his brown waves, and he began to move his mouth down to the lower part of her neck. Amanda gently slid down Alex's sturdy frame. Looking at him with a seductive smile, she grasped his wrists and led him into the bathroom. She turned on the water and turned back to face Alex. Staring at each other as the bathroom began to fill with heated mist they began to undress.

Amanda stepped in the shower and the steaming liquid stung as it ran over her tight shoulders, down her back and over her thighs. She inhaled and closed her eyes feeling a hand on the small of her back. Alex was behind her grinning lazily as he poured some shower gel in his hand.

He began rubbing it over Amanda's shoulders, trying to relax her aching muscles, calming the tension that lingered in her body. Kissing her neck he pulled her into him, and she could feel his cock hardening and twitching with each kiss. He gently ran his sudsy hands over her breasts. Her skin began tingling, and Amanda's body instantly responded to his touch.

A whimper escaped her firm lips as her body trembled. Lightheaded from the heat and Alex's hands gliding over her body, she managed to muster the words, "Alex, make me forget...*please*. Wash it away..." she breathed a deep sigh. "Wash it all away."

"Amanda," he whispered. "If I had my way you'd never be in pain." He searched her face running the pad of his thumb over her wet lips. "There would be no hurt to wash away, but that's just me."

She leaned into him and captured his mouth with hers. Alex moved Amanda away from the pouring water and lifted her onto him. He ran his lips down her jawline to the base of her throat. Her back was propped against the cool tiled wall and Alex began a slow, steady, rocking movement driving them both crazy. His hips ground into her while she gripped his shoulders tighter. Amanda let out a breathless cry as Alex delivered the final thrust that sent intense shockwaves pulsing through her entire body. Again the pain was gone. All Amanda felt was warmth spill over her. A smile slid across her lips.

Moments later Alex and Amanda found themselves wrapped in fluffy towels lying atop her bed. Propped up on her elbow she traced the lines on Alex's abs with her index finger. He weaved his long fingers through her damp wavy locks and brushed her reddened cheek with the back of his hand.

"Alex," Amanda said softly. "I saw my sister today and…well…I'm pretty sure she's hiding something from me."

"Oh," Alex said as he arched his eyebrow.

"Yeah, I was wondering if you could look into a guy named, Andrew Langston."

"Sure," he replied as his hand fell to her back. "Anything you need."

She curled up next to him resting her chin on his chest, and he wrapped his arms around her. Amanda let out a deep sigh and began to chew her lip. Alex could sense she was still troubled.

"Are you ready to tell me what had you so worked up earlier?" Alex asked softly and kissed the crown of her head.

"I also saw Vince today," she began. Amanda let out a deep sigh and rolled onto her back staring at the ceiling. "Alex, he was wearing a wedding band, and he told me he was going to be in New York until Thursday, but magically he's here and having smoothies with his wife and kids!" Amanda shouted at Alex in anger. "I'm so stupid. How, how could I have trusted him? This is karma, Alex."

Tilting her head back, she laced her fingers with his and said, "I feel so incredibly foolish, Alex. What am I going to do?"

He gave her a sympathetic look, which pissed her off. Amanda hates to be pitied, but it's a cause she's come to know quite well. Sometimes when desperation rears its ugly head, she uses pity to her advantage. It was beneath her to behave in such a way.

Punching her fist to the bed, she snapped, "Amanda Parsons is *not* mistress material—I'm the *goddamn* trophy. I'm the fucking gold, silver and bronze medal rolled into one."

Alex swallowed the lump in this throat and propped himself up leaning against the headboard. "Amanda, Vince *is* divorced."

Amanda sat up in the bed and drew her knees into her chest. Confusion flashed in her eyes. "What do you mean *is* divorced?" she asked, her voice brittle. "You sound pretty damn sure of yourself."

"Amanda, I'm with Vince a lot. I attend to all of his interests, personal and otherwise. I know more about him than anyone in the world. As much as it pains me to admit—he *didn't* lie to you."

"Okay, so spill it Alex. Tell me everything," she demanded.

Alex began explaining that Vince's kids did not yet know their parents were divorcing. He told Amanda, that

Vince and Jennifer, his ex-wife, were trying to figure out how to break it to them. In reality, the divorce was final.

Shock and embarrassment coursed through Amanda. She ran her hands through her wet hair nervously twisting the ends around her fingers.

"Godammit!" Amanda screamed as she jumped up from the bed. "Walking in a small pattern around her bedroom, she took a sip of the wine that Alex had brought her after their shower. She was breathing heavily, and the tears started to roll down her face.

"Amanda," Alex said, his voice soft and laced with concerned.

"I'm so confused," she said shaking her head back and forth. "Alex, you *need* to leave."

Alex stood up from the bed and walked towards Amanda. He reached for her, but she recoiled like a snake and backed away.

"Amanda," he began, his tone low. "Don't do that…*don't* push me away."

"Alex, we cannot do this anymore," she lectured. "This absolutely cannot happen again."

"Amanda, why…why are you with Vince?" his tone with her was sharp. "I know you feel this…connection…this heat we have between us."

Amanda thought about his question. Her mind was fogged. She had no real answer except that she needs Vince, but she also cares deeply for him. Amanda didn't know if she was *in love* with Vince but she knew she loved him. Amanda's feelings for Alex were confusing. He stirred mixed emotions in her. Obviously there was excitement and pleasure. There was also calmness. Alex grounded her, but he also frightened her, or at least the idea of him troubled her.

"Alex, I…I'm afraid of you…" Amanda confessed her voice was low and controlled.

Alex's brow furrowed.

"I mean, I'm afraid I'm using you as a replacement to take away the pain. It's like you're my drug of choice and I'm addicted to this thing that's ignited between us."

Alex inched closer to her locking his gaze with hers. Amanda felt her knees buckling beneath her and her skin began to prick with heat. Alex closed the space between them, and Amanda drew in a sharp breath.

"There's no need to be afraid." He grinned as he drew her palm up to his lips kissing her gently. "Amanda, I've never met anyone that gets my heart racing like you do. I go to work every day happy, because I know that at some point I'll see your beautiful face." He bent down and brushed his lips to hers.

His fingertips grazed the curve of her face. He says, "Your smile...it melts my heart and your laugh...I love hearing how it whimsically singsongs up and down."

"Alex," she pulled back breathless. Her bottom lip quivering, she replied, "but, we're hurting Vince. It's not fair. It will break his heart."

"I plan to win your heart and never break it. Vince has money, power and all that comes with that, but I can give you the one thing he can't—time."

Amanda reached her hands up and touched his face. No words were spoken, the glint in her eyes says everything. Alex swept her up, and she wrapped her arms around his neck.

"Our time is limited, Amanda," he whispered. "We shouldn't waste a second of it waiting for someone else's schedule to clear up to make plans."

Locked in a deep kiss, swallowed up in the warmth of their embrace, Alex pushed Amanda to the bed, where she surrendered to him over and over. They don't even notice the late afternoon sun had faded to darkness.

Chapter Thirty-Three
Emily

Emily arrived home after her morning work out to find Ethan's car parked in her driveway. She pulled into the garage as Ethan stepped out of his black Lexus looking as handsome as ever. He was wearing his favorite navy blue shorts paired with a navy, white and grey striped J. Crew oxford with the sleeves rolled up.

"Maybe, I should give you a key so you don't have to wait in the driveway," she said with a flirtatious smile.

"Did you think about me while you worked up a sweat at the gym, Em?"

"I always do," she hummed. "Although I would much rather be working up a sweat *with* you, Ethan."

As she began to walk towards the door, Ethan grabbed her by her wrist and pulled her back close to him. He pushed her back against the hot metal of her car, it stung a bit at first because it had been sitting for a while in the parking lot, under the blistering sun. Ethan let out a low groan as he kissed Emily. The vibrations sent a pleasurable shiver through Emily's core.

She heard her gym bag hit the garage floor as she felt Ethan's hands gliding down her thigh. Emily felt her knees go weak as she encircled her arms around Ethan's neck. He ran his index finger over her thigh making figure eights and zig zags, like he was drawing designs in the sand. Emily moaned softly. She became hot and cold all at once, her body ached for Ethan. She felt just how much he wanted her, too, as Ethan positioned his hips into her and hitched Emily's leg up around his waist while cupping her bottom. Ethan continued to kiss her neck, and Emily looked around to make sure no prying eyes were staring at them. She would die of embarrassment if her sweet neighbor, Mrs. Crenshaw caught Emily making out with her boyfriend in the garage like two horny teenagers.

Thunder rumbled in the distance. Emily took that as an opportunity to distract Ethan and suggest they go inside.

"Ethan, as much as I would love nothing more than to continue kissing you, I think we should take this inside away from such a *public* setting."

"Fine," he growled in her ear. "Besides, I have some news about the Cadillac that nearly ran me over," Ethan said as he scooped up her bag.

"Oh yeah?" her eyes widened and gleamed with hopefulness. "Did Alex find the owner?"

"They found the white Cadillac matching the description you gave down by the abandoned railway station on the southeast side near Wealthy Street. Alex said he and his team searched inside the vehicle and found nothing. It had been completely wiped clean. The license plate had been removed and the VIN number was stripped from the car"

A chill shot up Emily's spine upon hearing the news. "Seriously, nothing?" Emily scoffed as she dumped her bag by the stairs.

"I'm sorry Em," Ethan said while taking a bottle of water out of the fridge. "It looks like we've hit a dead end at the moment."

"We cannot catch a goddamn break," Emily said, her voice thick with anger and frustration.

"Alex isn't giving up, Em," he reassured her. Ethan slung his arms around her waist and hugged her tightly. "Okay, now don't you have to get your hair and nails done or something for tonight?"

"Yes, my appointment is in an hour."

"I have to go back to the office, but I'll meet you at my house to change. Then can we go to the gala together?" Ethan asked.

Shaking her head, Emily huffed, "I cannot believe Clark is making you come back to work on a Saturday afternoon, and before the fucking gala no less. Has he lost his damn mind?"

"Play nice, Em," Ethan joked and kissed her on the cheek. "I'll see you later, I love you."

Emily loved hearing those three little words pour from Ethan's perfect lips. She was on cloud nine. Everything seemed to be falling into place, well, except that she had a stalker.

"I love you, too," she said while walking him to the door.

Emily rushed to Ethan's house after her salon appointment to start getting ready for the gala at The Plaza de Grand. She was feeling a bit stressed, Ethan was at the office wrapping up a last minute meeting with Clark. Emily knew whatever they were working on had to important. She suspected it was something to do with LA Business Design and the store opening in Hong Kong next month.

Emily heard her phone vibrating in her bag. A text from Ethan read: CLARK PUSHED THE MEETING BACK ANOTHER TWENTY MINUTES.

Emily sighed and returned Ethan's text: THAT'S OKAY, WE STILL HAVE PLENTY OF TIME BEFORE TONIGHT'S EVENT. I WILL SEE YOU IN A BIT. I'M GETTING IN THE BATH.

After pouring a glass of red wine she walked upstairs and turned on the radio in the bathroom. A severe weather alert came across saying high gusts of wind were taking down trees, and there was a power outage in East Grand

Rapids. A possible funnel cloud was spotted near Kentwood. *Wow, we're in for a rocky ride tonight.*

Emily began to run the water in the tub, poured in some bubble bath and lit some candles just in case the power went out. Slipping out of her clothes Emily stepped into the tub and closed her eyes. Just then the power did go out, and Emily heard a rattling outside. She pulled up the Tune In app on her phone to find her favorite radio station and sat back in the tub. The wind was really picking up, and the lightning was intense, steadily streaking through the sky. Closing her eyes she took a sip of wine allowing her mind to relax.

Chapter Thirty-Four

Sparkling metallic stemware and sterling silver-rimmed place settings sat carefully atop pressed white linens that were surrounded by plush velvet chairs in the ballroom. Amanda stood with her arms crossed, very pleased at the sight of her surroundings. She drummed her freshly painted fingernails against her smooth skin and hummed to the soft music pouring through the sound system. George Michael was right in the middle of singing the chorus to "Kissing a Fool" when he was rudely interrupted by the intense rumbling of thunder that shook outside. The lights flickered a bit, causing the ornate chandeliers that hung above to jiggle slightly. Emma Sterling shot Amanda a worried look.

Amanda shrugged and said, "I don't recall inviting this thunderstorm to the event."

Emma giggled, "I definitely didn't put her on the guest list."

Amanda turned on her heel, moved out of Emma's line of sight and sighed with relief. She was glad this day had finally arrived. The Phillip Cooper Foundation was the biggest charity event of the summer season. Nearly three hundred prominent people would be in attendance for the glamorous evening—schmoozing and boozing. The silent auction items had all been delivered, and the hotel staff was currently setting up the banquet tables. Amanda's favorite florist, Anne Stephens, had just called and said she would be delivering the centerpieces for the tables and the rest of the decorations any minute.

"It's going to be a wonderful event, Amanda. I cannot thank you enough for pulling all this together," Emma gleefully hummed. "I'm very impressed with you, Amanda. You have quite the flare for event planning."

Her heart skipped a beat when she heard the thunder explode. It sounded like a bomb went off directly over their heads.

"Thank you for the lovely compliment. I think so too, Emma. Anything that could have gone wrong did, and we solved those issues. I'm sure tonight will be smooth sailing," she replied feeling a bit nervous. But she didn't let Emma see she was sweating bullets.

Ashleigh greeted Liam when he arrived at the Plaza de Grand.

"This weather is insane," Liam said as he kissed Ashleigh on both cheeks. "Hello my darling."

Ashleigh smiled warmly as Liam took her hand in his. "Hi handsome, how was your flight?"

"It was good. The flight from Detroit to here was a little bumpy. Luckily the strong weather didn't hit until after we landed. I am just glad to be here with you."

"I'm so glad you could make it here. Our suite is ready, and I have already checked in."

Ashleigh led Liam across the lobby to the elevator corridor. She jumped a bit when the thunder boomed again. Liam clutched her hand tighter and gave her a warm smile.

"This is quite a lovely hotel. Is this where you want to be married?" Liam asked smoothly while rubbing the pad of his thumb over Ashleigh's engagement ring.

Ashleigh had been thinking a lot about the wedding over the last few weeks. She could hardly believe how excited she was to begin planning all the details, she had already asked Emily to be her Maid of Honor. Her list of wedding invites was minute by modern wedding standards, consisting of a few close friends and her small family. Something intimate would be the perfect way to celebrate spending the rest of their lives together.

Ashleigh would be moving to London soon, her beloved penthouse was going on the market next week, and it she felt that it would be easier to plan a wedding in the country where she was currently living.

"Actually Liam, I think I want a small wedding. What do you think about getting married at Frost Castle?" Ashleigh heard the irony in her voice. Such an event at a castle doesn't exactly scream small wedding, but she had connections that could help make the event an intimate one.

A smile crossed Liam's luscious lips, "Of course, anything you want. I think it's a delightful idea. Have I told you how much I love you and how incredibly happy I am that you agreed to marry me?" He pulled Ashleigh in tight, delivering a long kiss to her full lips.

She knew, because she was happy, too. Finally, she let go of the past. In her mind Ashleigh had said goodbye to Nick and their baby, setting her free. Neither fear nor stubbornness would keep her from living her life to the fullest. The guilt finally escaped her mind, and for the first time in what seemed like years Ashleigh breathed again.

Taking a sip of scotch Alex peered at his notes then glanced out the window of the jet. Resting his head on the back of the seat, he closed his eyes, and his mind drifted to the enlightening conversation. As he replayed the exchange over and over, he realized there was nothing he could do that would prepare Amanda for the shocking news he was about to give her. Alex couldn't believe what he had discovered—it was all so devious and underhanded. Summer was coming to an end, and along with it, Amanda's world was about to be blown apart. Alex let out a deep sigh. "At least I can be there to help her pick up the pieces," he muttered to himself.

Emily's wine glass shattered on the tile floor. She tried to scream for help, but her head just went under the water again. Utilizing all her energy, Emily struggled back up for air and began coughing. She opened her eyes to find a woman with silky dark red hair dressed in black sitting on the edge of the tub. Wiping the bubbles from her eyes she realized who the woman was—Libby Westin, Ethan's ex-girlfriend. Emily began to feel dizzy, she felt drunk and tired. *How could I be drunk? It was only a glass of wine.*

"Libby? What…what are you doing here?" Her breathing was becoming shallow. Emily's body felt heavy. The power was still out, as darkness crept through the room.. Emily could hear the nonstop thunder, and the constant lightning sent electricity racing through the air.

"Emily," she began with a seductive icy tone. "So nice to see you again, I hope you're enjoying your nice warm bath, because it's the last one you'll ever have."

Emily tried to pull herself up in the tub, but she kept slipping. "Lib…Libby what…are…you saying?" Emily noticed that Libby was holding a kitchen knife. Emily looked around the bathroom and started to feel around the ledge where she left her phone. She accidently knocked over one of the candles. The glass holder cracked, and the flame was immediately put out by the melted wax.

"Looking for this I assume?" Libby purred holding up Emily's cell phone.

Emily tried to reach for her phone, but Libby pulled it back. "Ah, ah, ah. Not so fast. By the way, Ethan sent a message. He said he was on his way soon."

Libby stood up from where she was seated on the edge of the tub and crossed the bathroom to the door. "Where are you two headed tonight? Some fancy dinner?" Libby ran the blade of the knife up and down Emily's dress that was hanging on the back of the door. "What a pretty dress. Navy blue, huh? I'm not so sure this is your color, Em." Libby took the tip of the knife and slowly ran it from the neckline to the floor, slicing the dress in two.

Emily tried to focus as she began to slide under the water again.

"No, not yet Emily." Libby reached out and grabbed the top of Emily's head pulling her up by her hair. Emily tried to cry out, but the word *ouch* came out in a low voice.

"Libby, why… why are you doing this? I must…be dreaming."

"No Emily, I am afraid this is very real, but in a few short moments you'll be sleeping and you can dream all you like."

"Libby …did you…did you *drug* me?"

Heavy rain began to pour outside, and Emily could hear a loud thunder clap. She opened her eyes and saw flashes of lightning reflecting in the mirror.

Libby knelt down beside the tub and gently glided the knife over the top of the bubbles. "I just gave you a few of my sleeping pills and a muscle relaxer. You seemed stressed over the break-in and the scary phone calls you'd been getting, so I thought you needed to relax."

Emily's head bobbed, and she went under, face first. She felt soft hands pull her back above the surface.

"Emily, I told you to stay awake. It's *not* time to sleep yet. You have to listen to my bedtime story," Libby growled. "You see, once upon a time there was this beautiful woman named Libby, and she loves the most handsome man, whose name was Ethan. Ethan and the beautiful woman were living their lives happily ever after, until Ethan decides he wants to leave the beautiful woman for the wicked witch, whose name is Emily."

Emily shifted in the tub again. She could barely keep her eyes open. "Lib…Libby that's…not true…Ethan didn't… leave you…you for me…he said you wanted diff…different things."

Libby became enraged. She pushed Emily down in the tub again. Emily could hear Libby shouting, but it all sounded muffled. Emily tried to push back, but she just couldn't muster the strength.

"It's not nice to lie to people Emily!" Libby brought Emily up to the surface again pushing her back against the stone.

Libby crossed the bathroom to the mirror where she began to mess with her red hair. Reaching into the front pocket of her jeans, she pulled out a narrow tube of lipstick, which she expertly applied.

"Ethan belongs to me, Emily. He just needs to be reminded of why. When Ethan discovers you've died. I'll be there to comfort him in his time of sadness. He *will* love me again."

Emily's eyes began to close. She felt so tired, the urge to sleep was almost uncontrollable. Thunder continued rumbling loudly in the distance, reminding Emily of how much she loved watching storms roll in off the lake.

The warmth poured over her pale skin as Emily drifted lazily on the raft in her parents' pool. Her brothers began splashing her, and she yelled, "Come on guys! Stop it!" They just laughed hysterically. Emily saw her mom coming out of the house with a dishtowel in her hands. "You better come in now, the storm is approaching quickly. Emily did you hear me? Emily!"

Emily got out of the pool, but why was her mom still yelling at her?

"Come on Em, Emily please wake up….Emily! Oh God please let her be alright."

Chapter Thirty-Five

Ashleigh and Liam entered the Kensington Ballroom at the Plaza de Grand. Immediately Ashleigh spotted her old boss from *Maison Bleue* Magazine and paid him a quick greeting. She was impressed to see that the Mayor of Grand Rapids was able to attend the event and nodded a quiet salutation in his direction out of courtesy. Ashleigh began introducing Liam as her fiancé to many of the people she knew in the business community. After having their picture taken with several prominent community leaders, Liam and Ashleigh walked to the bar and ordered a couple of drinks.

"The Kensington Ballroom, huh?" Liam quipped with a throaty laugh.

"Ironic, isn't it?" Ashleigh replied taking his hand in hers.

"You look incredibly beautiful in this red dress. I cannot wait to peel it off you later."

"Thank you my handsome fiancé. You look fetching as usual. I *guess* I will let you peel this off me later, but carefully," Ashleigh teased.

Replying coolly, Liam asked, "Can men look fetching?" Handing Ashleigh her drink, he raised his glass and said, "A toast to you, my soon to be Mrs. Frost." He paused for a moment then asked, "Wait, will you be taking my last name?" He looked at her as if pleading, please say you will.

She giggled softly, "Yes, absolutely I will be taking your last name. I cannot wait to be Ashleigh Frost."

Relief washed over Liam's face. Looking at her phone she wondered where Emily was. It was unlike her to be late to an event. She scanned the room for Ethan, no sign of him either.

Amanda approached the podium to address the crowd and thanked everyone for their generous donations.

"Dinner will be served shortly. The silent auction will be closing in about fifteen minutes, so if there are any items that you wish to bid on, please do so as soon as possible. We will resume bidding after dessert has been served. Now, sit back and relax as we have prepared a short video to tell you a little bit more about the Phillip Cooper Foundation and how your donations will be helping so many of these wonderful families in Grand Rapids."

Amanda stepped down from the podium and felt someone tap her shoulder. She spun around to see her ex-husband, Brandon, standing inches away from her in a black tuxedo. Even though they'd been divorced for a while Brandon still managed to take her breath away. He was smiling at her. That put Amanda on guard, not knowing if there was wickedness behind his expression.

"Amanda," he greeted her, his tone was low and controlled.

"Brandon…" she swallowed hard then managed to find her tongue. "What are you…how are you?"

"I'm here with my fiancé," he said motioning to the woman in a dazzling white, crystal beaded gown sitting at their table near the podium. Amanda recognized her from the photos she'd seen on Facebook; it was Erica Hamilton. She nodded politely in Amanda's direction. A slow smile came across Amanda's lips.

"Engaged," Amanda sputtered out, managing not to sound too disappointed. "Brandon…truly that is wonderful news."

He inched towards her, placing his hand around her waist and kissed her on the cheek. The familiarity in his touch and his soft lips made Amanda's heart flutter. Memories of their relationship came flooding back. It was all too much for her to take in. She felt her breath hitch and her chest tighten. "Thank you, Mandy," he whispered. "It's good to see you, and by the way you look beautiful tonight, but then, you always do."

A shiver curled around Amanda, and her cheeks heated. She hated being called Mandy, but Brandon was the only person she allowed to do so.

"Thank you, Brandon," she replied squeezing his hand. "Now…go…be with that gorgeous fiancé of yours."

Giving her a quick nod, Brandon pivoted and walked away, while the scent of him lingered. Amanda felt her eyes prick with tears. She walked quickly to the table where Vince was finally seated, excusing herself to the ladies room.

Staring out the window of the plane into the evening sky, Alex thought about Amanda. Realizing that he was about to inflict pain on her would be soul crushing. He told her he'd never cause her pain. Technically, he wasn't the cause of the pain, but he was about to deliver news that would shatter her into a million pieces and break her heart.

Turns out, Amanda's sister, Julie, had orchestrated a series of events that changed the course of Amanda's life. Alex went to Chicago and met with Andrew Langston. Andrew was reluctant at first to give up the information, but Alex persuaded him that it would be best for his health to start talking.

The flight attendant approached Alex, "Would you like another beverage Mr. Robertsen?"

"Yes, another scotch would be just fine."

"You've been quite the frequent flyer these past few days, Mr. Robertsen," she said handing him the drink. "Your brother must love you a lot to offer you his jet at any time."

"Yes, I guess I have, and my brother is one of the best men I know. Thank you."

"Will there be anything else at this time?"

"No, thank you Scarlett."

"Very well sir. The pilot thinks he should be able to land in about thirty minutes. The storm seems to be falling apart now. You can change into your tuxedo anytime you like, Mr. Robertsen."

Alex felt a slight twinge of guilt as the flight attendant reminded him that he was falling for his brother's girlfriend, but he had made Amanda a promise that he could give her the one thing Vince couldn't—time. And, even though Alex couldn't give Amanda the time back that she'd lost with her family, with the revelations that came from his meeting with Andrew Langston, it was now possible he could give her time with them that she thought she would never have.

Ashleigh looked at her watch during the round of applause. *What could be keeping Emily?*

Taking note of the time, Ashleigh felt cold fear bubbling inside her. She had not received a single text message or voice mail from Emily all evening. Ashleigh tried to call her, but there was no answer. Next she tried Ethan—nothing. Her mind drifted to thoughts of Nick's accident. Flashes of Emily and Ethan meeting the same cruel fate twisted inside Ashleigh's panicked mind.

"Liam we need to go. Emily isn't here. She is never late, and I've not heard from her all evening. Something feels off."

They both pushed to their feet and headed towards the doors of the ballroom. "Try to call her again. Where is your car?" Liam asked.

As they had reached the lobby there was still no answer on Emily's cell. When they reached the valet stand Ashleigh tried Ethan's cell again. The humidity hung thick in the night air, steam billowed off the hot pavement, and the smell of wet mulch and fish enveloped their senses.

Dodging the puddles trying not to fall on the wet blacktop, Ashleigh instructed, "My car is the black BMW right there under the street light close to the door. Liam, have you ever driven a car in the United States before?"

"No, but I cannot think of a more perfect time to learn."

"Nope. Absolutely not. No way," she said shaking her head with a smile. "Not at night and especially not after it's been raining. Nice try, Liam."

Unlocking the doors to her car Liam slid into the passenger seat as Ashleigh pushed the ignition and sped out of the parking lot. Ashleigh knew Emily was getting ready at Ethan's house, so she had Liam pull up his address on the GPS. With all the calmness she could muster Ashleigh dialed Emily's number again.

"Ashleigh. Hi this is Ethan. Something," His voice broke. "Something has happened to Emily."

"Ethan." Her voice was shaky. "What…what are you saying? Is Emily alright?" Ashleigh's heart was pounding. "Ethan does this have something to do with the stalker?" There was silence on the other end of the phone. "Ethan!" Ashleigh shouted. "Answer me. Is Emily okay?" Tears were streaming down Ashleigh's face. Liam felt helpless. He could hear the fear and pain in Ashleigh's voice.

"Ethan, hello this is Liam Frost, Ashleigh's fiancé. She's terribly worried about Emily. What can you tell us?"

"Yes. Hello Liam. Sorry, I'm a bit panicked. I'm at Memorial Hospital. Emily was attacked and drugged. I'm not sure if she is going make it. Please hurry."

"Not sure if she's going to make it? Oh my God, Liam!"

Liam placed his hand on Ashleigh's, "Darling, I know you are scared, but let's think positively. That is the best thing to do for Emily right now. When we get to hospital you go find Ethan, and I will park the car."

His calm tone washed over her, mildly comforting her aching mind. She knew Liam was right. Ashleigh was scared, that much was true. The drive to the hospital seemed like an eternity. Ashleigh managed to hit every red light, which only made her feel more anxious. Finally she arrived at the hospital and hoped she wasn't too late.

Amanda walked slowly to the bank of elevators. She took another sip of her drink. She was breathing heavily, and the tears started to roll down her face. She never realized seeing Brandon again would conjure so many emotions. The last time she saw him, she was sitting across a cold glass conference table while their lawyers worked out the settlement of their divorce. Amanda and Brandon fought the entire time, he was relentless with his objections. Amanda begged for him to reconsider stripping everything from her.

The last thing Brandon managed to give her was a heated final screw on top of their divorce papers. Brandon asked for a moment alone with Amanda, and the lawyers left the room. Hiking up her skirt, he bent Amanda over the table and fucked her senseless.

When it was over, he said nothing except, "I love you, Mandy, but this is goodbye."

With that he zipped up his pants, fixed his tie, smoothed her skirt and ordered her to fix her ponytail.

After a few minutes, he opened the door and said, "I think we're done here, gentlemen."

Brandon walked away, and Amanda was left standing there shaken, with only her memories and a Gucci handbag. She thought because Brandon said he loved her, she might be able to win him back, but Brandon never took Amanda's calls or accepted any of her dinner invitations.

"Amanda!" Alex shouted as he came through the glass doors of the lobby.

A smile crossed her lips at the sight of him, "Alex, what are you doing here?"

Amanda wiped away the few tears that had fallen on her cheeks and Alex noticed she seemed upset.

"Are you okay, Amanda?"

"I'm fine. It's just very emotional hearing people share their stories of triumph and tragedy," she lied.

He took out the papers and said, "I went to Chicago, and I had a chat with Andrew Langston."

A look of disbelief came over Amanda's face.

"Can we go somewhere and talk?"

Amanda nodded and said, "My suite upstairs. We will have plenty of privacy there."

"Hi. My name is Ashleigh Preston. My friend Emily
Greene was brought in tonight. Can you tell me anything
about her condition?" The nurses at the reception desk
shuffled through paperwork. Ashleigh looked to her left
and found Ethan leaning against the wall. "Nevermind.
Ethan…Ethan, how is she?"

Ethan looked up at Ashleigh through red puffy eyes.
He muttered, "It was something with her heart. They…they
took her back to trauma. I don't know what's happening. I
gave her CPR when I pulled her from the bath, and she did
open her eyes. I called 911, and then she was in the
ambulance, and her heart started to beat uncontrollably.
The doctor said something about a possible heart
arrhythmia due to a lowered body temperature. The doctors
think the combination of drugs in her system and the time
she spent underwater may have caused this to happen."

Ashleigh reached out for Ethan, and he hugged her
back. Liam rushed into the hospital and saw Ashleigh
standing with Ethan.

"Oh Liam, I'm terrified," Ashleigh whispered to him choking back soft tears as she flung her arms around his neck. "Something's going on with Emily's heart. The doctors are with her now."

"Code Blue, Trauma Four. Code Blue, Trauma Four." Ashleigh, Ethan and Liam stood together staring at the swinging doors as nurses and doctors rushed past them. Everything was happening so fast, Ashleigh's heart sank. *Please don't let anyone die here tonight, especially not Emily.*

"I am afraid your sister, Julie, was behind your scandal. Amanda, she set the whole thing up. Andrew said that she approached him in the summer when she saw you were unhappy in your marriage. Julie instructed him to flirt with you and pay attention to you, especially when Brandon wasn't around. She paid him a considerable amount of money to do it."

All the color drained from Amanda's face. She walked to the bar and poured another drink. "Why? Did he say why she did it, Alex?"

Alex nodded, swallowing hard before answering, he walked over to Amanda. He placed his hands on her shoulders and said, "Julie was insanely jealous of you, from the love your parents showered you with, to your job, to landing Brandon Ford as a husband."

Amanda started laughing and looked at Alex as if he was crazy. "That is most ridiculous thing I have ever fucking heard— jealousy? Julie got my husband to divorce me, my parents to disown me and my trust fund revoked all because of *jealousy*?" she scoffed.

"There's more, Amanda,"

"Oh fucking wonderful. Lay it on me, Alex."

Alex went on to tell Amanda how Julie hired Jessica Clayton to take the picture of Andrew and Amanda and then post it on the Bloomfield Buzz. In exchange for her cooperation, Julie persuaded the station manager at WWSK to give Jessica, Amanda's job. Julie and the station manager were apparently old friends. More like he was in love with her and would do anything for her that she asked.

"After my visit with Andrew, I called Jessica Clayton, and she met with me in Detroit confirming everything Andrew had said. Jessica was quite cooperative. Apparently she was let go from the station a few weeks ago. She said she tried to call your sister for some help, to see if Julie could get her a job with another station or even at your family's company. Julie has not called her back. Needless to say Jessica was ready to rat your sister out to me with no regrets."

Amanda couldn't believe what she was hearing. Her own sister had fucked her over.

"There's more and this is the hard part Amanda." She looked up from her glass and Alex saw Amanda was sobbing. "Hey, it will be okay," he said placing his arm around her shoulders.

"Just, give it to me straight, Alex. Tell me the rest so I can figure out what I am going to do," she said wiping her eyes.

"Your sister is crafty. I will give her that." Amanda shot Alex a look of disapproval as she poured another drink. "I talked to your parents. They said they never wanted to disown you. They said they absolutely did not disown you." Amanda just stared at Alex. She was silent and motionless.

"You…you saw my… parents?" she inquired through a set of hiccupped sobs.

"Amanda, look at me," he said softly. "Hey, what happened after the scandal broke? The day the pictures came out, what do *you* remember?"

"I remember that Julie had emailed the post to me and called to give me a heads up. She told me that she was going to talk to our parents. It was Julie that suggested I tell Brandon the picture was taken out of context and see if he would seek legal action against the blog. I called Brandon right away and asked him if he could come home, and that I had something terrible to tell him and didn't want to do it over the phone. He, however, already knew what I was going to tell him and was on his way home when I called."

"But, did *you* ever talk to your parents, Amanda? Did you ever find out who leaked the information to Brandon?" Alex inquired.

Amanda never questioned how he found out, she figured one of the gossipy secretaries or his mother, who didn't care too much for Amanda, broke the news to him. Come to think of it, she never heard from her parents in their own words, either. It was Julie who informed Amanda about her trust fund, and that they never wanted to see her again.

"Your parents told me it was Julie who told them you were leaving for a month until everything blew over. She told them you stepped down from your job, and that it was your idea to have Jessica replace you."

"That bitch!" Amanda shouted. Her sobs had subsided, and she was now seething with anger.

"Your trust fund was never depleted. Your father said he never cut you off. Julie told them you were leaving Bloomfield Hills for good, and that you did not want them to contact you so you couldn't cause any further embarrassment or bring shame to the Parson's family name."

"Murder would be too good for my dear sister. Fuck!" Amanda shouted. "So where is *my* money, Alex?" she inquired, her voice brittle.

"Your sister has been taking it. Since Julie has been helping with the financials at Parsons Enterprises, she's been able to access your account. Looks like your sister reported your bank card missing last November and had a new card sent to her home address. Julie updated all your records with the bank and closed your account shortly thereafter. Your father never knew."

Amanda looked away from Alex. Hot tears ran down her cheeks. She was furious. She wanted hit something, more like someone, and that someone was her sister.

"At least this explains why my ATM card didn't work. And when I went to the bank and they told me my account was closed, I just assumed my father shut it down and that was the end of that. All of my information came from one source... Julie."

By now the anger had turned to relief. Knowing the truth and thinking about seeing her mom and dad again, she was overcome with happiness.

"Alex," she said. "I cannot thank you enough. What you did for me, this...you gave me closure, and you've given me my family back."

"Amanda," he came towards her lifting her chin with his finger. "I told you I'd do anything to take your pain away."

Lightning flashed and lit up the sky. She turned and gazed out the window. So many things were reeling in her mind. *How will I confront Julie? If the pictures never came out, would I still be married to Brandon? Vince...Alex...Vince...Alex.*

Chapter Thirty-Six

Five days had gone by, and Emily was still in a coma. Ethan had not left her bedside except for a few hours to go home and shower. He had set up a makeshift workspace in the hospital room but was barely able to concentrate on anything other than Emily pulling through. Ashleigh had been at the hospital every day, as well. Liam wanted to stay, but he had to go back to London. He felt horrible for leaving Ashleigh during a time of crisis, but he told Ashleigh if she needed him, he would return as quickly as he could. Emily's parents had flown in from Marquette and were staying at her house. So many people had come by the hospital to see Emily—including Amanda and Annoying Andy. Nearly everyone at Cooper Bentley had sent flowers or dropped by to check on her wellbeing. With Ethan at the hospital every day, it wasn't hard for their co-workers to make the connection that Emily and Ethan were a couple.

Ethan read the paper to Emily each morning keeping her up to date on current events. Even though Ethan did not want to leave Emily's side in case she woke up,

Ashleigh had managed to convince him to go home and sleep in his own bed for the first time since the accident. An accident, that's what everyone was referring to it as. Ethan and Ashleigh didn't want to think of it as attempted murder. They were too focused on Emily's recovery.

Ethan felt guilty leaving her alone in the hospital. He felt responsible for Emily being there in the first place. Libby was apparently more unstable that Ethan realized, or anyone realized for that matter. When she found out Ethan was dating Emily, she voluntarily went off of her medication, starting a downward spiral and showing her inner demons.

Libby was in love with Ethan, and she was convinced he loved her too. She told the police that Emily was a Wicked Witch, and she was only trying to save Ethan. Bottom line... Libby couldn't separate reality from fantasy. She lived in between the two, often getting the two worlds mixed up. There is no easy way to put it, Libby was mentally unstable and she may have taken a life in her disillusionment.

When Ethan arrived home that afternoon before the gala he noticed a trail of black colored clothing leading from his kitchen to the bedroom. He entered the room which was lit by a few candles and soft rays of daylight pouring through the windows from where the sun had managed to reappear. His eyes widening at the sight of Libby lying on his bed writhing around wearing nothing but her underwear and Emily's tattered evening gown. Libby had managed to construct the dress into some kind of wearable garment. She was muttering nonsense to herself, but when she saw Ethan standing in the doorway holding her crumpled clothes Libby spoke clear as a bell.

Crawling like a cat on the prowl she moved to the edge of the bed. "Welcome home darling," Libby said in a seductive purr. "Can I pour you a glass of wine?"

Shock fell over Ethan's face. "Libby, what the hell are you doing here and how did you get in?" he growled. "Better yet, where is Emily?" Ethan inquired as he threw her bra and the rest of her clothing onto the bed, ordering her to put her clothes back on.

"Oh Ethan," Libby began, as she lifted to her knees. "Emily is dead and I'm just so sorry for your loss. I'm here for you now." Libby replied sweetly, as she swung her long legs over the side of the bed.

The power had come back on by then, and Ethan heard music coming from his bathroom. That's when he flung the door open and saw Emily under the water. Ethan managed to pull her from the tub while Libby mumbled nonsense about Emily being bad and how Ethan was safe now that Emily was gone.

For someone who was as mentally distressed as Libby, she was lucid enough to put together her plans to stalk Emily. Social media made it easy for Libby to track the couple's every move. When Emily "checked into" the Farmer's Market that Saturday, Libby decided that was the day to break-in to her place and tape up all the pictures she'd taken of the two of them.

When questioned about her actions, Libby muttered incoherently to the detectives. She mentioned something about having a friend pick the locks at Emily's place. Later she changed her story saying that Emily was the one who opened the door and let her inside. Libby swore repeatedly that she never returned Ethan's spare key. Ethan guessed that Libby had more than one key to his place, but who really knows? Maybe someday the truth will come out.

With Ethan and Emily making plans and updating their Twitter and Facebook statuses the day of the gala, Libby had the information she needed to set her plan in motion. Emily's trip to the nail salon in the afternoon gave Libby plenty of time to drive to Ethan's and wait for her to arrive.

Alex came by the hospital with Officer Scott that afternoon to ask Ethan some more questions. Ethan had been putting off talking with the young officer because of the tremendous guilt he felt over Emily being nearly killed by his ex-girlfriend. He figured he had put this meeting off long enough, and Ethan was grateful to Alex for being there with him. The three of them sat in the waiting area a few feet from Emily's room.

Officer Scott removed her hat as she took a seat beside Ethan, saying, "Mr. Carlson thanks for meeting with me. I understand this is a difficult time. Again, I'm truly sorry this has happened to Miss Greene. We're all pulling for her to come through."

Ethan's eyes shifted back to Emily's room. "Thank you," he replied sighing deeply. Ethan eased back in the padded chair, his well-rounded shoulders slumping forward. The young officer opened her notepad while Ethan sipped the watered down coffee he had been drinking. Ethan looked completely wiped out, and Alex could tell that he'd barely slept.

"Now, Mr. Carlson the matter of Miss Westin breaking and entering your home. Do you want to press charges?"

Ethan's eyes darkened as he clenched his jaw. "Libby *had* a key," he huffed and ran his finger over his bottom lip. His eyes darted to Emily's room again and back to Officer Scott.

"Yes," Ethan muttered while shifting in the chair.

Officer Scott lifted her eyebrows, "Okay I'll get the paperwork started."

"Wait," Ethan exhaled sharply. "*No*, no I don't want to press any charges. I just…" his voice trailed off.

Officer Scott shot a confused glance towards Alex who urged her to continue with his expression, "Mr. Carlson are you completely sure?"

"I said no and *yes* I'm positive." Ethan's voice was thick with anger.

Her eyes widened and she flipped her notepad closed. Alex shook his head at her offering a comforting smile and mouthing, "sorry."

Officer Scott shrugged it off, knowing Ethan's anger was misplaced.

"Ethan, buddy, are you sure you don't want to press charges against Libby?" Alex inquired giving his friend a sympathetic nod.

Shaking his head, Ethan replied coolly, "It doesn't matter at this point, Alex." He pushed to his feet and stared into Emily's room. "Libby is in the psych ward, and she will be there for a very long time."

Placing her hat under her right arm, Officer Scott thanked them both for their time while offering Ethan a half-smile. She walked to the elevators leaving the two men standing alone.

"Hey man," Alex began while placing a firm grip on Ethan's shoulder. "I'm very sorry about Emily *and* Libby."

Anger flashed through Ethan and he pounded his fist against the wall. Letting out a string of frustrated breaths, he yelled, "Goddamn it!"

Two young nurses rushed over to the waiting area eyes-wide and nervous staring at Ethan. Alex waved them off speaking softly, "It's under control."

Their faces fell as they saw a frustrated Ethan bury his head in his shaking hands. They lowered their heads, and one of the nurses frowned as she placed her hand over her heart.

"Why the fuck didn't I see that Libby needed some serious fucking help?" Ethan paced back and forth running his hands through his dark brown hair. "And now, because of me Emily is there fighting for her life!"

Alex shook his head, replying, "Ethan, you can't let your mind go there. Don't you dare place the blame or any guilt on yourself."

Ethan stood in the doorway, his dark eyes raking over Emily lying motionless in bed. Alex could tell Ethan's emotions were bubbling near the surface ready to explode at any moment.

"Ethan, let's go grab some drinks and maybe something to eat," Alex suggested, treading lightly with this tone.

"I can't leave her," he protested. "What if she wakes up and I'm not here?"

Ethan darted his gaze towards Alex, who walked towards the nurse's station.

"Nurse," Alex began, stopping to view the nametag pinned to her white sweater. Nodding sweetly, Alex drew her green eyes towards a brooding Ethan. "Connie, will you make sure to immediately call Mr. Carlson or myself if there is any change with Miss Greene's condition?" Alex inquired as he handed Connie his card.

Smiling warmly at the two of them, she replied, "Of course, Mr. Robertsen."

"Come on Ethan let's go grub on some food," Alex said.

Ethan walked to the elevator with Alex and stood in silence. The shiny chrome doors opened, and they stepped into an empty car.

Ethan scraped his hands down his face, and turned to Alex saying softly, "I can't lose her, Alex."

Exhaling softly, Alex leaned back grasping the rails with his hands, "I hear you buddy."

"I'm in love with her, completely and deeply in love with her," his voice was shaky.

Alex felt a twinge of pain in his gut as he rolled forward when the car came to a halt. He offered Ethan a half-smile and said, "I'm glad you found Emily. Let's stay positive, okay?"

Alex's mind drifted to thoughts of Amanda, thinking he might fall apart at the mere thought of her lying in a coma unable to move or speak. Alex could see the hell Ethan was going through, suddenly grateful for the awkward situation he was currently dealing with in his own life.

Chapter Thirty-Seven

Across town Vince and Amanda were preparing to jet off to St. Lucia for a week-long vacation. The flight crew had just finished their pre-flight checks, and Amanda had settled into her seat with a glass of champagne before takeoff. Earlier that week Amanda had visited her parents in Bloomfield Hills and reconnecting with them after all this time filled her heart with joy. Emotions ran high as they discussed a range of topics, from what to do about Julie to restoring her trust fund.

One issue had been resolved, at least as far as Amanda was concerned. When she confronted Vince about seeing him with his ex-wife and kids he seemed visibly embarrassed. He apologized profusely for not being totally honest with her about the situation, confirming what Alex said about his kids not knowing their parents were divorcing was true. Vince told Amanda he and Jennifer, or Miss Tennis Whites as Amanda now referred to her, had decided there was no easy way to break it to them, but since

Jennifer was practically engaged to her new man, they needed to tell the kids soon.

"Alex," she announced startled to see him on the plane.

"Hey guys. Vince, here are those documents you needed," he said calmly while handing Vince a folder. "I got caught up at the hospital, with my friend, Ethan, whose girlfriend is in a coma."

"Are you talking about Emily Greene?" Amanda asked.

"Yeah," Alex had a puzzled look on his face. How do you know about that?"

"Well, I know Emily, we're...friends."

"Oh, well her condition is the same. I feel bad for Ethan. He's worried sick, but I worked with the police and they caught her stalker. So that's good news."

Vince handed Alex a glass of scotch saying, "Well brother, if anyone can catch a bad guy, it's you, Alex."

She arched an eyebrow in their direction, inquiring, "Brother?"

"Yeah, this slightly less handsome guy, is my little brother," Vince stated proudly.

Amanda bit her lower lip to keep from saying something she might regret. *Brothers? BROTHERS! You've got to be kidding me.*

Alex looked away from Amanda's icy glare and muttered, "Half-brother."

As they stood side by side, Amanda noted Vince and Alex both had the same trim build, but no other physical traits would link them as sharing DNA. Then she noticed they were both left-handed and cradled their scotch glasses the exact same way—two fingers underneath, two on the side with their thumbs moving from the rim to the side as they took a drink.

"Technically, yeah, we have the same mother, but my dad died when I was four and mom married Alex's dad. A few years later this little guy came screaming into the world followed by our sister, Amy." Vince said.

Suddenly Amanda felt nauseous like she might throw up. She placed her champagne on the table in front of her and rushed towards the bathroom. The smell of the alcohol was making her feel queasy.

"Amanda, are you alright?" Vince said looking up from his newspaper.

"I'm not sure Vince all of a sudden I don't feel so good. Oh…oh no." Amanda covered her mouth and ran to the lavatory where she proceeded to vomit.

"Amanda, are you okay?" Alex asked sweetly as he tapped on the door.

"Scarlett, tell Jim that we need a few minutes before take-off please," Vince instructed.

"Right away, Mr. Everett."

Amanda emerged from the bathroom pale as a ghost. Tiny beads of sweat had formed on the back of her neck. She felt a little better, but she was terrified she had food poisoning again.

"I think so. I might just need some sparkling water."

Alex led Amanda back to her seat gripping her arm softly. "Scarlett, can you please get Amanda some Perrier please?" Alex asked.

Vince sat in front of her gently rubbing her leg. Amanda reached out and touched his face as he kissed the inside of her palm. Settling back in her seat Amanda felt really tired. In fact the last week or two she had been overly exhausted. Looking out the window of the plane at the beautiful blue sky, her mind began to wonder. Reaching for her phone she checked her calendar. Her mind was screaming at her, and there it was in black and white—her period was two weeks late. *Am I pregnant!?*

Chapter Thirty-Eight

Ethan sat in Emily's hospital room after work staring out the window. It was a beautiful day, and she was missing it. She had missed so much already, and now Emily would miss the last weekend of summer.

"Emily, you'll find this interesting. Summer is considered to be from Memorial Day Weekend to Labor Day Weekend. So, I guess technically, we've spent fifteen weekends together as a couple. I know you wanted to rip my head off for causing you to work the majority of Memorial Day weekend, while all I wanted to do was rip your clothes off," he said and laughed to himself. "Happy Anniversary Em, we've been together all summer," he sighed." He stood silent for a few moments trying not to lose his mind over the agony of seeing Emily lying in the bed motionless. "I miss you," he whispered. "Please come back to me. Babe, you've gotta wake up." Squeezing Emily's hand, which was soft and cool, he laced his fingers with hers. The pricking of tears began to well in the corner of his eyes. Ethan took a deep breath kissing her on the lips gently, he stepped back and walked out of the room.

Ethan was overcome with emotion. His heart was aching for Emily. Standing at the elevator he took out the keys from his pocket as the doors opened. Ethan nearly ran into a tall guy with dark brown hair as he stepped forward, because he was looking down at the white tile floor.

"Oh…" his voice broke, he was distracted. "Sorry man, that's my fault," Ethan said as he entered the elevator.

The guy politely brushed past Ethan calmly saying, "Not a problem."

Ethan needed to get some coffee, but not the bland coffee from the cafeteria. He was tired of drinking that stuff. Arriving at the parking lot, he slid into his car and drove to the Bagel Beanery.

Back at the hospital, the nurses' station was relatively quiet. Two female nurses were seated at the reception desk on Emily's floor, and the waiting room only had one person sitting in a chair watching *Ellen*.

"Can I help you sir?" said a rather large lady wearing red rimmed glasses and carrying a clipboard.

"Yes, I'm looking for Emily Greene's room. I heard she was on this floor."

Tipping her glasses up with her index finger, she pointed to the right, directly at Emily's room. "Are you a friend of Miss Greene's?"

The man smiled at her nodding his head, "Oh yes...we've been friends for a long time. I've known Emmy since she was in grad school." The words dripped from his lips with a sultry smoothness.

"Emily sure is lucky to have such a good-looking friend like you come to visit her. Too bad she won't be able to see your fine self, she's been in a coma for a few weeks now. Maybe your sexy voice can bring her out of it," she said with a hearty laugh while winking at him.

"I'll see what I can do about that," he said, giving the nurse a wink with one of his piercing greyish-blue eyes, while revealing a sly half smile.

He walked past the nurses' station where all three women watched him intently as he entered Emily's room. Upon entering, he took his sunglasses and placed them in his shirt pocket. Standing at the edge of her bed he sighed deeply, placing both hands firmly in the pockets of his blue shorts. He moved to Emily's side and clasped her hand while rubbing his thumb over the top of her smooth skin.

"So Emmy, you've gone and managed to get yourself in a coma." He let out a deep sigh as he gazed at her sleeping peacefully.

The Emily he saw lying in the bed was not the same girl he saw the day he left. She looked pale, her flushed cheeks were hallowed and her normally svelte frame was boney.

"I read about the accident in the paper. I'm so sorry this happened to you, Emmy. I know you can pull through this. You're such a strong person." Looking around the room he noticed all the cards and flowers.

"You've got a lot of people that want you to come out of this, Emmy. Plus, I'm back now, and I want to tell you where I've been and why I couldn't see you all these years." He brushed a strand of hair out of her face and gently grazed her cheek with the back of his hand. "It's a pretty crazy story, but I know you'd be proud of me."

"Emmy, please come out of this so I can talk...talk to you. I have missed you so much. Being apart from you, every day was like a dagger to my heart. I didn't expect you to wait for me. Someone as beautiful as you…" His voice began to tremble, and he swallowed hard. "I had to stay away. My life depended upon it. *Your* life depended upon it."

He leaned over and touched his lips to hers, giving her a kiss and then whispered in her ear, "Emmy, if you can hear me, it's me, Craig. I need you to get well soon." He stood up and reached for the sunglasses in his pocket.

"Pardon me, but who are…are you?" Ashleigh's voice trailed off.

Craig turned around to see a woman with long brown hair holding a cup of coffee with a laptop bag over her shoulder staring at him. At this point Ashleigh's mouth was open, and her hazel eyes looked as if they were going to pop out of her head.

"Hi. I'm sorry… I wasn't trying to intrude. I heard Emmy…I mean *Emily* had been in a terrible accident, and I wanted to come by and see her. I'm Craig Walker." He walked to the end of Emily's bed offering his right hand to Ashleigh.

"Craig, yeah I know you," she said shaking his hand firmly. "Actually, Emily has told me quite the story about you—*Houdini*." She paused, waiting for his reaction. A ghost of a smile crossed his lips as he shifted uncomfortably. "Craig, I saw you at Heathrow airport a few months ago. You helped me with my bag."

Giving her a once over then cocking his head to the left, he replied, "I'm glad I could help you. Sorry, but I don't remember." His thick dark eyebrows knitted together as if he was trying to recall where he'd seen Ashleigh.

"Never mind that," she said firmly, releasing the grip she had on his strong hand.

Craig shot her a perplexed look.

"You know, Emily's a *bit* upset with you," Ashleigh said, placing her coffee cup on the table.

"I'm sure she is," he said with a light chuckle. "I have a perfectly logical explanation for my absence. And you are?"

"I'm Ashleigh Preston, Emily's best friend. I am on my way to the airport. I'm leaving for London to see my fiancé, but I wanted to spend some time with her before I left."

"Can you tell me anything more about her condition? I mean is she going to be okay?" Craig's voice was filled with concern. Ashleigh could see that he genuinely cared about Emily's status.

"I don't know, the doctor's aren't saying too much. The good news is that she is breathing on her own. The bad news is she has some brain swelling, and they don't know how it will affect her until she wakes up."

"How long was she under the water?"

"The doctors estimate about seven or eight minutes, but they have no way of being absolutely sure. Ethan was able to revive her in fewer than five minutes. If she had been under the water longer than ten minutes he might not have been able to revive her so quickly."

Craig shook his head and placed his hand on Emily's leg giving her two gentle pats. "I assume Ethan is her boyfriend?"

"Not that it's any of your business, but yes, and he will be back here any minute so you better move along," she instructed firmly. "Sorry Houdini, I'm not trying to be rude. I just don't want any tension in this room."

"I understand. Here's my card. Will you call me if there's any change with Emily?"

Looking at the card Ashleigh saw that Craig lived in New York City and was a Senior Energy Markets Analyst with CME Group. The mystery of Craig Walker had Ashleigh growing more curious by the minute.

"Okay Craig, if anything changes I'll call you. Take my card. Don't be a stranger—*Houdini*," she said with a hint of sarcasm.

Craig headed out the door and walked to the elevator. Ashleigh heard one of the nurses say, "Bye handsome." Ashleigh rolled her eyes.

"Boy Emily, he's completely in love with you," she whispered. "Goddamn it Emily, wake up out of this coma so we can discuss that Craig was *just* here." Ashleigh slumped down in the chair next to the bed and took a sip of coffee. She saw Ethan getting off the elevator and quickly placed the card in her laptop bag.

"Hey, Ashleigh," Ethan said, his voice was tight. "Did anything interesting happen while I was gone?"

Drumming her nails on her coffee cup, Ashleigh shook her head. Interesting was an understatement.

Chapter Thirty-Nine

Sitting on the balcony at Liam's high-rise apartment while enjoying a cup of tea, Ashleigh gazed across the London skyline. In a matter of months she was finally going to live in the city of her dreams. Liam had just purchased a fabulous two bedroom apartment in Central London a few months ago on One Commercial Street. The view alone was worth the money. Ashleigh had some of her stuff moved in already, what little she could bring with her from the states that is, which was mostly clothes and some smaller items. For now, she had held off on putting her place on the market, she wasn't about to leave while Emily was still in the hospital.

Looking at her laptop she began researching florists in Wales. Liam's mother, Paige, had sent her a sheet of vendors they frequently work with at the Castle to make the wedding planning a little easier. Even though they had yet to set a date for the wedding, she knew Emily would be pissed if she stopped her life just to worry about her being in a coma. The least Ashleigh could do was a little research, possibly start a Pinterest board. She was thinking of giving up social media altogether since Emily's accident, but instead she resolved to be more cautious of her posts.

It was nearly one in the afternoon. As soon as Liam returned home from work they would be leaving for Wales to visit his parents. They desperately wanted to throw her and Liam an engagement party, but Ashleigh did not want to have the celebration until Emily came out of her coma.

Ashleigh was pulled from her thoughts of Emily by the buzzing of her phone. It was a number she did not recognize, but she answered anyway.

"Good Afternoon, this is Ashleigh Preston."

"Miss Preston, hi, this is Connie at Memorial hospital. We have some news regarding Emily Greene." Ashleigh's heart started to beat rapidly, and she felt her throat tighten. *Please God, let it be good news.*

"Yes, is everything okay? Is Emily okay?"

"Miss Preston, Emily is awake. She has been awake for about an hour."

Ashleigh was overcome with emotion. She was utterly relieved, and tears sprang from her eyes. She composed herself and replied, "That's the best news I've heard in a long time. Have you called Ethan Carlson?"

"Not yet, he is next on our list."

"Thank you, Connie. Thank you very much. Goodbye." She hung up the phone to call Liam, but he walked through the door just as she was pressing his number.

"Hey! I was just about to call you. Emily is out of her coma!" she shouted at the top of her lungs. A smile crossed Liam's face. Ashleigh jumped into his arms and hugged him tightly.

"I'm so glad to hear your news, darling. Do you want to depart for Grand Rapids to see her?"

"You won't be upset that we aren't going to be able to see your parents?"

"Darling please, your friend just came out of a near month long coma. I think my parents will understand."

"Wait, why are you home so early anyway?" Ashleigh inquired.

"What? Can I not take off early to come home and spend the rest of the day with my gorgeous fiancé?"

"Okay, that's perfectly acceptable. Now we have to check the flights to Detroit. I cannot wait to see Emily." Ashleigh kissed Liam on the cheek and began to walk away, but he pulled her into him kissing her deeply. She looked up at him and he said, "Have I told you how much I love you?"

"Yes, but I never grow tired of hearing you say it. I cannot wait to marry you, Liam Frost, and the sooner the better. We'll set a date on our flight."

Ethan and Emily wheeled their carryon luggage through the hordes of people at JFK airport. They had at least an hour before their flight to London. It was the weekend of Liam and Ashleigh's engagement party.

"Can you believe Liam and Ashleigh are getting married in just a few months?" Emily said taking a seat at the bar.

"Em, they're getting married in less than two months. Is your memory still that fuzzy?" Ethan joked. She smiled and playfully punched his arm.

"I guess," she shrugged. "Ethan, since I missed the last few weeks of summer, I think you should whisk me away to a tropical island somewhere."

"Ms. Greene, you have some of the best ideas. I'd love to take you somewhere hot, where clothing is *optional*," he said, grinning wickedly.

Emily shot Ethan a playful smirk of her own then pulled up her phone and checked in to the bar at the airport. Ethan saw Emily with her phone and gave her a half smile. "I know what you're thinking Ethan. I refuse to let one sociopath bully me into giving up on social media."

"*Bully* you? You almost fucking died, Emily." He admonished.

"What are the chances of getting stalked again? I would say not likely," she scoffed.

Leaning against the wall, Amanda stared out the window of Vince's New York apartment. Watching the multi-colored leaves scatter across the sidewalk, she clutched her stomach then took a sip of her tea. The rain began to fall as she became lost in her thoughts. Amanda's mind replayed the events of last few months. The emptiness Amanda felt was filled by Vince's love and bubbled over with Alex's. She hadn't spoken to Alex in three weeks, she couldn't bring herself to pick up the phone or even be near him. The feelings she had for Alex were too strong and laced with complications. Her heart leapt into her throat as she read the message on her phone: AMANDA, I'M IN LOVE WITH YOU. I NEED YOU. I MISS YOU. WHY WON'T YOU TALK TO ME? Amanda let out a deep sigh and began to cry. Her stomach was in knots, and her emotions were all over the place. She was wrecked with guilt and confusion.

Emily finished the last sip of her chardonnay and told Ethan she needed to use the ladies room before they boarded their flight.

"Okay, I'll pay for the drinks and meet you at the gate," Ethan said kissing her on the cheek.

Emily flung her purse over her forearm and wheeled her carryon out of the restaurant towards the bathrooms. Handing the bartender his credit card, he never took his eyes off Emily as she exited the bar area. Ethan had made a point to keep a careful watch on Emily these days after what happened. He could not bear the thought of anything happening to her again. He knew it was silly and his fears would go away in time, but for now better safe than sorry.

"What are you doing here after work on a Friday night all by yourself?" Morgan Allen inquired as she shifted in her seat to face the handsome man seated at the bar. She was wearing a low-cut silk blouse and flirty micro-mini hoping her exposed fair skin would catch his eye.

"I just got in from Chicago, and I needed a drink. The flight I was on was a little nerve wracking, especially flying over the Lake Michigan."

"Oh? No kidding. I used to live in Michigan. I'm from Bay City, but I spent the last few years in Grand Rapids. I just moved to Brooklyn a few weeks ago."

"Grand Rapids is nice. I have been there a few times. I was there just a few weeks ago to see a friend," he said before taking a sip of his beer. His greyish-blue eyes entranced Morgan.

Emily emerged from the ladies room and began walking towards the gate. There were a lot of people in the airport that day. Her mind wandered as she walked through the crowd. She checked her purse for her boarding pass, but it wasn't there. *Oh shoot! Did I leave it in the bathroom?* She stopped dead in her tracks and started to frantically search her purse. After a brief moment of fear, relief washed over her as she remembered that Ethan had it. She was so forgetful lately, but the doctors said that her memory would return to normal in time. *Normal.* Emily laughed to herself.

She felt like a damaged freak, not being able to recall the simplest things in her daily life.

She started down the terminal again, and that is when she saw him—he was sitting at the Irish Pub. Emily blinked and gasped. Her eyes were not deceiving her—it was Craig Walker. She tried to move but couldn't. At that moment, Craig had spotted her standing there looking at him. Her pulse was racing, and she stood motionless as people hurriedly passed by her. She knew she was in the way, but she didn't care, he was more handsome than she ever remembered. He looked almost the same, only more sophisticated, just like Ashleigh described from her encounter at Heathrow.

Sitting at the airport bar, he was wearing a maroon and navy striped button down paired with a paisley print maroon tie and navy pants. The sleeves of his shirt were rolled up to his elbows, and his semi-curly hair was subtly spikey. He looked hot. *How was it possible for someone to be this gorgeous?*

The buzzing of her phone caused Emily to momentarily take her eyes off Craig. It was a text from Ethan:

OUR FLIGHT IS BOARDING NOW. SEE YOU IN A BIT. I HAVE YOUR BOARDING PASS.

Craig motioned to the bartender and said something as he stood up. He took a sip of his Miller Lite and then walked towards Emily, never taking his eyes off her.

"Emmy," he said softly.

The sound of Craig's voice melted over her, Emily's bottom lip quivered. He closed the space between them; she was trembling. Emily reached up and brushed her fingertips across his cheek. When she felt his skin, Emily's knees buckled beneath her causing her to draw her hand back briskly. It was really him. Craig Bennett Walker was definitely alive. After the initial shock wore off, Emily felt hot tears prick her eyes.

"Craig," her breath hitched. "I can't believe you're standing here… in front of me."

Craig's steely blue eyes washed over her, the pad of his thumb grazed her cheek wiping away the single tear that fell.

"It's me Emmy, I've missed you." His voice was shaky.

"I…I want to talk to you, but my flight to London is boarding."

Filled with tremendous waves of emotion, Emily dug in her purse frantically for her business cards. The tears were blinding her, and Emily thought she might crumble into a million pieces at the thundering beat of her heart inside her body.

The loudspeaker announced final boarding for her flight.

"Emmy, it's okay," Craig said reassuringly as he pressed his hand over hers. "Don't miss your flight. Your friend, Ashleigh has my number."

Emily blanched. Her wet eyes blinked at him spraying tiny droplets down her reddened cheeks. *How does Ashleigh have Craig's number?*

"Why are you peeling the label off your beer bottle?" Morgan asked as she moved a seat closer to him.

"It's just something I do when I want to remember a special moment in my life," he said. The icy blue hue in his eyes was completely dazzling. Morgan eagerly hoped the moment he was talking about was meeting her, and that he was going to jot down his number for her to call him on the back of that label.

"I'm Morgan by the way, Morgan Allen." She offered a flirtatious smile again while reaching her hand out to greet him, hoping he would take notice.

He did not. It was obvious she was desperately seeking attention, but he was polite to Morgan despite her rather anticipated behavior. Raking his eyes over her, he took note of her appearance. Unkempt was an understatement, slightly sloppy was too kind, disheveled was a better description with a chipped manicure and shade of lipstick that was too bright for her pale complexion. Morgan's green blouse had a stain on the right side near the third button. The tight black skirt she was wearing hugged her thighs, squeezing them, showing off every plump ripple. Her skin was oily, and her dishwater blonde hair was badly in need of a trim. The stench of her cheap dime store perfume was so overwhelming he figured she must have spritzed half the bottle on her.

"Nice to meet you, Morgan. I'm Craig Walker."

"So, Craig Walker, what brought on this special moment?"

"Well, if you must know, I just saw a woman I've loved for a long time, and I guess you could say that we re-connected." He took a sip of his beer. "Hey, you might know her, she lives in Grand Rapids—Emily Greene."

Morgan was overcome with shock. She felt like she just took a punch to the gut. *Of course it was, Emily Greene. Of all the men in all the airport bars he had to walk into mine. What should I do with this bit of information?*

The air was crisp, but a chilly fall afternoon couldn't stop Ashleigh and Liam from enjoying their tea on the terrace. Pulling her knees to her chest she wrapped the cashmere blanket around her tightly and pulled her chunky knit, ivory sweater down over her hands.

"Looks like it's going to rain again," Ashleigh remarked while looking towards the Thames. The fog was beginning to roll in, and in the distance she could see the misty clouds enveloping the Tower of London.

"Don't worry love, you'll get used to the rain," he said giving her a sly smile.

Looking at the time on her phone, she noted that Emily and Ethan's flight would be arriving in a few short hours prompting her to ask, "Liam, did you arrange a car for Emily and Ethan's arrival?"

"Yes, I sure did," he hummed.

Liam's phone buzzed. Looking up from his newspaper he said, "Sorry Darling, this is work. I must take it." Kissing Ashleigh on the cheek he walked into the living room and answered his phone.

As Ashleigh gazed out over the city skyline she sat back and took a sip of tea. She was feeling incredibly happy. Her life was practically perfect at the moment. Her penthouse sold quickly and the couple that purchased it wanted all of her furniture, too. That couple was Amanda and Vince. They wanted a bigger place for whatever reason, but

Ashleigh couldn't part with her beloved bed. That piece of furniture is in a safe storage space for now.

Her boss was very excited about her moving to London because it would save him on travel expenses. She received a raise for all of her hard work, and her article about the Le Petit Hotel & Café received three times the hits of any other piece, bringing in all kinds of advertisers from Montreal. *Thanks Xavier.* That was her little secret, and she intended to keep it that way. She wasn't even sure she would tell Emily.

Emily was doing well. The doctors seemed hopeful that her memory would return to normal very soon. She had yet to tell Emily about Craig coming to the hospital to visit her, but she knew she couldn't wait much longer. Most importantly, in December, Ashleigh and Liam would become husband and wife.

Liam finished his call and returned to the terrace. He looked to be anxious, or maybe he was distressed. She was still trying to read his body language.

"Everything okay, Liam?"

"Ashleigh, darling, I have some news." He was pacing briskly around the terrace and scratching the back of his head.

Oh this does not sound good.

Gripping the hemline of her sweater tightly, she asked softly, "What's the news, Liam?"

Liam's cheeks were flushed, and his body was stiff, "*Wanderlust* has been sold to a publishing house in New York City. They want me to move to Manhattan and serve as Editor during the transition period. After six months, I will settle into my new role as Vice President of Publishing."

Liam's jaw clenched. Every muscle in Ashleigh's body tensed as his words twisted recklessly inside her. The cashmere blanket fell to the chair as she stood up to face Liam. Finally, she was able to form the words.

"When do you, I mean *we,* have to move?" She stood there shivering slightly as the crisp air cut through the cotton fabric of her black leggings sending a chill up her back.

"In three weeks," Liam replied placing both hands on her arms while rubbing them gently.

The rain began to come down lightly. They quickly gathered their things and bolted inside. Ashleigh stood in silence scanning the London skyline. Liam carried the teapot and cups to the sink. From the kitchen he watched his fiancé stare blankly out the window. Liam ran his hand over the curve of his jaw as he approached Ashleigh from the kitchen.

"New York City," she muttered softly.

He reached over and took Ashleigh's hand in his as they stood in front of the sliding glass doors of his London apartment, *their* London apartment, watching the rain fall gently on the terrace.

Epilogue

One Week before Christmas
Grand Rapids
Amanda Parsons

Vince's frantic pacing in the waiting room and Alex's constant knuckle cracking were driving me absolutely out of my mind. Alex stood, as I excused myself to get a bottle of water down the hall from Dr. Sarin's office. The fourth floor of the hospital was relatively quiet. Only a few people were seated in the general reception area watching CNN or engaged in conversation with each other.

Moving to stand near the window, I watched cars pull in and out of the snowy hospital parking lot wondering what each person's story was— why were they here? Baby? Flu? Routine check-up? Surgery? Would they be getting good or bad news? Would their news be what they expected? Would the news be what they prayed for day after day or would it be life changing?

Swallowing a few sips of water, I contemplated for the millionth time my own reason for being here— paternity test results. With the cat out of the bag, both Vince and Alex agreed to blood work. Despite my best laid plans to tell Vince about my affair with Alex, one voicemail blew that plan to hell. The moment the words screeched out, I felt like I was falling, spinning down a drain and tumbling into blackness:

"Miss Parsons, this is Sami at Memorial per your urgent request. Doctor Sarin would like to schedule the DNA test regarding paternity three weeks from Friday. Doctor Sarin is extremely confident despite the candidates being half-brothers your results will not yield inconclusive. Please call our office to confirm a time that fits into your schedule."

I wanted to strangle that fucking nitwit receptionist for calling Vince's cell instead of mine. Why the hell the greeting didn't alert her it was the wrong number was beyond my fucking comprehension. The chance to be honest with Vince and Alex was something I wanted to do of my own volition. But, I had my chance many times to come clean, and I didn't. That voicemail changed everything, and with a front row seat, the events that transpired on that day were burned into my brain forever.

Moving to his desk, Vince leaned against it crossing his arms. "So, I will ask again, who wants to tell me what the fuck is going on?"

"Look, it just happened," Alex stood. "Amanda's not at fault here. This was my doing. I came on to her."

Before I could speak a word, Vince's fist collided with Alex's jaw, and his head jerked back. Looking at me, Alex rubbed the spot on his jaw where Vince landed the punch.

"I suppose I deserved that hit brother," his lips twitched into a wry smile. "Consider that your free pass."

They moved cautiously like two fierce competitors studying each other anticipating the next move. Daggers of heated anger passed between the two of them. Thankfully I was across the room out of the way.

"You deserve a lot more than one hit, brother," Vince spat. "So Amanda, tell me how long have you and my dear brother been screwing?" he asked snidely. Walking to the drink cart in the corner of his office, he poured some amber liquid into a glass.

"Don't talk to her like that."

There was a definite warning in Alex's tone. This was not at all the time or place to have this kind of discussion.

"You know it's funny," he stopped abruptly to take a sip of his drink. The brothers' eyes glared at each other with the same intensity. The two men shared blood, and they were alike in so many ways. They both exuded strength and confidence, but carried it in completely different ways. Vince was powerful outwardly, when walked into a room he owned it with intensity. Alex was reserved in his quiet demeanor I suspected that was dangerous to any opponent.

A gleeful laugh escaped Vince as he poked Alex's shoulder. "I never dreamed my own brother would hurt me like this. Tell me, when did taking things that belong to others become your thing?"

"I don't belong to anyone." I scolded.

"It's not my thing," Alex replied through gritted teeth.

"Stop it, now." A low roar of anger escaped me. *"Look, there's going to be a baby, and no matter who her father is, she would be lucky to have either one of you as a parent."* Tears filled my eyes and burned down my cheeks.

Alex cocked an eyebrow, *"You're having a girl?"*

"No, no way," Vince shook his head in protest. *"If I'm the father, he will not have anything to do with my daughter."*

I stalked towards Vince, *"You really want to start cutting people out?"*

"Amanda," he sighed. *"No, I don't."*

"I will do this on my own. Don't push me."

"I realize I'm dishing out low blows, but I cannot believe you'd sleep with him. And the baby could be his, my own brother." Blowing out a frustrated breath, Vince slumped into his leather chair.

"Yes, it's true we are in this messed up predicament, but that is because of me," I said pointing to myself. "Not Alex. And for all of this, I am so very sorry." I dropped back onto the couch. "I had this irrational fear of being alone— again."

Alex and Vince both stared at me softening their expressions, absorbing my words.

"Look," I sighed. "We're all tired and hurting, let's continue this conversation later."

Vince started to argue with me, but I explained I needed sleep and he needed to cool off.

"I'll make dinner tonight. I want the two of you here at 7:00 sharp. If you have meetings, conference calls or anything that doesn't involve life or death, reschedule it. Are we in agreement?"

In unison they both responded, yes. I went to the guest bedroom, my head hit the pillow and I was out like a light.

Emotions ran high that evening at dinner, more hurtful things were said but somehow after a few hours of difficult conversation among the three of us, we managed to forgive one another and made a decision to move forward with the paternity test. I admitted to Vince that I intended to tell him in St. Lucia I was leaving him for Alex. That was not something he was prepared to hear. He had no idea that his hectic work schedule was an emotional trigger for me. I harbored more pain than I realized, so I have started to see a therapist to work out my own issues. I don't think there is a pill you can take that makes you stop being a bitch in an instant, but I finally realized I needed to smarten the fuck up.

For the past few weeks I have been living on my own at the penthouse, not really in a relationship with either one of them. Vince has made efforts to take me to dinner on more than one occasion. We have talked at great lengths about our feelings and what we want from the other in a relationship.

My relationship with Alex is awkward at best. Aside from the occasional movie or tea date, our friendship is not what it once was. However, he has been helping me workout and showing me safe things I can do to stay in shape while I'm pregnant.

Alex or Vince— by the end of the hour one of them would be a father, and I would have a clearer picture of the future. More importantly, despite the grown-up issues currently on the table, the only thing that truly mattered is what the baby needed, a loving stable home to grow up in with two people who loved her unconditionally.

My gaze caught Vince's reflection in the glass. I turned around to face him.

"It's time?"

He nodded. Stepping forward he wrapped me in a tight embrace. I buried my face in his chest feeling all the muscles in his abdomen contract and release.

"How's Alex holding up?"

"He's doing just fine."

"And you?" I asked, as we made our way down the hallway towards Dr. Sarin's office.

"I'm fine."

"Liar." I joked, bumping him with my shoulder.

"Hey, fine you got me," he held up his hands in surrender. "Listen Amanda, I can do this. I can be the businessman my company demands me to be, the father my kids need me to be, but most importantly I will be the loving and kind man you can depend on even if this baby isn't mine."

Tears streamed down my cheeks. "But, I have caused so much pain and nearly destroyed your relationship with Alex in the process. How can you even want to be with me? God Vince, I am so sorry... for *all* of this."

"Shhh," he whispered, gently stroking his hand up and down my back. "Can I be honest?" He pulled back, cupping my face in his hands wiping away the tears, and I nodded. "You said you turned to Alex because I wasn't being the kind of man you needed. My ex-wife and I separated for many reasons, but one of them was because I was unable to manage my personal and work life with balance. Now, I see that life is too damn short. If you'll let me, I'd really like to try to make this work."

"What about Alex, how will we even begin to heal?"

"Let's get the results first and figure out the rest after." He brushed his lips to mine, and deep inside I knew that Vince was my second chance, too.

****

One Month Later

Alex Robertsen

I returned from my late afternoon appointment to find Amanda standing near the window of my office. Her blonde hair was swept up, revealing the smooth slope of her neck. I wanted to rush to her and kiss my way up and down that gorgeous neck. Instead, I walked to my closet and hung up my coat.

"Amanda."

She turned to face me, and a smile crossed her pink lips. "Hi Alex."

"This is a surprise. What are you doing here?"

"I just wanted to drop by and say hello."

"Okay, well then," I sat on corner of my desk, pushing up the sleeves on my dress shirt. "You've said hi, is there anything else?"

"Alex," she breathed taking a step closer.

I moved away rounding the corner of my desk and took a seat; she didn't follow. She eyed me for the longest time saying nothing. Immediately I felt uneasy; I couldn't get a read on the situation, which was a fucking specialty of mine. With her expressionless face, Amanda would make a damn fine poker player.

"Don't you think it's time we talked Alex?"

I shrugged. "About what? I'll be at the benefit Saturday. You received my RSVP right?"

Today was the first time in weeks Amanda had spoken to me other than polite pleasantries and greetings. I hadn't exactly made myself available for her either, or Vince for that matter, aside from a few charitable events, holiday parties and brunch at Mom and Dad's. My relationship with Vince was strained to say the least.

"Okay this is ridiculous. You know that is not what I am talking about. Please talk to me… *please.* I miss you. I miss our friendship."

And there it was, she missed our *friendship,* and I was in love with her. I couldn't blame her— the way she felt, the decisions that we all made. But, it didn't make things any easier or hurt any less. I played my part in this fucked up scenario, and in the end things for Amanda and I were just not meant to be. I moved from behind my desk to stand in front of her.

"Look, you know I only want you to be happy, that's all I've ever wanted. I am not what you need. Vince needs you and my niece will too, once she gets here. You look happy Amanda, really happy."

The paternity test revealed that Vince was without a doubt the baby's father. Of the twenty-three DNA markers tested, Vince hit all of them and I matched only eleven.

"Alex," she said clasping my hands in hers. "You offered me friendship, and in return I played on your feelings."

"Yes and I," pointing to myself, "played on *your* fears."

She shot me a knowing glance. She knew I was right. I felt the tension passing between us every time we were together last summer. It was completely avoidable. We both wanted to have our cake and eat it too.

She dropped her eyes to the floor, pinching the bridge of her nose. "Alex *no*, you're,"

"Amanda," I sighed, scrubbing my hands down my face. "Don't put the…"

Cutting me off, she shouted, "No! We were on a toxic path, and because I wasn't strong enough at the time, I let my insecurities play on *my* fears. Instead of talking to Vince, my emotions took over, and I made assumptions that could have easily been dissolved."

There was a long moment of silence, as if we were mourning the painful truth of our relationship. At least we'd finally been honest with each other.

"Alex, you'll always be special to me. I wish we'd made better choices, and I hope someday you can forgive me for hurting you."

On some level I anticipated those words were coming. Despite my best efforts, I was still holding some flicker of hope that Amanda would love me and want to share a life with me. The words cut, but this was the definite push I needed to finally close up the part of my heart that loved her. There was zero chance for the two of us.

"There is no need to apologize," I replied tugging at her arm. "Let's chalk this up to a life lesson and realize we're better people for it, but I forgive you if that's what you need to hear."

"Good, I'll see you at the benefit Saturday. Then I want you to be at our place for brunch on Sunday." She gave me a quick hug and skirted out the door.

Blowing out a breath, I dropped back into my chair. I had a ton of work to do and it was already after 4:00 PM. I pulled up my email clicking on the one that I had been putting off for the past two days and replied. Thirty minutes later, I received a confirmation with my flight and hotel itinerary.

All right Alex, let the next chapter in your life begin.

Change was good, but even more I *needed* it.

AFTERWORD

Thank you for reading! Did you enjoy *Fifteen Weekends* and want more? Hop over to my website and check out the bonus material. There's a bonus epilogue with Liam and Ashleigh. Plus, you can find out what happened to Craig all those years ago!

Need to know what happens next with Alex? Check out his story in *Bound to Me*.

About The Author

International Bestselling Author and self-proclaimed french fry addict, Christy Pastore writes sexy, contemporary romance books that contain no nonsense (mostly) heroines and swoony gentleman with a naughty side. Readers so overwhelmingly embraced one Wicked Gentleman, Jackson Hart specifically, turning many of her #AuthorGoals into a reality.

When Christy's not turning her risqué thoughts into something worth reading, you'll find her geeking out on all things pop culture, obsessively stalking Pinterest for home interior ideas, lunching with friends, or researching her next vacation destination.

She has strong opinions about folding laundry, fruity wines, the Oxford Comma, fashion, and mixed vegetables.

Christy lives in central Indiana with her husband and their three loveable cats, Cheeto, Dorito, and Brew. But as cute as they are, please send scratching posts asap because they're slowly destroying the furniture.

Books by Christy Pastore

The Scripted Duet

Unscripted

Perfectly Scripted

The Harbour Series

Bound to Me

Healed by You

Return to Us

The Gentleman Collection

Wicked Gentleman

Royal Gentleman

Dirty Gentleman

Standalone Titles

Fifteen Weekends (Women's Fiction)

The First Lights

The Cardwell Family Series

Beautiful March

Sweet Agony

Copper Lining

Novellas

Double Contact

Snowed In with the Quarterback

Snowed In with the Boss

Be sure to sign up for my newsletter at christypastore-author.com for the latest news on releases, sales, and other updates.

www.ingramcontent.com/pod-product-compliance
Lightning Source LLC
Chambersburg PA
CBHW050022030726
47506CB00001B/78